Caressa's Homecoming

by

Gabbi Grey

Caressa's Homecoming

Cover Art by *Diana Carlile*

The Wild Rose Press, Inc.
PO Box 708
Adams Basin, NY 14410-0708
Visit us at www.thewildrosepress.com

Publishing History
First Edition, 2024
Trade Paperback ISBN 978-1-5092-5324-1
Digital ISBN 978-1-5092-5325-8

Published in the United States of America

So, less than a day later, we sat in Save-On-Meats and chowed down on hearty breakfasts. I was glad to see Caressa digging into her food, although I wasn't completely surprised. We might've gone to bed relatively early, but we'd also woken repeatedly during the night to come together. A touch or a smell or just her presence was enough to rouse me from sleep and bring my body into awareness. Sometimes the lovemaking had been leisurely and soft, with us barely conscious. Other times, it'd been demanding and almost violent. As if we needed to crawl inside of each other. As if lives depended on joining our bodies.

"You two look tired," Cole commented as our dishes were taken away and we all settled in with our warm drinks. Cole and I drank coffee while Caressa nursed a caffeinated black tea.

I glanced at Caressa who glanced back.

"Oh, this is interesting." Cole's blue eyes were sharp on the two of us.

I wanted to reach out and take Caressa's hand but held back. Instead, I shifted subtly so my thigh was pressed against hers.

"We have something to tell you, Cole." She looked him in the eyes without flinching.

"Oh, I think I can guess." His voice dripped with sarcasm.

Rip off the proverbial bandage. "Caressa has moved in with me. We're together. As a couple." As if clarification is necessary.

"It's been two days." Cole slammed his mug down.

Praise for Gabbi Grey and...

Dedication

To Renae for reminding me how much I loved this story.
To Roseann for taking a chance on me.
To Josette for your unwavering faith in me.

Chapter One

Caressa

I placed the newborn infant on his mother's chest just as the paramedics made their way into the tiny, cramped bathroom of my favorite pub on Commercial Drive. A pub I'd never look at the same way again. "Full-term infant born three minutes ago. Mother's heart rate is steady and no signs of complications. The placenta hasn't delivered yet."

As the paramedic clamped off the umbilical cord, she eyed me. "You a doctor?" Her short-cropped brown hair accentuated her big smile while her blue eyes lit with obvious excitement.

"Nurse." I tried to extricate myself and return to my guys, easing my way to the exit. I'd done my part. The woman was in good hands now.

"You did a good job." The other paramedic was a bigger man, also sporting a wide grin. "Must've happened fast."

"I don't know what happened." The new mother gripped her baby tightly. "I came in here, and my water broke and…"

The paramedics prepared to move mother and child to a stretcher. Just before they lifted her, the woman waved them off. She turned to me. "I don't even know your name."

Gabbi Grey

"Caressa Klein."

"I'd name my baby after you…"

"But he's a boy."

The woman nodded and winced. Whether from residual pain or the fact I had a definitively woman's name, I wasn't sure. Then she asked, "Who are you here with?"

"My friends Michael and Cole."

"Michael Cole." She beamed incandescently. That little birth glow new moms got. "I think that's the perfect name." Finally, she allowed the paramedics to move her to the gurney and bundle her into the blankets.

What if I'd said Cole and Michael?

Surely, the woman, still high from the birth, didn't mean to actually name her son after my best friends. Yet even as I had the thought, I embraced the possibility. That some random woman named her newborn after the two people most important in my life.

As the paramedics left, the manager of the pub came in to survey the damage. She looked ruefully around the room. "I think the men's bathroom is going to be unisex for the rest of the night."

I grinned. "Yeah, probably a good idea."

She poked her shoe against a pile of towels I'd commandeered to make the bathroom as clean as possible. "I have to tell you, that woman's husband was useless. Apparently, this is their fourth child, and the guy was so pale your friends had to get him to sit down and put his head between his knees before he passed out. They in the medical profession as well?"

"Nah, Michael's an engineer, and Cole's an actor."

The manager's eyes widened as she snapped her fingers. "That's where I've seen him. He's the lead on

2

that superhero series, right? Man, he's hot."

Since I couldn't disagree, I offered a sheepish smile. Women had always found Cole attractive. Or at least they had since his braces had come off, he'd gotten contacts, and his gangly teen body started filling out. His late teens had been good to him, and he'd gone to theater school right out of high school. He'd paid his dues, working his way around productions for years, but this series was his big break. It'd been picked up by one of the major American networks and just renewed for a fifth season.

A chill ran through me, and I glanced down and grimaced. Amniotic fluid did not look or smell good on my favorite jeans and pale-blue blouse. The blouse I'd chosen because it matched my eyes. Not that I was dressing up for Michael and Cole. They wouldn't care if I showed up in a potato sack. But I hadn't been out since returning to Vancouver, and I'd wanted to look nice. Since Cole had complimented me on the blouse and Michael had admired my hair, I'd obviously cleaned up okay. After I'd spent five years in a little village in Africa, I was now sitting and having dinner in a first-world country with running water and cold beer. That felt weird.

"I think I need to get going."

"My chef has put together a takeout box for you and your friends. We didn't figure you were going to stay." She waved at my clothes. "Feel free to send me the dry-cleaning bill."

I offered her a smile and made my way over to the sink. I'd scrubbed as best as I could before delivering the baby, and now I was going to do my best to clean up. Then I was going home. A moment of disappointment flitted through me, though, because I'd been looking forward to catching up with Michael and Cole. Our meal had barely been served before the call to help came. Since I loved this pub's dishes, I'd enjoy whatever the chef prepared for me.

When I finally emerged from the bathroom, Cole and Michael sat at the nearest table, Michael holding my coat, Cole holding the bag of what I assumed was the food. I was barely out the door before my two men rose and applauded. Within moments, all the patrons of the pub were out of their chairs. A few whistles in the mix accompanied the cacophonous cheering and clapping.

I'd admit to being surprised. But maybe I shouldn't have been. Of course, the whole place knew what I'd done. So, despite my heating cheeks, I curtseyed to the crowd.

Pretty soon, the patrons returned to their barstools or slid back into their booths.

"Bravo." Michael pulled me close and gave me an enthusiastic hug.

"I'm covered in gunk." I tried to push away. Pointless, as he was a strong man with an iron grip.

"No matter." He squeezed my shoulder. "I'm just glad you're okay."

"Why wouldn't I be?" I'd hardly been in any peril in the bathroom. Oh. This wasn't about a bathroom on Commercial Drive—this was a South Sudan worry. I allowed him to pull me into an embrace that felt as familiar as coming home and laid my head against his chest as Cole ruffled my hair.

"You did good, kiddo." Cole lightly caressed my temple. He glanced down at his watch. "I really hate to do this, but my call time is at four a.m., which is about six hours from now. We're doing an early dawn scene. Hoping for mist off the river, and all that shit."

God, I'd been gone that long? It felt like minutes, although it'd clearly been longer than that. "I'm sorry you can't enjoy the food with us."

"So am I. I would've loved to invite you two back to my place, but I've got to get some sleep." He ran his hands through his black hair, which was longer than the normal style. It nearly swept his shoulders and framed a face blessed by the gods, with his high cheekbones, chiseled jaw, corded neck, and deep-blue eyes. I understood why women swooned over him week after week in his role of corporate raider by day and secret vigilante by night.

He pressed a kiss to my forehead, which was easy to do as he had a few inches over my five-foot-eight-inch height. "I'm glad you're back safely."

His voice hitched—the first chink in his armor I could ever remember. It stunned me, this visible demonstration of worry. What was I supposed to make of it?

I blinked back tears. Tears that often bubbled up after an intense experience. And delivering a baby was right up there in my book. "I missed you guys too." And I had. Just not enough to come back. I'd taken ten straight tours because I feared coming back to Vancouver and seeing my best friends would have caused my resolve to falter—resolve to help and give back to a world that had been so good to me.

Cole waved to Michael. "Soon."

Michael nodded. "Definitely."

With a nod, Cole turned and headed toward the door, not looking back as he stepped out into the cold and rainy

Vancouver evening. Mid-December and the weather had taken a turn into true winter, bringing with it days and days of unrelenting rain. After the arid and hot climate of South Sudan, Vancouver was a relief. A return to what I knew and loved. Rain had never been an impediment to having a good time with my two best friends.

"Why don't we go back to my place?" Michael made the offer with a smile. "You're staying out in the valley, right? No sense driving back there tonight."

I was staying with a friend from nursing school in Mission City, about an hour out of town. Now I was crashing from the adrenaline high. The promise of a hot shower and food was like a siren's song. Deciding a trek home wasn't top on my priority list and knowing I wouldn't be missed, I linked my arm with Michael's and gave him a wide grin. "Deal."

We left the pub and headed around the corner to the side street where he'd parked his late-model electric SUV.

At my raised eyebrow, he shrugged. "It's great when I have to go out to a job site." Then he grinned. "And sometimes it's just great to have my own vehicle." His last car had been a Honda that had seen better days. That he could now afford this small luxury spoke well of how he was succeeding as a structural engineer. He held the door for me, waiting until I was secure before shutting it.

He rounded the hood and slid into the driver's seat, then, within moments, he pulled out and headed downtown where his new condo was. He turned on the seat warmers, and the hot air was on full, trying to blast away the chill of the night. The SUV still had that new-car smell and was decked out with all the latest accoutrements and a few gizmos I didn't even recognize.

In the passing streetlamps, I stole greedy glances. Whereas Cole had the tall, dark, and dangerous look, Michael was more of a hometown golden boy. He had short, blond hair and beautiful hazel eyes. Eyes that had clouded with concern when I announced I was leaving for some war-torn country on another continent. Eyes that revealed his relief and pleasure at my safe return. Eyes that were as open and honest as he was.

Michael hid nothing.

Cole hid everything.

He glanced over while we were stopped at a red light, catching me staring unabashedly. "What?" Amusement laced his voice.

"Just thinking."

"About?"

"You…Cole…Africa…" I swallowed the lump in my throat. "I'm glad to be home, you know?"

He nodded, his attention turning back to the green light. Without looking, he reached across and took my hand, then squeezed it. I wanted to admonish him about keeping two hands on the wheel, but held myself back because the contact felt so good. Michael, despite his abusive upbringing, had always been comfortable— offering physical comfort to me and Cole. And emotional support as well. Of the three, his had been the direst of circumstances, yet he'd endured and had been a source of strength and support. He'd been the one to push us into studying hard and getting good grades. His encouragement had empowered me to go to nursing school on a scholarship. That same inner determination had enabled him to get a degree in engineering and encouraged Cole to go to theater school.

Wow, we'd arrived. Michael released my hand to

depress the button on the key fob to raise the gate for the garage. As he drove slowly down to the lower level, I glimpsed quite a few automobile brand names I recognized. Cars whose cost could feed a village in Africa for a year or two. That could bring desperately needed medicine and better healthcare.

The familiar band tightened across my chest. I'd done everything in my power to help, but it never felt like enough. And now I was back in a world of privilege and comfort. I might be just couch-surfing, but I had a warm bed with unlimited hot water. Things I'd never again take for granted. Right now, bags of warm, fragrant food sat on my lap, and the smell filled the SUV, making me salivate. Unlike those I left behind, I wouldn't go hungry tonight or be unable to find clean water.

Knowing what he expected, I waited for Michael to come around and open my door. He held it open for me, relieved me of the food, and helped me alight.

I shut the door.

For someone who grew up with monsters for parents, Michael'd somehow developed a true sense of chivalry and empathy—qualities that held him in good stead over the years, as the many women in his life had proven. But there'd never been a special someone. Or at least, not as far as I knew. Maybe that'd changed while I'd been away.

I halted our journey to the elevator. "Am I intruding on some other woman's territory?"

He stopped as well, meeting my gaze head-on. "No."

I waited, but no elucidation came. Nothing to give me a clue about the current woman in his life. Or if there even was one. Well, fuck. I'd never concerned myself before about his love life as the women had always been transitory. I'd assumed if he was to become serious with a woman, he'd share that news with both Cole and me.

He gestured for me to continue, and I did. Yet I still felt unsettled. Two years was a long time to have been away. We'd exchanged lots of letters and emails when I got to a computer with the internet, but truth be told, he wasn't much of a letter writer. Cole, on the other hand, with his dramatic flourish, had been a font of information about Vancouver and the goings-on. But his letters had always left me feeling empty, as he hardly talked about his personal life.

The elevator waited, and it whisked us to the seventh floor. Michael unlocked the door to the condo and ushered me inside.

"It's not much." He held the door for me, locking it after I walked through. Then he put the food on the island in the kitchen. He removed his rain-soaked coat, and I followed suit.

As he hung them up, I waved him off, stepping into the space. "It's lovely, Michael." The main living area with its kitchen, dining room, and living room were all in one large space. Ivory crown molding accented the soft-gray walls. A series of photographs in frames caught my eye. One was a cityscape of downtown Vancouver at night with the bright lights of the city.

"I have the same view from my balcony." He gestured. "But this print captures the vitality of the city."

Huh. The downtown core and not the Downtown Eastside where we'd grown up. Two miles might have been a million—the disparity a chasm between the two worlds. I gazed at the next print of the North Shore Mountains at dusk. Pink-and-purple streaks in the sky fell across the snow-dusted peaks. The shot had obviously been taken in winter, during ski season, since the mountains were bare of covering during the summer.

"I did the Grouse Grind last summer."

I whirled to meet his sheepish gaze. "That's how many steps up?"

"Two thousand three hundred and eighty." He smiled shyly. But I caught the gleam in his eye. "About a mile and a half to get up the mountain."

"Well, that's crazy."

He shook his head. "The trek took a while, but I survived. I wanted to be able to claim to have done it, you know?"

I did know. It'd been one of the things we always talked about but never managed to find time to do.

"We'll do it together."

I snickered. "Don't kid yourself, Michael. I might be leaner than I was before, but it's not from doing cardio."

He shrugged. "We have a year to get you in shape. The Grind doesn't open until spring."

Another reminder Christmas was a mere two weeks away. Regardless, the thought of serious exercise and training left me feeling weary. I was accustomed to hard work—but not actual physical labor. "What made you decide to do it?"

"I went up when you told me you were staying for your ninth tour."

My breath caught. What an odd thing to do in reaction to my decision to stay in South Sudan working with Médecins Sans Frontiers. The Grind was a challenge, sure, but not dangerous. "Why…"

"Because I was worried about you and I needed to let off some steam. What I really wanted to do was fly to

Africa and drag you home, but I didn't figure international authorities would turn a blind eye to kidnapping, so I went up the Grind. Cole went out and got wicked drunk."

Speechless, I sought words. I was slow in responding. Like I was in a fog. "I was safe where I was, Michael. I told you that."

"In a war zone, Caressa, really? You've never seemed like a stupid woman to me. Naïve? Yes. Stupid? No."

My hackles rose. "They needed me. They still do, but I knew the time had come for me to fly home. I might go back—"

"No."

The word was said in a deceptively quiet tone, but I couldn't miss the underlying message. I held his gaze and noted the flecks of gold in his hazel eyes that glittered in the lamplight. Never had his face been set in such stone. Never had I witnessed him so unmovable. Finally, he appeared to relent, his taut stance relaxing.

"I don't think I'll survive you leaving again, Caressa. Neither will Cole."

Words again failed me. Drawing a deep breath, I sought to find my center of calm. Michael'd always been a reasonable guy. The easygoing one. The strong one. The unflappable one. "Well, my contract at St. Paul's Hospital is for a year, so you can relax. I was able to get into the emergency department, even though most of my trauma skills are rusty. I considered applying for maternity, but I would've had to go through the qualifications, and by the time I do…"

"It'd be time to contemplate going back."

Nailed it in one.

"Why don't you show me the rest of your home?"

His lips pursed, but he gave me a quick nod. "There's not much to it. Vancouver prices being what they are, and not wanting to take on a huge mortgage, I opted for a one bedroom." He beckoned me along the short hallway. The door to the bedroom was open, and I stepped in as he moved to flick on the light.

"No."

He stopped mid-movement.

The blinds were open, and the room was bathed in the city lights. The building directly across the street had many of the apartments with lights on. Some blinds were open, and I could see in, looking at people who were getting on with their lives.

"Sometimes I sit in the dark and watch." He eerily read my thoughts. "I just sit and wonder what they're doing. What's going on in their lives? What tragedies and comedies are they enduring?"

"Sounds like something Cole would do."

"Probably." Michael laughed. "But wait until you see his place. He's really moved up in the world."

I tore my gaze away from the cityscape and turned, indicating he could turn on the light. The two bedside lamps illuminated on low settings, and the room had a warm glow about it. "I can't hear the traffic noise."

"Good soundproofing. If you go out on the balcony, you get a sense of it. I like living downtown. I like the vibe of the city."

Turning, I caught the fleeting look on his face. "No, Michael, you don't. Your dream was always to find somewhere nice and quiet out in the country. As far away from the city as you could get."

His eyes flashed. "Those were childhood dreams,

Caressa, nothing more. I work in the city and, therefore, have to live in the city."

"How very practical of you." I cringed at my tone. I didn't mean to taunt him with his former dreams—but he'd always talked about getting out of the city. Sure, we were far away from our childhood apartments, but he was still enmeshed in the city life he always claimed to detest. "I'm sorry."

He shrugged. "No biggie." He stepped over to the walk-in closet and came back a moment later with a terry-towel robe. "It'll be a bit big, but you'll manage. Toss your clothes out the bathroom door, and I'll put them in the laundry."

"En suite?"

"Yep." Now he offered a wry grin. "No more laundromats for me. Ever."

I flashed to a memory of Cole pushing me in a cart around the laundromat while Michael attempted to coax us into behaving. We'd been what…ten? But the owner had a penchant for hanging out in his back office and smoking joints and of not caring who was using the machines as long as they picked up the clothes before closing time. Anything still there wound up in the dumpster at the back of the store. For that reason, and the ever-present threat of theft, the three of us had never left the clothes unattended. In later years, we brought our schoolbooks, and under Michael's steady tutelage, Cole and I studied to learn everything we needed to know to get out from under the crushing poverty.

I pointed to a door. "Bathroom?"

He nodded. "I'll wait out here for your clothes."

"Thanks, Michael." I hesitated, then moved closer. I placed my hand on his muscled forearm and leaned over, tipping my head up to press a kiss to his cheek. "For everything."

I was slipping away when he turned to face me. "Please don't go back, Caressa." His voice hitched on my name. "I think I'll go out of my mind if you do." Then he stalked over to the windows—his back to me. "I'll break."

Words escaped me yet again because I'd no notion he felt this way. In all his correspondence, he'd always told me to stay safe but never mentioned his fears for me. No mistaking the tension in his hunched shoulders.

He reached out and placed a hand on the window pane.

A gust of wind sent a lash of rain against it, matching the tumult inside me. "I'll toss my clothes out." Without another word, I fled.

Chapter Two

Michael

I hadn't meant to be so blunt. In psyching myself up for her return, I'd planned on sweet-talking her into staying. She had the new job at the hospital starting in a few days. I figured I'd bide my time and wait until she saw Vancouver needed her as much as some far-away country in Africa. She'd chosen St. Paul's, after all. That hospital served the elite of the downtown core, as well as the downtrodden from our old neighborhood. Overdoses, stabbings, and shootings were commonplace. As were the sick and desperate. Canada might have universal healthcare, but many people didn't see a doctor until they were truly ill and in need of urgent intervention. She could help those people.

And she could stay safe in the city. Cole and I could watch over her and make sure she took care of herself. She had a nasty habit of working lots of overtime to cover for others. Had once wound up with pneumonia after pushing so hard. She'd argued the illness was caused by a virus, but I knew in my heart she wouldn't have wound up so ill if she'd had reserves. She had a habit of pushing herself as if she had something to prove. And she was thinner than she'd been five years ago. True, the food in Africa wasn't as bountiful and plentiful as here, but I planned to help her put back on some of the weight she'd lost.

As I was closing the blinds, the bathroom door opened. Moment later, a thud resounded as her clothes landed on the floor. I scooped them up and headed to the laundry closet.

Once the machine was turned on, I headed for the kitchen to heat up our food. Caressa didn't dally in the shower. As a practical person, she washed her hair and her body, then got out and dried herself. Even with her long hair, she rarely took more than a few minutes. That was another thing I'd noticed—her hair. It'd barely brushed her shoulders when she left, and now the braid was almost to the small of her back, indicating she probably hadn't gotten it cut. Typical Caressa. Pull it up in an elastic and ignore it.

When the microwave beeped, I pulled out one plate of ribs and wings and put in the other, then set the timer. I retrieved the cut carrots and celery from the second container and put them on a plate, along with a good dollop of dressing. God, she loved salad dressing. The creamier the better. As creamy as her skin. Cole used to tease because she had virtually translucent skin that required great care to protect it from the damaging effects of the sun. I'd wondered if she'd be tanned or at least have some color when she came back, but she had the same pale skin she'd always had. Perhaps the girl had remembered to use the sunscreen I'd sent in her care packages. Sure, she'd probably rolled her eyes, but I was now glad I'd done it.

Woman, not girl. Caressa was a woman of thirty-two. If I felt big-brother tendencies toward her, that was my problem. Technically, she was three months older, Cole a month younger than that, but I'd always been the responsible one—the one who'd grown old before his time.

"Michael?"

Caught unaware, I turned toward her voice. She'd rolled up the sleeves because the robe swamped her, but that wasn't what drew my attention. She was towel-drying her hair, and the robe dipped dangerously open. I spotted the swell of her right breast, and instead of averting my gaze, I let it linger. A light dusting of freckles covered her collarbone—angling down toward her sternum and spreading out from there. Would they go all the way to the nipple? And how would her skin taste as I licked a journey from neck to shoulder and then down to her breast? Would her breath hitch? Would she run her hands through my hair and writhe in ecstasy, or would she duck her head—trying to protect her modesty?

"Michael?"

I startled and met her gaze.

She looked…confused. Pointing behind me, she said, "Microwave. I'm hungry."

"Helping deliver a baby will do that, I'm sure." I cringed inwardly, hoping I'd managed to save the situation.

She smiled. Phew. Maybe she'd see my wandering gaze as the aberration it was. Because this was Caressa. My best friend Caressa. Having lascivious thoughts about her was completely inappropriate.

She sat at the breakfast bar as I put a plate before her.

"Let me know if it's hot enough."

"I'm sure it'll be fine." She took the first bite, and her eyes closed in bliss. "I've missed these ribs. No one makes them better."

Since she was right, I didn't bother to reply. Instead, I sat next to her and dug in as well.

We consumed the meal in silence, and Caressa didn't glance over at me until reaching for a wet napkin. "We left my car on the street."

"Overnight parking," I assured her. "We have to move it by nine."

She glanced over at the microwave. "Michael, that's barely eight hours from now."

"Your point?"

"I'm tired, but I'm also wired."

"You still need eight hours' sleep to function?"

"And then some."

I smiled. Her nature was to work hard and then crash even harder, and she'd taken some ribbing over the years for falling asleep in unusual places. Like the time we'd skied on Grouse Mountain with rented skis. She'd easily beaten Cole and me in just about every run, and then she'd fallen asleep in the gondola on the way back down the mountain. She'd been so exhausted Cole carried her to the car, and she'd only roused when we got back to the city.

After wiping my hands on a napkin, I rose and took the plates to the sink. I put the bones in the compost and the plates in the dishwasher. I turned back, then rested my hip on the counter. "So what do you want to do? We can watch television. I have a few newer movies on my recorder. You can watch until you fall asleep." I indicated the bedroom where I had a second television. I rarely used it except to watch the news while getting dressed in the morning and just before bed. Yeah, I knew I wasn't supposed to watch television in bed, but I had little else going on in that room.

She stared at me—again, with confusion in her expression.

"Do I have sauce on my face?" I tried for a light, joking tone, but no doubt my attempt fell flat.

Opening her mouth, she began to speak, then closed her mouth. She again opened it, again hesitated.

I closed the distance and took her hands in mine. "What is it? You look upset. Is it something I've said?"

She pulled her lower lip through her teeth, leaving little indentations. "I…I think I'm crashing, that's all."

"So we'll put you to bed." Without hesitation, I tugged her off the barstool and into my arms.

She let out a startled gasp and twined her arms around my neck. "I can walk, you know."

"I know. But let me do this for you, okay?" She was a lightweight, and I required only a few strides to reach the bedroom.

"I need to brush my hair."

I laid her on the bed before going to my dresser and pulling out a T-shirt that swamped me. "You put this on while I turn off the lights in the living room. When I get back, I'll brush out your hair."

And since her beautiful curls were already fighting with gravity, I recognized the challenge. As a child, she'd always cursed her curls, often hacking her hair off because her drug-addicted mother rarely had funds for things like visits to the hairdresser. By the time she got to college, she'd begun to embrace those luscious locks and would spend extra attention on them if she was going on a date. Of course, any guy who wanted to date her had to go through Cole and me first. Since that fact was well-known at the high school, fewer guys made moves on her than might've otherwise.

I left the room and made a quick round of the condo, which admittedly took little time at all. I'd only turned on a couple of lights when we came in, so turning them off was no big deal. I knocked on the bedroom door, then heard her muffled invitation to come in.

She sat cross-legged on the bed, the T-shirt overwhelming her slight frame, as predicted. Holding the brush out to me, she shifted so I could sit behind her. "I can do this myself—"

"Shush. I know you can. You can do anything you put your mind to. But I see you're tired, so let me do this, okay?" When she nodded, I grabbed a fistful of hair and began to work out the tangles.

We'd done this a few times over the years, and she'd always been clear that brute force was required. Although I rarely went that far, I couldn't be gentle either. Not unless we wanted to be here all night. Her hair was still a little damp but silken in my hands. I longed to bury my nose and inhale, but that probably wouldn't go over well. Instead, I consigned myself to the torture of touching without tasting. Soothing rather than rousing. Just the thought of what I wanted to do had me growing hard. We'd created an intimacy, but I wanted more. I wanted to bury myself in her and let oblivion reign.

Fucking hell. Unacceptable. Would only lead to a world of hurt. I steeled himself and applied effort to the task. As the last of the knots gave way, I stroked from root to tip.

She moaned.

"Good?"

"Glorious. It's been a long time—"

"Long time?"

Her shoulders hunched.

The tension built within her. Where'd this come from? I was about to offer a shoulder rub when she finally answered.

"Since someone has touched me."

Touched her? Like a hug in a friendship kind of way or like an embrace in a lover's arms? Fearing I'd regret it yet knowing I needed information, I probed for answers. "How long?"

She shrugged, keeping her back to me. "A guy on the logistics team—but it never amounted to anything. Before that…" She appeared to consider. "That doctor at the free clinic where I used to volunteer."

I stiffened at the casual reference to the *married* doctor who'd coaxed Caressa into a relationship before telling her he had a wife and two kids. What she didn't know was Cole and I had taken the doctor aside one day and had a little *chat* with the man. I doubted the man's dick was ever going anywhere other than his own fist or his wife's vagina again.

I didn't miss the somewhat wistful tone in her voice. As always, I was completely in tune with her emotions. That bond existed between the three of us—had almost from our first meeting. Three lost souls.

"You'll meet someone, Caressa, if that's what you want. All the single guys at the hospital will be knocking each other over to get to you."

My proclamation was met with resounding silence. Her shoulders were still rounded—her body still radiating tension. Again, I fought the compulsion to reach out and rub those tense muscles. I'd done it more than a few times over the years when she came home from a tough shift at the hospital, all the while carrying the weight of the world on her shoulders. She took her work personally and felt the losses as acutely as she rejoiced in the victories. Lives lost, lives saved. She felt all of it. That made her damn good at her job—and was also her greatest liability in a career that required objectivity.

"I'm tired, Michael. I think I've been tired for a long time."

"So we'll tuck you into bed." I moved to pull down the covers with the thought of coaxing her under them.

Finally, she turned to me, and her pale face in the low light looked fragile. Like a breath of wind could knock her over.

"Where are you going to sleep?" Her brow wrinkled as she looked from me to the bed.

"The couch." Wasn't this the most obvious thing in the world? Of course she'd get the bed. It'd probably been a long time since she slept on a top-of-the-line mattress like mine.

"Michael, I can't take your bed. You'll never be comfortable on the couch. You're too big."

"Been a while since a woman accused me of that." I said it with a grin. Clearly, she hadn't gotten the joke. She must really be tired, because she could be as bawdy as Cole and me when it came down to it.

"Sleep with me, Michael, like we used to."

Her coaxing was barely comprehensible through her slurred voice.

An hour ago, it would've been a no-brainer. How many nights had the three of us cuddled in my bed, unbeknownst to my parents? Caressa's mother was usually passed out from drugs, and Cole's dad was working the night shift at the docks, leaving his son to his own devices. We three hated to be alone, so we'd gather in my bedroom—an easy trip up the fire escape and my parents had never been the wiser. Of course, by the time I let Cole and Caressa in, I was usually sporting several bruises under my clothes. From both parents. They'd believed in equality when it came to beatings, and when they finished, they'd send me to my room and then hit the liquor cabinet. Usually, I heard nothing of them until morning.

Now, though, in the early hours of this morning, sleeping with Caressa felt hazardous. I didn't answer as I was caught between desire and practicality.

She turned her head to meet my gaze. "Throw on a pair of pajama bottoms and get under the covers with me. You can talk to me until I fall asleep."

When she put it like that, it sounded quite reasonable. I could do this. I was a grown man whose hormones were well and truly under control. Okay, a long time had passed since I was with a woman, and yes, I hadn't shared a bed with Caressa in twice as long, but all I needed to do was strip and get into bed with her. Once she was asleep, I'd sneak back into the living room and crash on the too-short couch.

As if sensing my desire for modesty, she turned her back and crawled under the blankets. But the T-shirt rode up her thighs, and I almost swallowed my tongue. Yep, no underwear. I hadn't noticed them when I tossed everything into the washing machine. Should I have washed them separately on a delicate cycle? Nah, she'd have said something, and in my gut, I figured she wore serviceable cotton briefs.

Cursing under my breath, I unbuttoned and removed my dress shirt, shucked my shoes, yanked off my socks, and pulled down my jeans and briefs. From the dresser,

I retrieved a pair of pajama pants and yanked them on before heading to the bed.

I banked my raging desire and gave my stiffening cock a quick lecture before I got under the covers. After turning off the light, I lay on my back and pulled the blankets over my tenting erection and up to my chest. A long moment passed before Caressa rolled over on her back, bringing her arm to rest against mine—her thigh touching mine. At length, she threw an arm over her eyes and sighed. Even in the dark, a little light filtered in through the blinds.

"What is it?"

Another long moment and another heartfelt sigh. "Images. That's all. Just images. I can't get them out of my head."

"Do you... Would talking about it help?" Powerlessness swamped me because I heard the pain lacing her voice.

"I appreciate the offer, Michael, I really do, but not tonight. I guess..."

Wait for her to come to you.

"The birth tonight reminded me of all the ones that went wrong."

I knew the statistics—had read up on them before she'd headed to Africa. I'd almost tried to use them to talk her out of going, but quickly realized it would've been a fool's errand and I might've pushed her further away. "But there *were* saves, Caressa. Times when you made a difference. Times your intervention helped save a life."

"Not save." Caution laced her tone. "Assisted in the save. I was more focused on prevention of illness and disease. Healthy pregnant mothers are more likely to have healthy births. But in the end, it all felt like a crapshoot."

And she'd been in that game for five years.

I reached out and pulled her toward me.

She rolled on her side and pressed flush against me, tucking her head against my shoulder and resting her hand on my chest as if it were the most natural thing in the world.

And since I'd managed to put a leash on my libido, it felt right. Caressa in my arms felt right. So I'd hold her all night and try to help her keep the demons at bay—if that was what she needed.

The silence stretched. Had she slipped into sleep? Nope, those were tears wetting my chest. I pulled her closer and pressed a kiss to the crown of her head.

"I was reminded of Thana. Seventeen years old and pregnant with her third child. She was so tiny it was hard to believe she'd successfully carried two other children to term, although the babies had been small."

"Seventeen? Really?" A stupid question to ask, but I wanted to make sure I understood the story she was telling. Here, safe in this room and away from poverty, it felt surreal. I buried my nose in her hair, fragrant from my shampoo, far from her normal floral-scented product, yet it still teased me with tantalizing possibilities.

Fucking pay attention—especially since she's oblivious to your internal war.

"She walked three days to get to us. She knew something was wrong. I don't know how, but she sensed it. A quick physical exam showed me she had dangerously high blood pressure. Fearing eclampsia, I wanted to induce and get the baby out as soon as possible. I'd barely made the suggestion to the doctor before Thana went into convulsions." A shudder wracked Caressa's body.

I tightened my grip, silently willing her to purge herself of some of the grief.

"We managed to induce labor, and it went as well as could be expected. The baby was underweight, but he rallied, and everything seemed like it would be okay." She let out a short breath. "Two days after the birth, Thana's kidneys failed. She was dead three days later."

I'd foreseen this sad outcome, given Caressa's distress, but my heart still hurt. Three children left motherless in a country ill-equipped to care for them. What chance did they have? Living under crushing poverty and so close to a war zone?

Apparently, she wasn't finished.

"Two days after that, the baby contracted what we figured was malaria. You do your best to keep the mosquitoes away, but there's only so much that can be done. He had no immune system, so he was gone within a few days." She sighed. "No one came to claim either of them. I don't even know how word got back to her husband or what happened to her two other children. I'd like to think everything worked out, but I know it probably didn't. I suspect Thana's death spelled the end of her entire family."

Since I knew nothing of social support networks for children left without mothers in third-world countries, I let the silence spin out. With all my heart, I hoped she'd pull from my strength and come back to me—away from those horrific memories.

"I shouldn't have said anything."

"No." *Make her see.* "You can tell me anything, Caressa, and I'll listen. I just...I don't know how to comfort you. How to help you obliterate those images."

Well, I can think of one way.

Oh, asshole, that's so wrong.

Maybe I'm the one who needs life-affirming passion.

Never going to happen.

But slowly, her shaking eased, and the tears dried.

After a few minutes and a few snuffles, I was grateful that the crisis seemed to have passed.

"Michael?"

"Yes?"

"Why are you alone?"

Where the fuck did that come from? "Cole's single as well, you know. And I'm not alone. I have friends and work colleagues. You and Cole."

"But you're thirty-two." She turned her head, resting her pointy chin on my sternum. "Aren't you thinking about settling down? Starting a family?"

"I don't know if I'd be any good at a family, Caressa, given my upbringing."

She pushed away and propped herself up on her elbow. She poked my ribs. Hard. "What kind of shit is that?"

"Shit?"

"You'll make an amazing husband and father, Michael. No bullshit. You're the most compassionate and caring person I know. You're a nurturer who's meant to share that gift with someone special. Are all the women in this city blind?" Exasperation tinged her voice.

Despite everything, I smiled, rolling my eyes at the same time. Although uncomfortable, I preferred this topic.

"Don't roll your eyes." She sounded cross.

"It's practically dark in here." Only a bit of light filtered through the blinds. Light pollution, they called it. That perpetual pink glow the city had all night long. Since I'd only ever lived in the city, it didn't bother me. The three of us had gone camping the summer between high school and university, and we all found the profound darkness on a moonless night downright unnerving.

"Fine, don't say anything," she taunted. "I know you rolled them. I know everything about you."

No doubt. I believed no secrets existed between the three of us. Too much crap in our lives to bring anything but absolute trust to our relationship. "You do know, Caressa—nothing's changed since you went away. I'm still the same guy."

"But you're not."

Huh? "What do you mean?"

"I don't know how to put it into words. You seem more mature. More settled."

"Spending five years worrying about one's best friend has a way of aging one."

She stilled. "Was it really that bad?"

Downplay it or be honest? "Caressa, every day was excruciating. I waited with bated breath for each letter, each phone call, each email. Cole and I'd message back and forth daily, asking if you'd made contact. I haunted the internet, looking for stories, and watched the news every night."

"I was safe—"

"Not to me." *Damn my wavering voice.* "Not to me. You weren't with me, Caressa, and I couldn't keep you safe. If something happened to you, it would've broken me." The words echoed what I'd said an hour ago. But she needed to understand their importance.

I sensed her moving even before she pressed her hand against my cheek.

She stroked it gently, a soothing motion.

When she reached across my chest and her breasts pushed against my side, all rational thought headed for the exit. Before it hit the door, however, I dragged it back. I cupped her hand, pressed a kiss to her palm, and reluctantly pulled it away from my face, suppressing the sigh of regret the loss of contact created.

She did sigh. "Can't we go back to the way things were? I'm home now. I'm safe now…"

I didn't want things to go back to the way they'd been. Because what had been surging protectiveness was now surging need. It thrummed through my body, and my cock hardened. "Just go to sleep, okay?"

Her sharp intake of breath was likely the result of my brusque tone.

"Sorry. I know I have to move on." *Lame. Truly lame.*

"What's really going on, Michael? Something tells me this isn't the only issue."

All or nothing.

"I love you, Caressa."

"I love you too." Her response came quickly. "I always have. You and Cole mean everything to me. You're my family—"

"No. I mean I *love* you." *God, have I just made the biggest mistake of my life?* I hadn't meant to be so blunt, but now that I recognized my feelings, I had to admit them to her. *Let the chips fall where they may.*

The stillness was oppressive. *Why can't there be traffic noise? Like when we were kids.* Waiting for her response was almost as tough as waiting for her the past five years.

She cleared her throat. "When…"

"Always. But when did I realize it? Genuinely see that I want more than your friendship? Just now." I sat up. "I've screwed this up. Let me crash on the couch, and maybe in the morning this'll all seem like a bad dream."

"Ha." The word came out on a laugh. "Fuck you. You can't drop a bombshell like that and then sneak away with your tail between your legs, Michael. You have to give me a minute."

I would, of course—for whatever that was worth. *I don't see what difference it'll make.*

Chapter Three

Caressa

Stunned.
Beyond stunned.
Shaken to my core? Blown away? Irrevocably changed?

Michael'd just professed his love for me. His *love* for me. Yet somehow, along with the surprise came the feeling of rightness. As if a missing piece finally clicked into place. I loved Michael. Of course I did. Loved him since I was five and he'd snuck me into his bedroom because my mother'd disappeared on one of her drug-fueled benders. I'd been alone for two days and was hungry. He'd talked to me after school and encouraged me to come home with him where he raided his kitchen, offering me cheese, crackers, and sliced ham. I'd devoured the meal with zeal and desperation. He hadn't tried to talk me into going to the cops because he understood I'd been raised to fear authorities. Plus, my mother'd come back. My mother always came back. Soon after, Cole had joined our group, and a burgeoning friendship became a three-way of sorts.

Cole.
How would he react if things changed between Michael and me? Because despite the warning bells going off in my head, this felt right. Hadn't I thought

about Michael every day I'd been away? Missed him terribly? Was that love? For that matter, what did I know about love—true romantic love? Just because I'd never been in love didn't mean I wasn't capable of feeling it. And I was attracted to Michael. He was a hunk. But that wasn't why I wanted him. He was kind and gentle and the best friend a girl could ever ask for. And what was the worst that could happen? We'd bomb in bed, and then we'd move on with our lives, knowing we'd made a mistake.

So how to begin? I knew how to have sex. I just didn't know how to have sex with *Michael*. And since I hadn't really responded to his proclamation, this was up to me. My hand rested on his sternum, warm to my touch despite the chill in the air. Leaning over, I pressed a kiss to his chest.

He had a light smattering of chest hair as opposed to a pelt. It turned golden blond in the summer. Was it darker now? As I ran my hand across his chest, his muscles rippled. He had a runner's body, all lean and tight. He kept himself in shape, and he didn't have an ounce of fat. I pressed another kiss, this one to his nipple. It pebbled, and he sucked in a breath.

His skin was softer than I might've imagined. In my experience, men's skin was tougher, less supple to the touch. Placing a kiss to his stomach, I breathed in his scent. Soap and something less tangible, less easily explained. His breathing hitched, encouraging me to trail my hand lower across his taut abdomen and even lower still. Unerringly, I grasped his cock—pleased to find him as hard as a rock. Suddenly, desire swept through me, and my libido, long dead, kicked into high gear.

Lightning fast, he removed my hand from his

erection and flipped me so I was flat on my back and he lay over me. One thigh insinuated between mine. He was hard against my hip.

"A kiss first, I think." His voice was deeper than I'd ever heard. "If you're sure."

God, he's such a good man. "I am, Michael."

"And you understand that you can stop this at any time, right? *No* stops everything."

His fervor and adamancy caught me off guard. Of course I understood that—he and Cole had drilled it into me when I went on my first date. I hadn't had sex until four years later when I was nineteen, but I'd always understood the rules. "I understand."

He relaxed just a fraction, then his weight shifted.

"What are you…"

"Condom."

At least one of us is thinking clearly. I heard the tear of foil, and the bed shifted as he rolled it on, but where I expected him to press himself between my thighs, he swept in for a kiss. No tentativeness to this. And I opened to the invasion. His tongue stroked me, coaxed me, encouraged me, but the demand was almost violent. Heat and lust like I'd never have known to anticipate overwhelmed me. He was singeing me from the tips of my toes to the roots of my hair. I was more turned on than I'd ever been.

He caressed my body, tugging the T-shirt up, clearly impatient with the impediment.

I gave him a quick shove, and as soon as he shifted, I sat up just enough to yank up the offending garment and throw it over the side. At some point Michael'd shucked his pajama pants, and now, as he came over me, skin met skin.

His mouth slanted over mine again, this time in a carnal mating dance. He slid his hand along my throat, across my collarbone, and then to my breast.

I'd believed I was prepared, but that'd been a lie. His touch was electric, shooting desire through to my core. My nipple pebbled, much as his had under my ministrations. He was gentle yet demanding, not grabbing, but securing my breast firmly in his grasp. When his mouth left mine, I knew what was coming, so I arched my neck, giving him the long column of my throat. He took full advantage, nipping along my jawline, down to my pulse point where he sucked none too gently. Not enough to leave a hickey, but enough to get my full attention. Next was the hollow at the base of my throat.

He was fervent in his attentions as he latched on to my right nipple. Funny, I'd always thought of him as the relaxed one. The odd times my mind wandered that way, I had assumed he'd be a gentle lover. But he was showing me that he could also be a passionate one. And when he ran his hands down the seam of my thighs, I opened instinctively. His hand insinuated itself between them. He parted my labia as if we had all the time in the world while I was desperate for him to get to my clit. I angled my hips to make the tiny bundle of nerves more available to him, but he only rumbled a chuckle as he moved his wonderful mouth to my left breast, giving it the same attention as the right.

Desire pooled as yearning ratcheted to a fever pitch. My nipples were sensitive from his sucking and biting, and I groaned in frustration. I verged on giving up when he did as I wanted and brushed my clit. But he didn't linger, and the light touch wasn't nearly enough.

"Please, Michael."

"Please what, Caressa? What is it you want?"

He was going to make me say it? *Sadistic bastard.* "I want you. I want you in me now. I want you to fuck me senseless."

Again, he chuckled. "There's nothing I want more, but I don't think you're ready."

"If I were any more ready, I'd explode." *Why is he doing this to me?*

"Patience, sweetheart. You've waited this long. I'm sure you can hold out a little bit longer."

I was in no way convinced of this, but I acquiesced because he had the equipment, and short of rubbing one out myself, which would probably be quite rude, this was his game. And evidently, we were going at his pace.

Busy with my inner monologue, I nearly missed his shift, and suddenly, he was between my spread thighs. My first instinct was to clamp them shut. No one went down on me. *No one.* One of my nonnegotiable rules— one of very few. His actions were way too personal, and anyway, most guys were relieved when I spared them the task. One had grumbled, but I'd cut him off by giving him a mind-blowing blow job. I liked giving head because it gave me a modicum of control in a situation that so often lacked any. Sex was messy. Sex was dirty. Sex was something I enjoyed but was just as happy to go without for years on end, not particularly noticing.

But Michael's mouth settled on me. Nudging my pussy lips apart. *Will I ever see sex the same way again?* He was thoroughly examining me with his tongue, lapping up the juices escaping my pussy. Again, I expected embarrassment, but when he nipped my clit, I nearly bucked off the bed. His hands were firm on my ass, and his shoulders had my thighs securely apart. He had a talented tongue, for sure. *Why have I refused this before now?* Honesty required me to admit that beyond the embarrassment, the act also required intimacy. He was releasing all kinds of desires within me. And that scared the shit out of me.

Then he nipped my clit again, and I cried out. My legs stiffened, and I tried to stretch them, but his grasp was too strong. Grateful for the soundproofing, I came hard and fast, the orgasm ripping through me. Instead of letting me go, however, he kept up his ministrations, milking each spasm like a thirsty man who'd just discovered a creek of cold water.

Had it ever felt like this before? That question barely crossed my mind before he moved up and settled between my thighs. In one thrust, he was inside me. My pussy, not having been used for quite some time, felt stretched and overfull. The discomfort was transitory, and soon need built within me again.

His chest rubbed against my sensitive nipples as he set a demanding rhythm. I'd only felt him through his pajama pants, and although I'd recognized he was hard, I hadn't registered his size. I'd never bought the adage that size mattered. Now, however, as he ground his pelvis against my clit with every thrust, I rethought that as well. He was large and thick and stretched me, forcing my muscles to accommodate him without giving me time to get my bearings. Soon, however, I was building back up to the summit of some foreign peak. I'd never been able to come again so quickly, but his body was demanding it of me.

"Come, Caressa." He commanded it through gritted teeth, obviously reading my body and mind perfectly.

I'd never had someone demand this of me, but his

words were enough to push me over the edge again into a violent orgasm that had me bucking against him, seeking more friction, more pleasure.

After just a few more thrusts, he held himself still for a long moment before relaxing his arms.

Thank God. Although he all but collapsed on me, I held him close, our perspiration-slicked bodies sharing heat. We smelled of sex, and instead of being turned off, I was intoxicated. I fingered his sweat-dampened hair.

"I'm crushing you."

I tried to let out a little laugh, but my lungs were still drawing in air after the mind-blowing climax. "It's all good."

"Just good?" A teasing tone.

"Well, *fucking rocked* would be a better descriptor, but I was trying to be polite." A joke, of course. The three of us had discovered crudity early on and often shared it in private. But when we were with others, we avoided any vulgarity.

"I have to get rid of the condom."

As he rolled off me, I managed a chuckle. "Always practical."

Before he did the complete roll, however, he leaned down and placed a hard kiss to my lips. "Fucking awesome for me as well."

He was gone, but the city lights illuminated him in the shadows. He went to the bathroom, and I turned away from the glare when he flipped the light switch. The water ran, and soon he was back with a warm washcloth. He washed my thighs and my mons, and what should've been soothing was again kicking my libido into gear. The cotton abraded my sex, and my body began making demands. A third time? Really? I couldn't ever remember having two orgasms back to back, let alone contemplating a third.

But the towel was gone, and he crawled under the covers, nudging me so I turned on my side away from him. We were going to spoon, of course, but this felt alien to me as well because it involved an intimacy I rarely shared. Most of the time, I went to the guy's place or a hotel and left soon after the deed was done. Yeah, usually, the guys wanted to get out of there and to avoid cuddling—but I'd taken on the persona of someone who wasn't looking for long-term attachments. *Except with Franklin, and look how that turned out.*

In truth, I was a bad bet. I was the daughter of a drug addict who'd overdosed mere days after her daughter graduated from high school. Had her death been suicide rather than accidental? My mother hadn't ever seemed to care about me, and her death had been just another callous reality I dealt with. Understanding genetics and predisposition to addiction, I avoided attachments because I wasn't worth the effort. Yet in the span of time it took Michael to make love to me, my whole way of thinking had changed. *Maybe I am worth the effort.*

"What is it, Caressa?"

"Nothing." *Don't go there.*

He threaded his hand beneath my arm and secured it under the shelf of my breasts. He pressed a kiss to my shoulder and cuddled us farther under the blanket. "We'll talk in the morning, okay?"

"Yeah, okay." I didn't really want to talk in the morning, because it might spoil what had been an amazing night. He might regret his impetuous declaration of love, and I might regret having let him get so close. But hadn't he already been that close? There had never been any air between the three of us, but that was about to change. We'd have to tell Cole, of course, but I wanted to wait at least a day or two before we made that overture. First, I needed to come to terms with the fact my best friend was now my best lover.

Nothing's ever going to be the same again.

Chapter Four

Cole

"Good morning."
I held back the biting remark.
But barely.
Last night's late adventure with Caressa and Michael—coupled with very little sleep—meant this morning I was running on adrenaline and caffeine.
Not a good combination.
"Good morning, Seamus."
If anyone could put me in a good mood, it'd be this young man. Okay, young was relative. But he was half-a-dozen years younger than myself, and most days I felt like a much-older brother to him. His work as a production assistant on *Vigilante Justice* was superb, and his unending enthusiasm and kindness warmed even the coldest of hearts. Oh, and his charming Newfie accent that pushed through occasionally. His red hair wasn't shining this early in the morning, but once the sun came out, it'd be brilliant.
"Kelci's waiting for you in makeup. I think she said minimal today as you're supposed to look exhausted. After a night of fighting bad guys," he added.
What he tactfully didn't say was I already looked like shit, so the makeup artist's job would be easy this morning.

I patted Seamus on the back and headed to the tent. Kelci stood inside near the heater.

"I thought you were a prairie girl. Hearty in winter."

"Fuck off, Hamilton." The robust woman pointed to the chair.

Obediently, I plopped down on my ass.

"Saskatchewan thirty years ago doesn't make me a prairie girl. I've been Vancouver ensconced for all this time, and I don't like cold. I don't mind damp and rainy, but cold and snowy? No thanks—that's what the mountains are for."

"Grouse's got a good snowpack."

"You planning on skiing anytime soon?"

"My contract's pretty clear—no dangerous activities." Didn't mean as soon as we wrapped that I wouldn't be heading up. Maybe I could convince Caressa to come. And Michael, of course. We needed time to bond again. Five years was a fucking long time.

As Kelci smoothed the foundation, my heart constricted again. Caressa was home. She was really home. I'd despaired of that ever happening, and yet it had.

The key was convincing her to stay. Crashing with Kendall in Mission City was impractical—she couldn't work an exhausting twelve-hour shift and then make the hour-long drive. More if traffic was heavy. No, she needed a place in town.

Why not with me?

Something I'd considered and dismissed, but now the idea swirled in my mind.

Michael's place was too small. Too cozy. My house? Five bedrooms, seven bathrooms, open living space, a den, a media room, and a workout room. She

41

could have all the space she needed. And I used a meal preparation service, so she wouldn't need to worry about cooking. Basically, I could take complete care of her.

Her contract with St. Paul's was for a year. The key would be making her see the city needed her. And it did. Nurses were in high demand. As were all healthcare workers. I wanted to coax her into a nice plush high-end clinic where she'd be safe, but that'd never fly. If she wasn't helping out the downtrodden, she wasn't happy.

An icy hand pressed to mine, and I glanced over.

Elouise Hynes bestowed her trademark beautiful smile upon me. Her expressive gray eyes sparkled. "You were a million miles away."

The actress, like Seamus, came from the Rock. But where his accent still broke through, hers had been carefully eliminated. She'd wanted Hollywood to take her seriously. And they had. She refused to talk about it, but the film that debuted earlier this month had Oscar buzz, for the production, the director, and herself.

I respected her desire not to jinx things. I never talked about being nominated for a Golden Globe twice for the role of Justice. Probably because I hadn't won either time. And I was nominated again this year. Maybe I could convince Caressa to come with me to the awards show. Maybe she'd let me pamper her in the luxury she deserved.

"You're far away this morning."

"Huh?"

Elouise tapped my nose. "You've got that dreamy look on your face."

"Dreamy?" I sputtered the question.

"Like I get when I think about Kelci."

Her girlfriend snorted.

Elouise feigned hurt. "But I love my sweetie kins."

If I hadn't known she was joking, I might've gagged.

"Sit your ass down so I can do your makeup as well." Kelci pointed. "At least I'm making you look pretty." She indicated to me. "He's supposed to look like shit."

Elouise cocked her head. "Well, you've done a superb job. Although you always do."

"I've hardly done anything." Kelci shrugged. "He came in looking haggard. I'm just playing it up."

"Long night?" Elouise winked.

Damn.

I didn't have a reputation as a ladies' man. Or of a man's man. I was intensely private and, for obvious reasons, kept my own counsel. Kelci might be worldly, but I sensed a fragility in Elouise sometimes.

Hence keeping my kinky proclivities to myself.

"Saw an old friend who's been out of town for a long time. And things got interesting."

Elouise perked up, and even Kelci cut me a glance as she coated foundation on her girlfriend's flawless skin.

I grinned. "She's a nurse and been working overseas—in refugee camps mostly. Anyway, a bar patron went into labor last night, and before we knew it, Caressa delivered the baby."

"How exciting." Elouise clapped. "A real-life hero."

As opposed to the one I played on television. She didn't mean it cruelly, but the comment felt like a jab. I only pretended to be a good person. Caressa was one. And yet she'd wanted none of the praise. None of the accolades.

Kelci adjusted her cap. Her normal bald pate was covered in deference to the cold. "That's quite a story. You should share that with the writers. Maybe Lyric could do something heroic like that."

"Or Montgomery could," Elouise pointed out. "I think that'd be even more interesting."

Montgomery was my character. Corporate raider by day and the superhero Justice by night. Lyric was my nemesis.

"Well, Julie'd be up for it. She'd be up for anything." I said the words with surety. My co-star was a pint-sized dynamo who'd take on the world if it meant saving it. She was the complete opposite of Lyric—and yet also another side to the same coin. She'd never admit it, but she shared some of Lyric's qualities as well. Dogged determination being the main one. "And she's tucked into her bed this morning." Assumedly alone, but I couldn't be sure. She'd been cagey recently about her love life. The gossip rags always tried to make it out like we were a couple. We weren't.

Because you love Caressa.

My chest constricted. Yeah, because I loved my best friend. The best friend who'd never love me back the same way.

Seamus poked his head in. "The sun's about to crest the horizon. You two ready?"

Elouise, playing Mirela, my trusty executive assistant, was going to confront me about my profligate lifestyle. She believed my nocturnal adventures were carnal in nature—but she was starting to question that. In this moment of desperation, after having gone toe to toe with Lyric the night before, I was on the verge of revealing everything.

But she had a secret of her own she was about to reveal—something that would irrevocably change our relationship. Something I'd never seen coming.

This morning's shoot was down by the docks of Vancouver's shipping terminal. A place of eternal movement. A place of ever-shifting elements. A place where things could change in an instant.

A place I truly loathed.

But I'd never speak up. Lisette, the director, and her production crew. They didn't know about my complicated relationship with this place. My father'd worked as a longshoreman for thirty years until he died. And he'd been neglectful, sometimes abusive, and a general asshole. I was grateful he hadn't turned me over to social services when my mother walked out, but I also was resentful of the way he raised me.

Hell, I didn't even consider him family. Caressa and Michael'd been all I needed growing up. Caressa the fierce defender—daughter of a drug addict. Michael the nurturer—son of horrifically abusive parents. I'd been a hanger-on. Even after all these years, I still felt I had something to prove. That my father'd been wrong. That I wasn't a worthless excuse for a human being. I'd left home the day we graduated from high school, and I'd done just fine on my own. My father, on the other hand, had died a bitter old man, felled by the cigarettes he smoked and the alcohol he drank all his life.

Elouise snagged my hand as we walked over to the makeshift set. The extras milled around in their hard hats, plaid jackets, worn blue jeans, and steel-toed boots. God, they reminded me so much of my childhood.

Maybe I should've spoken up when I saw the location. Except I'd never do that. I wasn't a prima donna who made demands. Julie and I might star in the show, but we worked hard to ensure we were just two of the gang. That being said, people treated us differently. With a deference that made me uncomfortable. I hadn't become an actor for the fame, fortune, and glory. I did it for the love of the craft. The set and stage were where I felt most like myself. While portraying someone else.

"I want to meet your girlfriend."

"She's not my girlfriend."

Elouise arched an eyebrow at my quick denial.

"Friends. Really good friends, but just friends."

"If you say so."

She gave me the enigmatic smile that audiences swooned over. I knew that beatific expression did it for Kelci as well. The two had met back in April but had only recently come out as an official couple.

Elouise and I took our positions after Lisette explained what she wanted from the scene.

As the sun crested the horizon on this cold December day, I listened as Montgomery Daley to Elouise, Mirela Stork, explain how she knew my true identity. How she was going to leak it to the media if I didn't give in to her blackmail demands.

My character was, of course, stunned. This woman, who'd been in my employ mere weeks, had ferreted out my identity. And although I knew my lines, sinking into the panic proved easy. Flashing to the perpetual panic for the past five years that Caressa'd been away, and the unrelenting stress that brought, was easy to find within myself.

After a mere five takes, Lisette called an end to the shoot. The next scene took place in my office, so we headed back to the studio. I'd brought my car, and since

Kelci'd already left, I offered Elouise a ride.

"Only if you tell me about your friend."

My new co-star used air quotes.

You asked for it.

Yes. Yes, I had. And since I needed a discreet sounding board, I spilled my guts.

Chapter Five

Michael

God, but Caressa was beautiful.

I didn't remember her being a stomach sleeper, but she lay on her belly now, arms wrapped around my pillow. The dislodged blankets exposed her exquisite back—the curve of her spine, the extension of her neck, and the mass of raven-colored hair. I longed to kiss every one of her vertebrae, from skull to ass. I wanted to nip and lick and elicit more moans of pleasure. Just because I wanted to prove last night hadn't been a fluke.

The light filtering through the closed blinds was muted, but I'd needed sunglasses when I went out. Last night's rain was a long-distant memory, and brilliant December morning sunshine poured over the wet pavement of the city. The nip in the air reminded me Christmas wasn't far off. Organization being my strong suit, I'd already purchased all my presents for Caressa and Cole.

You went overboard.

She's home where she belongs. Plus, she doesn't have a lot of stuff. She needs to set up her own place.

Unless she moves in with me.

The force of the thought nearly brought me to my knees. Would she? I lived close to the hospital, so that'd be a bonus. I was a decent cook and could take care of her. Like rubbing her neck and feet when she worked those ridiculously long shifts. I could hold her when she cried over the loss of a patient. I could be there for her in a way I hadn't for a long time.

On the other hand, my place was small. She wouldn't have much space for herself if she needed to retreat. Which she sometimes did. But I could hunker down at the office or go for a run to give her the time she needed to recharge. Or, even better, I could find a way to help her through the rough patches. I didn't kid myself—she hadn't begun to scratch the surface of her pain. Her letters had always been circumspect. But I'd read enough to have some idea what she'd gone through. She'd done mandatory counseling when she came back, but that'd been more of a debrief. And only three sessions. Had she told the counselor about Thana and her baby? Likely not. She wouldn't bounce back without more help—no matter how resilient she could be.

She shifted, brushing hair from her face, and I caught the hint of the curve of her breast. I'd never considered myself much of a breast man, but last night I'd been dying to do more than just taste. I'd wanted to look, to admire, to salivate over. She might've lost a few pounds while she was away, but she'd kept some of her luscious curves. What color were her areolas? Pert pink or dark mauve? Would they come to attention under my gaze or would I need to use my hands and mouth to bring them to hard peaks? Did she enjoy having her breasts played with, or did she go along with it because she thought I enjoyed it?

Needing to know, I shed my clothes and eased into bed behind her. Although she needed her rest, eight o'clock had come and gone, and my body was making demands I wasn't willing to suppress. So I took up where I'd left off last night and pressed a kiss to her shoulder.

"You're cold." Barely a thread of sound.

"It's chilly outside. A cold front has moved in, and although the sun is out, the temperature dropped overnight."

She glanced over her shoulder. "Thank you for that very succinct weather report." Her smile softened, and her eyebrow arched. "All I was going to say was let me warm you up."

Clearly, she meant that invitation. So when she turned in my arms and pressed herself against me, I took her mouth in a long, sensual kiss. Tangling my hands through her thick, soft hair, I used that as leverage to bring our bodies closer together. She yielded against me, and I reveled in the little sighs of pleasure she made when I reached down to capture one of her nipples. It pebbled immediately, evidently enjoying the attention I was giving it. Straying lower, along her hip and across her abdomen, I caressed down to her thighs. Unlike last night, however, she didn't open them at my unspoken request.

"This is my show." She stated it like she was talking to a recalcitrant patient.

I gazed into her pale blue eyes with their pupils large and dilated. *Ah.* I allowed her to roll me onto my back.

"Hands up."

Oh, the imperious tone I loved so much.

I bit back a retort and complied with her request, placing my hands behind my head and interlacing my fingers. I lay against my pillow so I was able to look down and see her still-naked body.

She pulled down the sheets, exposing us completely.

My cock was almost purple as it strained, curving up toward my abdomen, with a bead of pre-cum on the slit.

I want her so much.

I'm going to die before I have her.

She stroked my cheek with her long, delicate fingers.

I'd shaved the morning before, but my beard grew quickly, and I needed a shave again. I'd debated doing it before coming back to bed, but I'd been too anxious to see if we'd take up where we left off the night before, or were things going to be awkward and uncomfortable?

She caressed down my sternum to my belly.

Answers that question.

Her lightly callused fingertips traced my ribcage, and I sucked in a breath when she placed a kiss to my belly.

She swirled her tongue in my navel and then blew across the wetness.

My cock strained for something just beyond reach, but if she kept up her ministrations, I'd likely explode right here and now.

Those questing fingers trailed lower still, tracing my pubic bone and then grasping my cock.

I sucked in another breath and let it out slowly as she took the bead of pre-cum and swirled it around the head with her thumb. The secret smile she gave me was all the warning I had before she took me in her mouth. I'd hoped this was coming, but her boldness surprised me. I never asked my partners to go down on me. I always let them make the first move. I loved getting head. What guy didn't? But I'd never put a woman in the position of feeling she had to just because I asked. Maybe those women I hadn't asked thought I wouldn't enjoy it, and maybe I'd had fewer blow jobs than I might've otherwise, but my principles came before my body's desire to have a woman fuck me with her mouth.

Caressa's movements were awkward. Sometimes, she went at it with gusto, but other times she was tentative. As if this wasn't natural to her. Of course, if there hadn't been anyone since… Jesus Lord, why the fuck was I thinking about other guys when *my* cock was in her mouth? She was giving me everything I could ask for, and fucking hot described it perfectly. Then she cupped my balls, and I nearly bucked off the bed.

"I'm going to come." Was that enough of a warning? Was I clear in my words?

She stopped and gave me a quizzical look.

"I want to come in you." I gritted my teeth so hard the muscle in my jaw ticked.

Her smile was beatific. Still holding my cock, she straddled me.

"Condom." I wheezed the word out, fighting the need to just come right there and then.

She arched an eyebrow. "Do you think…"

"Think?" Who could think at a time like this?

"That we could…"

Holy crap. I'd never gone bareback. Never. In all my relationships, I'd never done it without a condom. My parents had drilled it into me that I'd been an accident and they'd only married because their parents insisted on it. My folks had taken every opportunity to lecture me about how I'd ruined their lives. I was never going to risk having a child with a woman I didn't love and couldn't see spending the rest of my life with. "I've never…"

"Neither have I." She gave me a tentative smile. "But I want—"

"I do too." I never wanted her to feel insecure about asking for what she wanted. "But—"

"I'm protected. I have an IUD."

Which had a failure rate of less than one percent. If she said she was protected, then she was. "Okay." Somehow the word came out on a sigh, as if a great weight had been lifted off my chest as opposed to something I should be concerned about.

She straddled me tightly. *Is she ready for me?* She ran my cock through her folds. Yep, she was soaked. In fact, the musky scent of her desire swirled through my nose, and my nostrils flared. When she positioned herself over me, I held my breath as she eased down on me. As soon as she relaxed at the intrusion, I bucked and managed to seat myself to the hilt. She was tight and slick and hot. So fucking hot.

I'm going to go out of my mind.

She began to move up and down my shaft.

I'd never given much thought to the difference between bareback and latex. Fucking was fucking, right? *Wrong.*

I felt every tremor, every movement, every stretched muscle. I felt her rubbing her clit against my pelvis in an attempt to get enough friction to make herself come. "Let me touch you." I'd beg if I had to, but I was running out of time. No way was I coming before she did.

She seemed surprised at the request—probably having forgotten she'd ordered me to keep my hands off. "Yes, please."

In less than a heartbeat, my hands were on her thighs, guiding her up and down, delivering a punishing rhythm we both desperately needed. I sucked in air, desperate to try to slow things down and savor them, but she was having none of that. Resting her hands on my abdomen, she levered herself up and down. Her nipples were a light, dusty rose. Her breasts jiggled with her frantic movements, and I cupped them in my hands, using my fingers to tease her nipples. That seemed to be all that was required to push her over the edge.

Thank fuck. Two pumps later and I emptied myself into her. Something elemental existed in knowing my semen, my sperm, was inside her. Not going to result in conception. But a way for me to make her mine in the most primitive way possible. I wanted to put a sign on her, warning off all other men—claiming her for my own pleasure and enjoyment.

My mind flashed to Cole, and mentally, I swore viciously. In the abstract, loving Caressa romantically was a world full of possibilities and wonderful things. In the real world, a good chance existed we'd likely hurt Cole. Or maybe our friend would understand. Maybe he'd just be happy for us.

She collapsed against my chest, my limp cock slipping out of her.

I wrapped my arms around her and pressed a kiss to the crown of her head. "Good?"

"I would say fucking amazing again."

I smiled. Yeah, I'd say that too. I tugged the blanket over us and held her as if she were the most precious thing in the world. Of course, to me, she was.

Chapter Six

Caressa

The shower took much longer than it should have, but given our exploring hands, roving fingers, and another pair of mind-blowing simultaneous orgasms, I wondered we didn't run out of hot water.

Oh yeah. Condo.

Although Michael'd brought work home, he assured me that he didn't need to complete it on this lovely Saturday morning. "I was just planning to get a head start. Monday'll be soon enough."

Since I didn't want our time to come to an end either, I chose to believe him.

Breakfast was eggs Benedict, and yet again I was reminded of his culinary skills. Mine were more basic. Although now that I was back in the city, I planned to take cooking classes.

After we cleaned the breakfast dishes, he loaned me a coat so we could go outside for a walk. We had yet to actually talk about what'd happened, breakfast chatter having been about inconsequential things. He'd taken a taxi to retrieve my car that morning, and it now sat in a guest parking spot in his secure garage. I'd sent a text to Kendall saying I wasn't sure when I'd be back. *Hope you're getting laid* had been the reply. I'd wanted to send back something pithy, but getting laid implied this was just about sex…and this was so much more than just sex.

The air was chilly, and when Michael reached for my hand, I offered him a wide smile. "I didn't think you liked PDA."

He gave me a solemn look. "Because I never found someone I wanted to show off as mine."

His? The feminist in me railed against such a primitive statement while the woman in me reveled in the thought I belonged to him. That he was willing to tell the world to back off because he'd staked a claim.

We continued to walk in silence, and the city blocks got eaten up as we avoided being bumped and jostled by Christmas shoppers. After about fifteen minutes, I ventured a question. "Where are we going?"

"We're just walking."

Huh. Defensive much? "True. But we're walking up Burrard."

"So?"

"So we're heading toward St. Paul's. Why are we going to my new workplace when I don't start for another four days?" I suspected I knew the answer, but I wanted him to confirm it.

"Just figuring out how long of a walk it is." He wouldn't meet my eyes.

"From your place."

"From my place."

I slowed my steps and nudged him out of the way of most of the pedestrians. "We both know it's about twelve blocks or five minutes on the bus, Michael, so what's the deal? What's really going on?"

"I want you to move in with me." He spoke in a hurry, as if to prevent me from objecting. "I think it's the right thing to do, and you might as well do it before you find a place of your own. I live close to your work, so it'll be convenient. It'll be safe for you to live at my place. And living in this city is so expensive. If you get a place on your own, all your money will go for rent and you'll never get ahead. It'll be hard for you to save enough to get your own place. And you need to get your foot onto the property ladder to ensure you've got a nest egg for retirement. Pension plans are all well and good, but equity in your own home—"

I silenced his ramblings with a finger to his lips. He wasn't given to rambling. His comments were always thoughtful and deliberate. He was just as prone to contemplative silence as he was to making a casual observation.

"Moving in together is a big step. Twenty-four hours ago, we were just friends. Now we're friends with benefits—"

This time it was he who cut me off with a hard kiss. His tongue demanded entrance, and I granted it, more out of surprise than anything else. He dug his hands into my hair, pulling on it so he could angle me perfectly to deepen the kiss.

I ruffled his hair, reveling that it felt short and soft. He didn't wear cologne, so I sniffed a combination of soap and elemental Michael. A stronger aphrodisiac, I couldn't remember. When he nibbled and then bit my lower lip, desire raced through me, and I was tempted to pull him into a back alley, but a whistle came from a passing car.

In the end, he pulled back, pressing his brow to mine. "This is more than just friends with benefits, Caressa. I don't need a fuck buddy. I need a lover. I need someone I can love and support through everything she's going through. I need someone who'll be there for me through the monotony of my daily life. I need someone to be by my side, and I think you need that too." He took a deep breath and met my gaze. "I need you."

After high school, we'd gotten a two-bedroom apartment, the three of us. Even on scholarships, Michael and I had little cash to spare, and we worked to pay our fair share. On top of attending theater school, Cole worked two jobs, ensuring we always had a roof over our heads. But this was different. Cole and Michael wouldn't be sharing a bedroom in a platonic way. Cole wouldn't be part of this at all.

I wanted to argue. I wanted to shout *too soon*. But in my heart, I knew that to be a lie. This was how things were meant to be.

Chapter Seven

Cole

It *had* to be the underground.

Plenty of perfectly good dark alleyways, abandoned lots, and deserted parks in this fucking city, but, no, the production team had to pick the underground.

Not that I was complaining. I never complained. About anything.

Still, on this brisk December day, I would've preferred being above ground. We saw so little of the sun that I cherished every moment. Hell, even if the day was gray, I still tried to get out. Daylight, so at a premium this time of year, needed to be revered.

Julie tucked herself into my side. "It's freezing."

We were in a seldom-used area of the SkyTrain, Vancouver's rapid transit system. This area was supposed to be off-limits to all persons, but a distinct foul scent lingered in the air. Urine? Rotting rodents? I wasn't sure and wasn't going to comment, but I'd be glad to get above ground.

"Once we get going with the action sequence, you'll warm up."

Easy for me to say—I wore a dress shirt, business suit, and shiny leather shoes.

She wore a skin-tight spandex dress that barely touched the tops of her thighs, had a daring bustline, and barely covered her assets. Her legs were also bare, and she wore three-inch stiletto heels.

How she didn't teeter over was beyond me.

Our stunt doubles had done some of the more daring work, but Julie and I had a sequence Donovan'd created for us. Our stunt coordinator was one of the best in the business. He also knew how to put us through our paces.

Seamus, the production assistant, approached us. He wore a wool coat, thick jeans, and winter boots.

"Thought you were a hearty Newfie."

He arched an eyebrow. "Yeah, I'm from Newfoundland. That means we know how to dress for the weather or we die." His accent was light but unmistakable. He eyed Julie. "Would you like me to get you a blanket?"

She shook her head. "Imminent, right?"

"Well, yes." He gestured his head.

We followed to where the action would take place.

All I wanted was to go home, put my feet up, eat some food, and hunker down. Could I splurge on junk food tonight, or did I need to be good and eat something wholesome? Chili might do. And surely, I could find a hockey game on television. Or an old film I had yet to see. Even as I had the thought, I felt myself sinking into my comfy sectional couch.

Instead, though, I was about to expend an excessive amount of energy to produce twenty seconds of film.

"You coming out with us afterward?" Julie took her appointed position as our director of photography gauged the shot.

"Hadn't thought about it."

A lie. I had. What I really wanted was to see Caressa, but by the time we'd be finished, she'd be hunkered down in her place in the valley. She wasn't due to come back to Vancouver for several days, and I didn't have another day free for a bit, so coordinating schedules was going to prove challenging.

I'd manage.

Somehow.

"Hamilton, move to your left."

I did as the DP asked, and soon she grinned.

As she stepped back, Lisette, our director, stepped forward. She pointed to me. "You don't want to die."

Pretty much Justice's motivation in every scene.

She pointed to Julie. "You want to kill him, but you know you'll miss him when he's gone."

Pretty much Lyric's motivation in every scene.

After a moment, she stepped back. "Give me your best."

And we did.

Chapter Eight

Michael

Moving Caressa into my place took all of four hours.
An hour to drive out to her friend's place in Mission City,
an hour to explain to her friend that the decision wasn't
really all that sudden—and that she wasn't just shacking
up with some guy—ten minutes to pack her bag, an hour
back to the city, and fifty minutes to find a place where
she could store her car until I could secure a spot for her
in my building.

Once we had her settled, I took her out for lunch at
one of my favorite bistros, and then we went grocery
shopping. After we finished putting away the groceries,
she unpacked her one bag of clothes and toiletries. My
walk-in closet was large, and since I was on worksites
more often than not, I tended to wear jeans and casual
shirts that fit in my dresser. My three suits hung in the
closet. Caressa owned one dress, two pairs of jeans, three
shirts, and four pairs of scrubs.

"We need to take you clothes shopping." I held my
breath, waiting for the protests to start—she hated
shopping.

I was rewarded with a long-suffering look. "It's a
waste of money. I work more than half my life, and I
have four pairs of scrubs. We bought the detergent that
gets blood out of them, so what's the big deal?"

I'd yield on this. For now. Unless… "How about we go to Value Village or one of the other secondhand clothing stores? Their earnings go to charity, and you can pick up a few other things."

She arched an eyebrow. "Do my clothes embarrass you? Are you thinking you can't go out with me?"

"Caressa, you know me better than that," I grumbled. "You can wear the proverbial potato sack, and I wouldn't care. If you don't want to go—"

"I'm being churlish. It's just…" She looked down and picked at a nonexistent piece of lint.

"Just?" I wanted her to open up so badly I could taste it.

"I've lived so sparingly for so long that the thought of spending money is intimidating." Her voice sounded a little off.

"You have some money saved, though, right? I mean, it's not like you had many expenses when you were away." Even as I said the words, I wondered if I was venturing into dangerous territory. We hadn't talked finances, and wasn't that one of the main reasons couples split? I'd just assumed I'd be paying for everything because I made a good salary, but that probably wouldn't go over well with Caressa.

"My salary wasn't that big, and I spent every penny on paying off my student loans. I'm free and clear of them."

"That's great news. And now you'll be living with me, so you can begin to save up for retirement." Why didn't she sound ecstatic, knowing such a big debt was paid off?

"You and your obsession with retirement." She rolled her eyes. "I'm thirty-two. I'm more worried about…" She winced.

"About being poor." The lightbulb finally clicked on.

Mutely, she nodded.

"So we put together a savings plan for you. I don't know what your salary at the hospital will be—" Finally, a plan of attack.

"You're thinking about paying for everything, aren't you?" Her tone was accusatory.

"Well, yeah. It's not like I don't have the money—" In my enthusiasm, I'd forgotten to be careful about her prickly pride.

She shot off the couch and paced. "That's not going to work for me, and you know it. I have to contribute. I can't be living off you, or it'll feel like charity. I make decent money and was planning to pay rent. So it's not like I can't pay my fair share."

"Then we can set up a joint account for household expenses." I couldn't see what the problem was.

Her eyes narrowed. "Just like that?"

"Just like that. We can both contribute every month." I hesitated. "And I want to make you co-owner of the condo. We'll have equal equity in it."

She stopped mid-stride. "Are you nuts? Twenty-four hours ago, we were having dinner as friends, and now you want to give me half a condo?"

"Half a condo with a mortgage—"

She cut me off. "Nuts, Michael, nuts. No lawyer worth their salt will let you get away with something like that."

"You and Cole are already my beneficiaries, so what's the big deal?"

"Because you're not dead." A shot with accurate

aim.

I shrugged.

"One year." Said with great reluctance. "*If* we survive for a year, then we become common-law. At that point, I'll consider something as insane as this. Until then, I pay you what I would've been paying in rent."

Yield. I planned to put it into a savings account for her anyway, so if this was what was necessary for her to feel comfortable, I was okay with that.

"One year." I nodded at her and smiled.

"That was too easy. You've got something up your sleeve." She narrowed her eyes. "I know you. I know you probably better than you know yourself."

Since she knew I was a terrible poker player, I was aware I'd have to work hard to conceal my plan. "I'm making Cajun chicken, fried rice, and roasted vegetables." These were all her favorites, and hopefully, she'd see it as the peace offering it was.

"I'm going to get fat if you cook like that for me every day. I don't have your metabolism." She shook her finger at me.

I refrained from pointing out she'd bought plenty of low-calorie foods for the lunches she planned to take to the hospital. I also decided now was *not* the time to point out how much weight she'd lost while overseas. *Should talk to Cole about it.* Before I broached it with her. He'd know what to do.

Cole.

Moving Caressa into my condo had taken about four hours. Telling Cole was going to be a whole different situation. I wanted to wait, but it wouldn't be fair to our friend—and wouldn't make it any easier to deal with the situation.

"Why don't you give Cole a call while I start dinner?"

"I'm not telling him over the phone."

"Of course not." *Duh.* "But we need to tell him. Find out the next day he's not filming, and we'll see what we can do." I rose and moved toward her, then took her face in my hands. "This is going to work out, Caressa. This was meant to be. *We* were meant to be."

She didn't look convinced, but she accepted my kiss—not fighting when I pulled her into my embrace. *At least it's something.*

So, less than a day later, we sat in Save-On-Meats and chowed down on hearty breakfasts. I was glad to see Caressa digging into her food, although I wasn't completely surprised. We might've gone to bed relatively early, but we'd also woken repeatedly during the night to come together. A touch or a smell or just her presence was enough to rouse me from sleep and bring my body into awareness. Sometimes the lovemaking had been leisurely and soft, with us barely conscious. Other times, it'd been demanding and almost violent. As if we needed to crawl inside of each other. As if lives depended on joining our bodies.

"You two look tired," Cole commented as our dishes were taken away and we all settled in with our warm drinks. Cole and I drank coffee while Caressa nursed a caffeinated black tea.

I glanced at Caressa who glanced back.

"Oh, this is interesting." Cole's blue eyes were sharp on the two of us.

I wanted to reach out and take Caressa's hand but held back. Instead, I shifted subtly so my thigh was pressed against hers.

"We have something to tell you, Cole." She looked him in the eyes without flinching.

"Oh, I think I can guess." His voice dripped with sarcasm.

Rip off the proverbial bandage. "Caressa has moved in with me. We're together. As a couple." *As if clarification is necessary.*

"It's been two days." Cole slammed his mug down. "Two fucking days." His tone was low, probably in consideration of the two families in other booths, but the disdain and anger were clear. "You couldn't wait one more day and talk to me first? What was the fucking rush?" He paused, and his eyes narrowed. "Or has this been going on all along? Did something happen while Caressa was in Africa, or even before?"

"You know there was nothing." Her voice was just as quiet. "And yes, we probably should've waited to talk to you… It just happened."

"His cock didn't just sort of happen to fall into your pussy." Cole's expression chilled me to the bone.

"That's none of your business." My tone was just as cold. "And don't talk about Caressa that way."

"Or Michael." She sounded resolute, like she was daring Cole to argue with her.

Cole slashed his hand through the air. "You two need your heads examined."

"I have to get out of here."

Caressa's pronouncement took me by surprise. She struggled to leave the booth and almost tripped in her haste. I barely had time to register what was going on before she was out the door. I escaped the booth and was heading for the door like a shot before I felt a vise-like grip on my wrist. Trying to shake Cole off proved impossible because my best friend was much stronger.

"Sit," he growled. A combination of plea and demand.

"I have to go after her." I hated we'd shaken her up like this.

"I'll go." Cole sighed and rubbed his neck with his free hand. "But she needs a few minutes. It's not like we don't know where she's going."

Which was true. Caressa was nothing if not predictable. We were, after all, just a half mile from our old neighborhood. I'd been surprised she suggested this place, but it held special memories for us. Once a month, from the time we'd been old enough to hold down part-time jobs, we'd come here—proof we were going to make it out of the Downtown Eastside and on to a better life. A metaphorical bridge between where we were and where we wanted to be. Not that the place was anything to write home about. An old-fashioned diner. Just a diner. But to us, it'd been everything.

When Cole released my wrist, I briefly considered abandoning him and going after Caressa, but we had business to discuss. So I sat.

"Couldn't keep it in your pants?"

My anger flared, but I held my tongue.

"She's been home a week, Michael. Her head is still spinning, and now she's living with you? How is that logical?" Cole seethed, his voice a snarl.

"Well, she would've been commuting from the Valley to the hospital until she found a place to live, and we both know rentals are at a premium in this town. We also both know she could've been forced to take something unsafe or substandard because she was in a pinch."

"I was going to offer her a room at my place." He blew out a harsh breath. "That night at the pub. But other things happened, and I didn't want to drop it on her. I didn't foresee you swooping in and taking over."

"I didn't take over." *Why am I arguing this?* "I offered an alternative."

"Friends with benefits?"

I chose to ignore his snarky tone. "I'm in love with her. I've always loved her, but her time in Africa made me see that I wanted to be with her. Romantically. Did I plan this? Hell, no. Do I have any regrets? Hell, no. Am I asking your approval? *Hell, no*."

He appeared to consider as he sipped his coffee and then flicked off a nonexistent piece of fluff from his jacket. "This changes everything."

"I know. Your friendship means everything to Caressa and me. Please, Cole, cut us some slack. Be happy for us."

His mouth twisted. "And if I told you I was in love with Caressa?"

Oh shit. "Are you in love with her too?"

"Would it change things between the two of you? Would you be willing to give her up to me?"

Jesus Christ. "It's not my decision to make. If Caressa tells me that she wants to be with you, I wouldn't stop her, of course. I'm not going to hold her to our agreement—if that's what you're asking." Recklessly, I continued. "If you think you're the better man. If she's meant to be with you, then go for it." I'd never been a competitive person, but right now I was itching for a battle. A battle for Caressa's hand. A battle I intended to win.

Cole nodded. "I think I've given her enough time."

"I want to come with you."

"You can, but you have to let me talk to her first."

I wanted to rail against his high-handed behavior, but somehow this seemed like the fairest way to do things. If our friend wanted to proclaim a romantic love for Caressa, then she deserved the chance to listen. If she chose Cole…

A reality I couldn't contemplate.

Then why did you challenge him? Give him permission to try to take her away from you?

Both good questions. Questions I didn't have answers for.

Chapter Nine

Caressa

"Caressa?"

I jumped. Being so into my own head about what was happening, I hadn't even realized Cole had sat down next to me. *So much for being on guard.* "How did you know where I was?" The Dr. Sun Yat-Sen Classical Chinese Gardens to be exact.

"Really? Obviously, I knew where you'd be." He shook his head.

"I renewed my membership." Which had given me unlimited access. This place was only about a mile from Michael's condo and open year-round. Of course, that was if I was still going to be at Michael's. The gardens were another one of those locations straddling our old lives and our new ones. From the time I was eleven, I'd scrimp and save to get a membership. Being able to come here and be by myself with my thoughts meant everything. Thoughts that'd never been good. Unless I'd been dreaming of getting out of the hell I lived in.

The silence between us stretched. While Michael'd eventually break any silence between us, Cole could sit without saying a word until the sun went down. The patience of a proverbial saint. And since he wasn't due on set until tonight, we might be there until closing. Because I wasn't going to be the one to break. I shivered when the sun dipped behind a cloud.

"You need a winter coat." He frowned at me.

"And other clothes, according to Michael." There. I'd said his name. Brought up the subject, even if only tangentially.

Cole sighed. "I wish you'd stayed at the diner so we could've talked. Hashed things out."

"You're angry."

"Disappointed." He crossed his leg casually. "And that's not the same thing."

"Disappointed, angry, disapproving…it all amounts to the same thing. You're not being supportive." *Do you have to needle him?*

"Do you need my approval, Caressa? My support? If this is what you want, my opinion and feelings shouldn't matter."

He was right, of course, but he was also wrong. Our bond was supposed to transcend things like this. "I never meant to hurt you."

"Are you doing this because you need security? Is it because you're still off-balance from your time away?" His voice was level but carried an odd note in it.

No point asking him how he knew I was still so unsettled. He knew everything. Well, not *everything*. He hadn't realized Michael loved me. He hadn't realized I might return those feelings. "Can we get past this? Or is this a deal-breaker in our friendship?"

He barked out a laugh. "You think I'm that capricious? Jesus, you know me better than that. I could no more cut you and Michael out of my life than I could cut off a limb. I love you both. The kind of love that binds people together forever."

He sighed and ran his hand through his beautiful,

thick, black hair. "I'm worried, okay? Don't you see how that might be? How I might think you're both moving too fast and for the wrong reasons? Michael spent five years worrying about you every day. Getting you to move in is a way for him to watch over you. But that concern could quickly become suffocating." He paused, letting those words sink in. "And you're unsettled and unsure of how to reintegrate into civilization, so to speak. You left part of yourself back in Africa, and you're wondering if you'll ever be whole again."

As always, he'd summarized the situation succinctly and correctly.

So where does that leave us?

"I can move out…" The mental gymnastics required to work out a solution proved challenging.

He cut me off. "I'm not suggesting that. You know your heart—and I think despite everything, you love Michael in a romantic way. You can see yourself having a future with him—and I respect that. What you can do, however, is go into counseling. Find someone who'll respect you and help you deal with the trauma you've been through." Before I could protest, he held up his hand. "We both know you've been traumatized, Caressa, so don't try to argue that point. What you saw over there was both life-fulfilling and tragic. You saw the good and the bad. You felt things as acutely as if it was your life— not just that of your patients. And I know you haven't told us everything. Whether because you think you could protect us or because you're protecting yourself, I don't know. But does the reason matter? You need to sit down and talk to someone. I'll pay, of course."

Again with the high-handedness. Did neither man believe I could handle things on my own? "My work offers counseling through the insurance. Since my benefits kick in the day I start, I can make an appointment right away."

"You've looked into this." His voice betrayed his surprise.

"Actually, HR did. They like the staff to have a relationship set up with a therapist and even have a list of counselors who are familiar with PTSD. They aren't saying there'll be problems—but they like to have that line of communication open. They suggest seeing the psychologist or social worker at least once a year to keep in touch. More, if needed. I plan to call on my first day off."

"Well…that's good. That's really good. And you'll tell him or her about Michael?"

I nodded. "I'll tell the counselor about everything. My mom, my childhood…everything. While I was away, I realized my life choices have been made based on what happened to me when I was younger. Do I regret any of them? Of course not. But I want to make sure I'm doing things for the right reasons, not out of a sense of obligation."

"Obligation?" He seemed to turn the word over in his mind. "Is Michael an obligation? Am I?"

"Of course not." *Make him understand.* "I'm good with my decision to move in with Michael. I've talked him into taking the rest of it slowly. I think he'll respect that." I hesitated. "I'm asking for your blessing, Cole."

"Do you need my blessing? Do either of you really care what I think?"

His expression was grim, but I caught the hurt. He looked crestfallen, with sad eyes, and it broke my heart.

"No. Yes." The words made my chest tight. "Yes,

we do care, but no, we don't need your blessing. Still, we'd like it just the same."

Cole put his arm around my shoulders and pulled me close. "You have it, Caressa. You'll always have it. And if things fall apart, God forbid, I'll be here to pick up the pieces. I'll never take sides, though, so don't ask me to. Unless he does something unforgivable like abusing you. Or you abusing him."

Physical abuse was probably absurd, but I understood, as I always had, that I had the power to hurt Michael's feelings. Like I had the ability to hurt Cole's. Like I just had.

Cole shifted and raised the arm that wasn't still gripping my shoulders. I glanced up and spotted Michael step out of the shadows. He was far enough away so he wouldn't have been able to hear our conversation, but he would've been able to see our body language, and I had no doubt he'd have stepped in if Cole upset me.

Michael came over and sat next to me, taking my hand.

Cole moved his arm from around my shoulders and took my other hand.

His hand was icy, and given the weather, that was to be expected. But the chill still hit me in the gut. I wasn't sure everything was okay. "I love you both." I fought to keep my voice steady.

"We know." Michael was quick to assure me. "If you want to change things—"

"That's not what she said." Cole was quick to clarify. "She's trying to tell us she doesn't want anything to come between the three of us."

"*She* can speak for herself." I wanted to knock their heads together and see if any sense could be jarred loose.

75

Both men chuckled.

"The department store is open now." Cole slid in the comment as if everything else was settled. "Let's go get you a winter coat."

"About time. I've been standing there watching you shiver," Michael groused.

Was it really that simple? Could we move forward in this new dynamic? Testing the new relationship, I let go of Michael's hand and leaned over to press a kiss to Cole's cheek. "Friends forever, right?"

In return, he pressed a kiss to my forehead. "Of course."

Then I let go of Cole's hand and turned to Michael, taking both of his in mine. I was staking my territory. Telling the world who I loved. "No matter what, I'm happy, okay? We'll make this work."

"Damn straight we will." He pulled me forward, catching me off-balance and tugging me into his lap. He thrust his hands in my hair and used the grasp to pull my mouth to his. No preliminaries as he thrust his tongue into my mouth. He tasted of coffee and desperation, and I responded. How could I not?

"This is a public park." Cole's voice was tinged with annoyance. "Maybe you two can wait until you get home?"

Michael ended the kiss and pressed his lips to my temple. "We can. But barely."

My heart was about to burst from happiness. I had everything I could've wanted. Life was damn good.

Chapter Ten

Cole

"Hamilton, get your head out of your ass!"

Donovan's invective had my head snapping up. The stunt coordinator looked displeased, and as I quickly scanned the room, several other crew members gazed at me with curiosity. Since my reputation as always being professional, and having my head in the game, was stellar, I must be really falling down on the job. So to speak.

Julie held up her hand. "Can we take five? I want to review that sequence in my head again before we shoot. I think I made a misstep." She directed the question to Donovan, but her green eyes were laser-focused on me.

"Yeah, okay." Donovan held up his hand to indicate five minutes, and people scrambled over each other to make themselves scarce.

Seamus gave me one long look before indicating with his head.

Since he probably wanted to check in with his husband Val and their foster son Jason, I nodded that I'd be okay.

He gave me the thumbs-up and made a beeline for the exit.

Donovan turned to Julie and myself. "Lisette is directing the shoot tonight and is going to be here in a

Gabbi Grey

few minutes. I thought we had this nailed, so what the fuck is going on?"

On an easy day, Donovan pulled off intimidating without effort. Six foot three and two hundred pounds of pure muscle, he could be as sleek as a panther and as lithe as a gazelle. His skin was black and his eyes nearly as dark. For effect, he shaved his head—and the ensemble made him look more like a bouncer or a linebacker. Only an idiot would underestimate his speed, though. Instead of being hampered by bulk, he was light on his feet. Nimble as an alley cat.

"So I do the roundhouse, then duck left?" Julie's question was clearly an attempt to refocus the three of us.

"Because he's going to pivot right." Donovan's response to Julie's question was automatic, but his gaze never left me. As if the man could see in my mind, I squirmed under the scrutiny. We'd been friends for twelve years, since theater school, and he'd never tolerated any bullshit between the two of us, so for me to hold back…it felt wrong.

"It's Caressa." Even as I uttered the words, I wished I could pull them back.

Donovan's expression changed instantly. Gone was the pissed-off coach—in his place was an empathetic friend. "Is she okay? I thought you said she was coming back from Africa. Did something happen to her plane or something?"

Oh shit. Donovan knew Caressa. Likely considered himself her friend because of her position in my life. Friend of a friend and all that. "She's fine." I slashed my hand through the air. "Forget about it, okay? I never should've said anything."

"Who's Caressa?"

Both of us turned to find Julie, hands on hips and looking to be a mixture between confused and annoyed. *Ah crap.* Julie would have never met Caressa—my friend had left town weeks before *VJ* had started shooting and hadn't been back the entire four seasons. And apparently, I hadn't talked about her either.

"Best friend since grade school," I mumbled, averting my gaze.

Julie had a way of seeing into me, or at least thinking she could. Since she was such a damn talented actress, sometimes I wondered if she had mind-reading abilities or if she was just great at reading people. Me, in particular.

"So why's she on your mind?" She had an open countenance, making it clear she was willing to hear whatever I had to say. Especially if that got us back on track.

"She's back in town." I evaded, not wanting to admit the truth—least of all to myself. "I think I'm just so relieved she's back safe from Africa that I can't wrap my head around it." I ground the heel of my expensive shoe into the concrete floor. My character didn't always have time to change into army boots before saving the day. The shoes had good treads, but slipping was always a possibility.

Donovan placed a hand on my shoulder. "I know you tried to act like her leaving was no big deal, but I knew different. But she's back and safe, right? So no more worrying."

I wanted things to be that simple, but instead of worrying about Caressa's physical safety, now I worried about her mental health. What had possessed her to agree to move in with Michael so quickly? What would've been the harm in waiting a few days or weeks? What was the fucking hurry?

But now wasn't the time or the place to think about this. I was renowned for my ability to focus and be one hundred percent present. Today, that concentration simply wasn't here. Shaking it off, I gave the others a smile. "Okay, let's do this." I aligned myself with the mark and waited for Donovan to give the cue.

Only when Julie's foot connected squarely with my thigh did I remember I was supposed to pivot right, not left.

Chapter Eleven

Caressa

"I think that went well. With Cole, I mean."

My gaze snapped from my food to Michael's face. After leaving Cole in the park, we'd gone over to Value Village on Victoria Drive where I'd bought a winter coat and a few other clothing items to replace ones that had gone missing when I was in Africa. No call for wool socks there. But I definitely needed them now. I tried to argue about spending the money because I was sure I had a box somewhere with my winter clothes. The problem was I couldn't remember where that box was. Michael said he didn't have it and he was pretty sure Cole didn't either. He offered to call Cole to find out, and I acquiesced to the request I stock up with warm clothes. The last thing I wanted was to call Cole over something as stupid as a few pairs of socks and a couple of sweaters. I could still see the hurt that had flashed in his eyes when Michael told him we were together now.

I arched an eyebrow. "Define *went well*."

He held my gaze, shrugging. "Well, we're all still friends, so that's something, right? I…" With his brow furrowed, his gaze shot toward the photo of Vancouver on his wall. "I…was surprised at how angry he was."

"Disappointed." I echoed the word Cole had used earlier. Did I want to go there? Except Michael had provided me the opening, and I wasn't known for being a chickenshit. "He did sort of have a point."

Now Michael's eyebrows arched. "Are you saying we were wrong? That you regret your decision to move in with me?"

Did I? Was that the reason for this unsettled feeling deep in the pit of my stomach? I'd hoped it was just hunger, but now that I'd eaten most of my food and the feeling hadn't abated, I had to admit there might be something to it. "Not wrong, Michael, just…hasty." I laid my knife and fork at the five o'clock position, then slowly rotated the plate forty-five degrees, adjusted the knife and fork back to the five o'clock position, then rotated the plate again. On the fourth turn, he stilled my hand.

"I can rent you a hotel room, if that'd make you more comfortable. I mean—"

"No." *Christ, I'm fucking this up.*

I tried to pull my hand away, but he held fast. His grip was tight, and he ran his thumb along my knuckles. He meant it as a soothing gesture, but it only stoked my anxiety.

"I hurt him, Michael, really hurt him. He's always so strong. Always comes across that nothing can touch him. But we both know that's not true. Inside that façade is a little boy who grew up feeling unloved and uncared for. His mother's abandonment, his father's indifference…"

"But he had us. Don't forget that. We all had each other."

His words were true, but they weren't enough to tamp out the flame of doubt in my heart. I'd had no father to speak of and a drug-addicted mother—so Michael and

Cole's friendships had been gifts from a god I didn't believe in. I'd never have thrived, let alone survived, if not for them. The first day of my friendship with Michael, he'd given me much-needed food. The comfort he offered had become the cornerstone of our relationship. Cole had hooked up with us just a few weeks after that. We'd been all of five years old— already weary of the world we were living in. People called it grinding poverty for a very good reason.

I rose from the table and attempted to pick up the plates.

"I'll do it." He rose as well, reaching for them.

"But you cooked…"

He brushed me off. "You're tired, Caressa, and although I'm not going to tell you what to do, why don't you lie down for a bit or watch television or read a book? Or how about a bath? Just relax, you know? You start work in two days, so you need to rest while you can."

I wanted to argue, but weariness enveloped me, and although I should be doing the dishes because Michael'd cooked, I respected that, at this moment, he wanted to take care of me.

"A bath sounds heavenly." This time, my smile was genuine. "Kendall only has a shower, and I've only had a handful of baths over the last five years." Kendall who'd expressed serious reservations about me moving in with Michael after so little time. Except time was relative. I'd known Michael for twenty-seven years but had only known him carnally for one day when I made the decision. Although Kendall had a point, I was doing what was best for me, and maybe this was one of those times when I deserved to be selfish.

Michael pulled me into his arms, and I went

willingly, letting him grasp me—allowing him to press a kiss to my temple.

"Enjoy those bath salts we bought."

On impulse, I'd asked if I could buy them when we were stocking up on groceries and other necessities. I'd tried to pay, of course, but Michael had become recalcitrant, and I hadn't wanted an argument in the grocery store.

Running the water as hot as I could stand it, I stripped out of my jeans and blouse, then folded them nicely with my bra and underwear. Everything was serviceable and practical. I didn't own lacy or satin things meant to entice a man. Plain cotton and well-used, which meant I had another thing to consider. Michael never seemed like a guy who needed fancy lingerie to turn him on, but I should put in an effort, right?

The lavender scent from the bath salts assailed me, and I slid into the fragrant water, uttering another little thanks for indoor plumbing that was accompanied by an endless supply of hot water. Using so much water felt decadent, but I was just going to have to learn to live with that nagging voice in the back of my head that reminded me I was using luxuries and might soon come to rely on them. A girl could get addicted to a hot bath and the heat soaking into her tired muscles. Not that I'd done anything strenuous today. Okay, last night Michael and I had fucked like bunnies for most of the night, but that only accounted for some of the soreness. The rest, I suspected, was from the stress of telling Cole what had happened. What had changed.

Still, I couldn't banish the look of hurt in Cole's beautiful blue eyes. We hadn't just surprised him—we'd wounded him. Deeply. Did he think we didn't value his opinion? Had he thought he should have a say in the direction our lives were going to take? Well, that should've been a big, fat, obvious *yes*. Even though the decision to become lovers and move in together was between Michael and me, we should've spent more time concerned about Cole and his reaction. He had every right to be pissed. He'd accused us of having a sexual relationship even before I'd gone to Africa, which was patently ridiculous. Until three days ago, I'd never seen Michael as anything other than a best friend as dear to me as a brother.

Interestingly, though, I'd never equated him to family. As close as the three of us were, no familial binds existed whether theoretical or actual. People would tease me about having two protective brothers—it'd never felt that way to me. Just two best friends there to pick me up when I fell. There to nurse my wounds. There to love me through everything. Most especially, there when my mother died of an overdose mere weeks after we'd all graduated high school.

If Michael hadn't arranged for the three of us to rent a two-bedroom apartment, I'd surely have wound up homeless or in a shelter.

As it was, Michael and I both held down part-time jobs while studying nursing and engineering, respectively. Cole held down two jobs as well as theater school.

As there hadn't been money for luxuries, the bond between the three of us deepened as time had marched on. Cole's graduation had been first, then mine and finally Michael's. I'd been the first to leave that apartment, instead opting to get a house with two other nurses I'd gone to school with. A tough decision, but I'd felt constricted by my life. Cole and Michael were reminders of where we'd come from, and I was trying to look toward the future. Plus, I told myself, the guys wouldn't have to share a bedroom anymore if I was gone. The lease had been up a couple of months later, and for reasons I'd never been privy to, the men had decided to strike out on their own. Michael, although crippled with student debt, landed a good entry position with an engineering firm in town. By that time, Cole worked as a waiter at a five-star downtown restaurant—The Georgian—and was pulling in serious tip money. Plus attending to every go-see his agent could land him.

We'd coasted through the next few years, seeing each other whenever possible, texting and emailing constantly. But life wasn't the same as when we'd lived under one roof. Conflicts in timing would come up, other priorities would apply pressure, and the time between when we'd get together grew longer and longer.

Until I announced I was going to South Sudan.

Then all hell had broken loose.

In the past.

I squeezed a large dollop of shower gel into my palm before recapping the container and putting it back on the side of the tub. The very large tub. Easily double anything I'd ever seen—let alone had the pleasure to luxuriate in. After rubbing my hands together to create some lather, I ran my hands along my arms. Lavender scented, the gel was cool against my overheated skin, but as I soaped my body, a languid sensation overtook me. Memories of Michael's fervent lovemaking flashed through my mind, and my nipples tightened in remembrance. My body shivered in anticipation with memories of his ardency.

He'd made no promises or suggestions for tonight, but I optimistically suspected we were going to make the sheets dirty again.

As I rubbed the soap against my breasts, my fingers grazed against my areolas. My pussy contracted in pleasure. I'd never given my breasts much consideration as they were practical things I owned in case I ever needed to breastfeed. Men in my past had showed interest in them, but Michael'd worshipped them. His mouth and talented tongue elicited more of a reaction from me than any man who'd come before. Not big on self-pleasure, I'd never spent much time figuring out what made me feel good. What I liked and didn't like. Instead, I'd let guys take the lead, and I'd take everything I could but never gave all of myself. With Michael, the opposite was true. I was driven to give as much, if not more, than what I received.

Moving away from my breasts, I lifted first one leg out of the water and then the other, soaping and scrubbing as I went. I used the moisturizing gel, not that I was convinced it made any difference, because my skin was so dry. Michael had continued to supply me with sunscreen while I was in Africa, and he'd chosen the thickest stuff out there, but it'd been a losing battle. My skin had always itched and peeled.

Knees and thighs were next. More gel as I moved farther down. Stomach, hips, pelvis, and lower still. Flashes of Michael between my thighs that first night crossed my brain like a movie being played on an old projector, the image not quite steady. I'd never let a guy go down on me before and had almost done the same with Michael, but something had stopped me. Sure, I was curious, but this was more than that. My fear of intimacy seemed to have vanished with him. He'd been showing me the way physicality was supposed to be between two people in love, and in that moment, it'd felt like the first time I ever made love.

My skin heated, and it had nothing to do with the warm water. No, memories of Michael caused my skin to turn a rosy shade of pink and my breath to hitch. My eyes drifted shut as my hand slid between folds already slick with more than just water. What if I touched my clit? Could I recreate the magic from last night? Would it feel just as good?

The knock on the door had me sitting up abruptly and sloshing water over the side of the tub. I cursed under my breath. "Yes?"

"I have some chamomile tea for you."

Of course he did. Because he was just that kind of caring guy.

"I can keep my eyes averted."

Given everything we'd done over the past three days, the idea was ludicrous. "Come in, Michael. Don't worry about not looking. Nothing you haven't already seen." I pitched for just the right wry tone, and the look of mock shock he gave assured me I nailed it.

Then his gaze raked me from big toe to crown and back again, lingering on my breasts. And, of course, my nipples responded to the attention. Instead of tired, like before, I was now invigorated. Frisky even.

Cupping my breasts, I tweaked my nipples. I met Michael's gaze, and I curled my lips into a sly grin. "You interested?" My voice was husky, my breathing shallow. Then, very deliberately, I looked down at his crotch.

Oh, he was definitely interested.

He held up the mug, and I sat up, reaching for it. I

figured I could have a few sips before he joined me. Easing back, I took the first sip. The drink was hot but not scalding, and it suffused me with a warmth from within.

Where I expected Michael to strip with due haste, he arched his eyebrow and reached for the hem of his sweater. He pulled it over his head and folded it. He raked his hand through his short-cropped blond hair, causing his biceps to flex. I'd seen his bare chest before, of course, but not in such bright light. His chest hair was a few shades darker than the hair on his head, and his abdomen was flat and lean. His skin was light but not pasty white like mine. And in the summer, he always went a golden brown, even if it wasn't healthy to tan under the sun's rays.

He had a runner's body, not an ounce of fat on him. He sat, with deliberate slowness, on the closed toilet-seat lid and removed his shoes. Eventually, his laces were undone, and he slipped out of his shoes. Then came the socks. One at a time, with deliberation. Nice gray wool socks. Nothing to write home about. But they left little indentations from his ankle up under his jeans, and I longed to touch the ridges. And finally his feet. Michael was a big guy—and he had big feet.

I licked my lips.

He rose, finally meeting my gaze.

Bastard.

He knew exactly what he was doing and didn't care. He was happy to just keep going with the floor show, increasing my arousal and yet managing to hold his own desires at bay. He undid the button on his jeans and eased the fabric over his slim hips. He wore gray boxer briefs and sported an enormous erection.

My nipples tightened with desire, and my pussy clenched, preparing for him. An ache between my thighs tempted me to alleviate it myself, but delayed gratification had its advantages.

His folded jeans hit the pile of clothes, then his hands moved to his erection. One hand cupped his balls while the other rubbed up and down the length of his cock. The fabric was so tight I saw every contour of the beautiful extension of him, capable of bringing such pleasure. His eyes drifted shut, and the pleasure he was bringing himself robbed me of breath.

No fair.

I wanted in on the fun as his cheeks flushed bright pink and his breath hitched. His eyes opened, and the gray and green of his hazel eyes were almost gone, his pupils were so large.

I swore. "Jesus, Michael, get over here."

He inclined his head in question, all the while keeping up the steady rhythm.

After sitting up abruptly, I started to get out.

"What're you doing?"

Is he an idiot? "I'm tired of watching the show. I want in on the action." A petulant child demanding candy sounded less whiny, but I didn't give a shit.

At that, he smiled. He stopped fondling himself, and his thumbs hooked into the waistband of his briefs. With due care, he pulled them down over his erection. He kicked them aside and moved toward the tub. Instead of coming to me, however, he put a few fingers in the water. He met my gaze and frowned.

What? Oh, duh. "You had me overheating."

His wicked grin suffused me with another flush of longing. He pulled the plug and let the tepid water drain out. I shivered as the cool air hit parts of my body previously submerged.

"I'll warm you up."

"You'd better." I snapped out the words because the ache of longing in my body was painful. I didn't just want him; I needed him. And that scared me. I was fiercely independent, and this need to possess and be possessed was foreign to me. When the tub was fully empty, he turned on the taps and fidgeted with them a bit before he found the temperature he seemed happy with. Not the scalding hot I preferred, but I couldn't complain because the look he gave me scorched a path along my skin and arrowed right to my pussy.

I almost came then and there.

Still, he rose, urging me forward so he could get in behind me. Grudgingly, I obliged, and he slid in, pulling me back against him. His cock was rigid against the small of my back, and my only logical thought was we couldn't fuck in this position.

Michael, seemingly oblivious to my frustration, hooked his feet under my ankles and pushed them against the side of the tub—opening my thighs. His hands cupped my breasts. My skin was so sensitized his chest hair was abrasive against my spine. Had I ever been so teased and unfulfilled in my life?

When his fingers twisted my nipples, I didn't hold back the gasp of need.

The hand on my left breast moved, and I felt bereft until he took my hand and guided it so I could replace his.

"Show me how you like it."

His whispered words in my ear made me powerless to disobey. Previously dexterous fingers fumbled as I twisted my nipple in a way that made my pussy wet, hot, and ready for him. With his now-free hand, he swept my wet hair aside, placing his lips against my neck. Instinctively, I turned my neck farther, giving him the invitation. He rumbled his approval, nipping and licking, taking particular note of my pulse point. My heart hammered as fast as any runner completing the hundred-yard dash—the thundering in my ears making it hard to hear his little noises of appreciation.

Hard, but not impossible.

And speaking of hard—

"Christ, Caressa…" The hiss became a groan as my solid grasp of his slippery cock took hold. He'd been so focused on me he'd lost track of the game, and I'd slid my hand down to the persistent hard-on pressing into my lower back.

Fair play and all that.

If his intention was to torture me until holding back wasn't possible, I could do the same.

"I need you, Michael. I need you to *fuck* me."

The emphasis in the sentence must've left him in no doubt what I needed because his hold on my hand tightened, pulling it into the warm water and urging it along my belly and lower still. Through my pubic hair and even farther down. His whispered "show me" shot electricity up and down my spine, and the butterflies in my belly—previously dormant—woke and fluttered around. I'd never been asked to do this, but because this was Michael, my Michael, I'd do as asked.

Reluctantly, I released my hold on his cock, not missing his groan. Of relief? Of anticipation? Would I get a chance to pleasure him or—

"I love your mind, Caressa, but sometimes you think

too much. If you've changed your mind—"

"Oh, hell no," I spat because in no goddamn way was I not getting off. I eased my right hand over his and guided him down to my core. I didn't do this often, but over the years I'd learned that tension, especially caused by work, could be relieved by rubbing one out. Some days I took my time, teasing myself and touching everything except my clit until I was horny as hell, and other days I got straight to the task.

Today was one of *those* days.

His finger against my sensitized clit shot another electric shock through me, and my legs tightened in a protective stance as I tried to pull them together. His legs were firm against me, and I wasn't moving. Instead of being panicked at the bondage, it gave me permission to be wanton and demanding.

"Vigorous, Michael, I like it fast." Well, in fact I needed it *hard* and fast, but I still held back that little secret part of myself. Maybe in time I could give him all of myself—but I wasn't there yet. He was an ardent lover, but his inherent kindness and consideration was driving me crazy.

As if sensing my need, he picked up the pace. His dexterous fingers applied pressure as he rubbed, and despite the slipperiness inherent with water, his rubbing never faltered.

The orgasm came hard and fast, and it relieved the ache. With little ceremony, I thrust his index finger in me, wanting him to feel what he'd done to me. Of course my body going rigid, my legs convulsing, my head being thrown back probably had the same effect on him.

A grunt reverberating through his chest snapped me out of my post-orgasm languor.

"Michael?"

"I don't think it's broken…"

I tried to twist, but his hold on me was strong and unyielding.

"I said I don't think it's broken."

At least his nose didn't seem to be whistling, but I needed to get a look.

"You get out first, and then I'll follow."

An inauspicious end to what had promised to be such a good night.

Chapter Twelve

Michael

My nose wasn't broken. Small mercy, but Caressa's hard head had definitely connected with my nose, and as I examined myself closely in the mirror, I was grateful to see no sign of black eyes appearing. Along with the unrelenting teasing I was bound to endure from my work crew and the clucking hens of several of the older women in the office, I'd have to face Caressa's horror-filled eyes every time she looked at me.

Shit.

A black eye would've been a small price to pay for having given Caressa such pleasure. Even if she hadn't tossed her head back involuntarily, my finger deep in her pussy assured me of the violence of her orgasm. My diligence as a lover was something I took great pride in. I wanted the companion I entertained to enjoy themselves and my creativity as a boost to my ego.

I had to reassure her the injury was no big deal, but seeing as she was a woman rarely distracted, this was going to be challenging.

Still, I girded my loins and opened the bathroom door. Only the threat of pissing in front of her had convinced her to leave me alone. Although her hesitation assured me that she wouldn't be so dissuaded in the future were the situation any more dangerous by her calculation.

"Oh, thank God, Michael." She clucked, holding up an ice pack. "Still, just to be sure."

"Really? We're all good." My tone wry, I tried for humor, but she was having none of it.

Handing me a cold pack, she guided me over to the bed and encouraged me into it. The high-handedness would normally be intolerable, but she was my Caressa, and nursing was in her blood. Caring for those who were in need was as instinctual as breathing.

At least she allowed me the dignity of sitting up against the headboard.

Whatever dignity she'd allowed me when crawling into bed was gone when she began a thorough examination of my orbital socket. My need to be perceived as tough in front of my new girlfriend was quickly overridden by my desire for comfort from my best friend. "It hurts, Caressa, but it'll heal. No broken bones, I promise. I don't even think I'm going to get a black eye."

Her delicate eyebrow arched. "And where did you get your medical degree?"

"I know what a broken bone feels like. I also know the difference between an inadvertent love tap and a fist thrown in anger and meant to cause serious damage."

The light from her eyes died a quick death, and I cursed. My intention had been to assure her that I held no ill will—and was trying to make light of the situation. Instead, I'd opened the door to a flood of painful memories. For both of us. My body had been abused by the people who'd given me life, but it'd been Caressa's soul that had borne the true toll of the torture and cruelty. I'd learned to go elsewhere when my parents were in one of *those* moods. Often, I'd purposely trigger them earlier in the evening. Their anger was manageable when they were sober—they could exercise some restraint and keep the punches to my torso and legs. Later in the evening, when they were well into the bottle, or bottles depending on the night, they'd get sloppy. They'd grab an arm too hard and leave fingerprint bruises, which forced me to wear a turtleneck in the height of summer. Or they'd shove me down, taking a couple of solid kicks, several times causing hairline fractures of my ribs.

Or if they were really drunk and really careless, a fist would connect with somewhere clothing simply couldn't hide, like my face. Once the beating had been so bad that in the morning, I convinced whichever parent was less hungover to call the school and tell them I had a very contagious case of measles. A good lie because anyone at the school who might give a shit wouldn't want to be around me. The fact there was an effective vaccine wouldn't matter because authorities knew how irresponsible my parents were. The people in charge were more than capable of believing my parents had forgotten to get me vaccinated. The principal hadn't even requested a doctor's note but had insisted I get vaccinated before returning to school.

Thank God for Caressa and Cole. They'd come over every day after school, bringing my class assignments and loving support. Whichever parent had thrown the damaging punch hadn't broken my cheekbone, but the bruise had been vicious and, to my young mind, had taken forever to heal.

Now I looked back upon the nightmare of my childhood as being painful but not unbearable, and that was entirely due to my two best friends.

"We should call Cole."

Startled at seeming to be on the same wavelength as Caressa, I tried to arch an eyebrow but failed miserably. Caressa and Cole shared that particular ability, and they had completely left me behind. I was a decent runner, but dexterity was Caressa's specialty, and ambidexterity was Cole's. My great accomplishment was hitting a home run in the third grade.

"We don't need to call Cole. This isn't a big deal. He'll get a kick out of it the next time we see him and tell him."

"I meant to see if he's okay."

Ah. Shit.

"That's a nice idea, but I think we need to give him time and space. We can text in the morning."

We. No longer was I on my own; I had someone to consult. Someone whose opinion I needed to garner.

Someone who truly gave a shit.

Except hadn't I always had that?

The past five years had taught me that I needed to have my friends closer to me. Making a vow to bring Cole closer as well, I encouraged Caressa to slide under the covers.

Tomorrow. I could deal with all this shit tomorrow. And even though eight o'clock had barely come and gone, we were out for the night.

Chapter Thirteen

Cole

The ice pack against my thigh did little to alleviate the ache. Most guys equated a charley horse or a kick to the groin as the most pain a man could face, but a solid connection with the IT band was almost as good. I'd gone down like a proverbial ton of bricks, surrounded by gasps, groans, one horrified shriek, and one thunderous *fuck*. Whatever I might've said on the subject itself had been cut off when I hit the mat flat on my back, knocking the wind from me. For just one unguarded moment, I'd wished I was dead.

I was no longer lying humiliated on the concrete, as several technicians had helped me to the first-aid room. Helped me? They'd practically fucking carried me. My right thigh was so tight straightening it—or even trying to—was liable to have me passing out from the pain. Donovan had nixed me simply hopping on my right leg to the cot. Something about more liability, stupidity breeding insanity, an insult to my long-gone deadbeat mother, sons of bitches and all, an invective toward a deity, and finally, a long stream of curses directed at me.

Donovan's importance to the show couldn't be overstated, but I was the star, and some lead actors would've thrown their weight around to get Donovan reprimanded or even fired. My instinct was the exact opposite. I deserved every word of frustration and anger. Depending on how bad the damage was, this injury had the potential to throw the show's filming schedule into chaos. As much as I didn't want to believe the show revolved around me…it kind of did. And for all that I lauded the group effort and teamwork when speaking to anyone about the show, I was the vigilante in *Vigilante Justice*.

The cold concrete against my back was nothing compared to the icy stare from Donovan's black eyes. Our gazes held as Meggiebeth, the onsite first-aid person and caterer extraordinaire, examined my leg. Her hands steadily probed the muscle, and her bland expression almost could've fooled me, but I knew better. She had a huge crush on me and knew better than to show anyone because Lisette, our director, ran a tight ship, meaning all dalliances were kept to a minimum. Or better yet, none at all.

That being said, a couple of years ago, while filming a gay movie for Lisette, my co-star, Peter Erikson, was caught in a semi-compromising position with our production assistant, Thomas Walsh. In spectacular fashion, they'd made the tabloids and fueled tons of speculation because neither man was out. In the end, they'd gone from fake boyfriends to engaged to married in mere months. Now they had two adopted children and lived a picture-perfect life. Peter starred in another series while Thomas worked in production on *VJ*.

I might've been a bit—okay, incredibly—jealous of them. They'd built a life together while I dallied and waited patiently for Caressa to come home.

"Cole."

The shot of pain that ricocheted through me when

Meggiebeth hit the sweet spot was unmaskable as I gasped. I cursed my weakness, relenting a little when I saw the gleam of vindication in Donovan's eyes. Smart enough to know I was in deep shit, I took some comfort that my friend would be able to lord this over me. Ironically, it eased much of the tension of the situation.

"I'm not a medical professional…" Everyone knew this to be true, but the first-aid people were good at what they did, and Meggiebeth was no exception. Still, a light blush stole across her cheeks. Cheeks as pale as Caressa's had been this morning over breakfast.

Wrong thought.

"But?" Donovan's impatience yanked me back from wherever I'd been headed.

"But I can feel the tension and inflammation." Her hand was cool against my heated skin, and I'd been arrogant enough to believe she was nervous around me. In retrospect, maybe I'd read the whole situation wrong. Maybe—

"Hamilton." Lisette's shout carried from down the hall.

Meggiebeth's hands literally clenched as she was startled, while still holding my leg, gripping with the ferociousness of a wolf sinking a death grasp into her prey's neck. To my utter dismay, I cried out in pain. More like howled. Meggiebeth stepped away, holding up her hands in apology, and nearly tripped over Donovan who still hovered close.

Donovan might be built like a brick shithouse, but his litheness compensated for the bulk, and he righted her quickly, allowing her more than a modicum of dignity— rather than letting her fall ungraciously to the floor on her ass as I'd done. No one was worried about *my* dignity, or manhood for that matter.

The cause of the commotion had yet to step fully into the room, but her presence already loomed large over all of us. Lisette Grenier was a power unto herself. A force of nature to be reckoned with, and if one was smart, afraid of. She wasn't a tyrant. Perhaps she was the exact opposite. And no one on the crew or in the cast would dare say a bad word about her. Again, not a fear thing. Not afraid of her, but afraid of *disappointing* her. Because enduring her anger was nothing compared to living with the knowledge one had let her down. I, and most of the others, went out of our way to not disappoint. To please her. To even, dare we admit, make her proud.

She was a lioness in the industry in Vancouver, having worked her way up from production assistant in the mid-eighties until now when she was atop her throne as director of a television series. The pint-sized woman, affectionately nicknamed *Pipsqueak* behind her back, was all of four foot ten and maybe ninety pounds soaking wet. Steel-gray close-cropped hair that matched her silver eyes gave her a vaguely butch-dyke look, enhanced by her leather vest, worn by age. A rumored gift from an old flame. Someone who'd broken the woman's heart.

"Clear the room."

Although small, the room wasn't overly full. The three technicians who'd carried me and hung around to see if they were still needed headed out quickly—attempting to be unobtrusive despite their size. Meggiebeth also tried to duck, but Lisette placed a hand on the much-younger woman's arm. She stilled, looking down at Lisette yet still ducking her head in respect.

"Excellent soup today and"—Lisette indicated to

me—"good job."

Meggiebeth's gaze shot to me, and my breath stuttered. Before I could fully grasp the meaning in that look, she was gone. Donovan and Julie both attempted to follow her, squeezing past Lisette.

"Not you two."

Julie's eyebrow arched, and Donovan might just have sighed…but surely not because one did not do that in Lisette's presence, Pipsqueak or not. He did, however, scoop up the abandoned cold gel pack. After pulling a chair beside the cot, he lowered himself—angling so he could hold the cold against my thigh.

Enough babying.

"I can do that, man."

"You could, but you're going to let him do it so I have your full and undivided attention." Unlike Lisette's two previous utterances that had been more like proclamations, this statement was made quietly and without fanfare.

While she held my gaze, Donovan subtly flicked his head to Julie, indicating she needed to move closer to the bed. If there was to be a discussion, the fight coach understood, as I did, that Julie'd need support. We all would. Safety in numbers and all that. When Julie's hand brushed my shoulder, I gave a silent thanks to Donovan's wisdom. We three were now a unit. We had each other's backs.

"You know this is totally unacceptable, Cole."

I do.

I also held my tongue.

"You've put the shoot in jeopardy."

Well, duh.

"What's up?"

The pivotal question was asked very innocuously. Conversationally. Implicit, though, was the threat—my answer could make or break me.

"Momentary lapse of concentration." Not a lie. "Donovan tried to warn me, and Julie tried to keep me focused, but my mind wandered, and I went down. My fault, no question. I take full responsibility."

"As you should." Her erect posture didn't alter. Statues could learn from her stillness. "I've rearranged tonight's shooting so the stunt doubles can do some of the work. I want Julie doing some voiceover work, and I want you to go home. We'll shoot some outdoor backdrop scenes tomorrow, and you'll see our physiotherapist who'll determine your rehabilitation schedule. For God's sake, Cole, don't push yourself to get back sooner than you're able. I run a tight ship, but something like this must be taken care of. Not a word to the press, either. I'll inform the higher-ups because they need to know, but that's it. We keep this news in the family, and you recover as quickly as possible. Anything I did not make perfectly clear?"

"No, ma'am." Without question, I spoke for all three of us.

"I'll drive him home in his car and take a taxi back." Donovan's contribution. "He'll need help to get settled."

Lisette's mouth twisted. "See if Codi is working tonight. She can follow you in an SUV and bring you back." She pivoted to me. "No girls, no boys, no parties. You do everything to get healed fast."

Like I ever had girls or boys or parties. I'd attended a few events to see and be seen, but those weren't my scene. I preferred...private and intimate events. Nights that'd never make the gossip columns or websites noting celebrity spottings.

With a chopping motion, Lisette dismissed Donovan and myself. She held one arm up and encouraged Julie to step toward her, then slung an arm around the younger woman. "We have much to do, ma petite. You up for the challenge?"

"Yes, ma'am." She meant it.

They left the room together.

I almost felt sorry for my co-star as the director shepherded her out of the tiny room, leaving just me and my tormenter.

Within moments, though, Meggiebeth returned with a wheelchair. "Prop."

"Very handy." Donovan flashed her his toothy grin that made many a woman swoon.

Letting Donovan lift me into the wheelchair was humiliating but nothing less than I deserved. As with Julie, I did as many of my own stunts as I could. At thirteen I'd approached the owner of a local dojo. Martial arts training in exchange for cleaning services. Tired of being bullied and scared, I'd decided I needed to take my future into my own hands. Plus, I'd had some crazy notion I could protect Caressa and Michael as well— should the need ever arise.

Nothing dire had ever happened, but my agility and strength had built. A fight instructor at theater school had honed those skills, and now I was able to handle many of my own stunts. Except apparently when I was to pivot one way and did the opposite. We were almost to the car, and well out of earshot of everyone else, when I ventured to ask the question I dreaded. I didn't want to hear the answer, but I worked better with information than existing in a vacuum. Like I'd endured all the years

Caressa was gone. "How long?"

Donovan lowered the lever to lock the wheelchair in place. I hit the remote to unlock the car door and watched helplessly as Donovan opened the passenger door and frowned.

"You just had to buy an electric sedan. Couldn't you have sprung for an SUV?"

"Wasn't working on *VJ* when I bought the car—it's economical and environmental."

After snagging me under the arms, Donovan half carried, half dragged me and then plunked me unceremoniously in the car. Somehow, all that maneuvering and he hadn't tapped the bad left leg.

Impressive.

Before Donovan could do it, I slammed the door closed with a bit more force than was necessary, but, hell, this was my car, and I could do whatever I fucking wanted. Just as quickly the door re-opened, and before I could curse, he unceremoniously dumped an ice pack in my lap. This time he was the one who slammed the car door with more force than strictly necessary.

As he pushed the wheelchair back toward the building, I had a moment to think, to reflect. To curse my stupidity. I'd made it, hadn't I? *Vigilante Justice*'s ratings were climbing week over week, the series had just been picked up for a fifth season, and the American network had moved the show to its favored Thursday nighttime slot. Now I, Cole Hamilton, was watched in millions of households in North America every week.

Not bad for a kid from the Downtown Eastside of Vancouver.

Not bad for a kid who'd lived in poverty growing up.

Not bad for a kid who'd worked two jobs while going to theater school in order to get an education and a foot in the door.

I'd paid my dues—in life and in the business. Now, at thirty-two, I was on top. Professionally, anyway. Personally? Well, yeah…not quite.

Now this injury threatened everything.

Stupid, stupid, stupid.

"Six weeks or longer if you don't do what you're told."

Donovan's words yanked me out of my mind and to the realization the car was moving. We pulled out from the lot and onto the main road.

"I take it we're heading to your place?"

"Where else would we be going?" Despite myself, and knowing better, I snarled.

"I don't know…maybe somewhere you can get your head out of your ass?"

I wanted to argue, but I'd totally earned that smackdown.

"Like maybe Caressa's?"

Caressa.

My breath hitched, and a band tightened around my chest. As it did every time I thought about my best friend. Well, one of my best friends. And wasn't there a problem contained in the definition? One was supposed to have *one* best friend. One person who knew their heart, kept their secrets, accepted them the way they were—and loved them unconditionally. But I had two best friends.

Michael and Caressa.

Whom I'd believed, until a few hours ago, were just best friends.

"No." Quick, sharp, and a knife to the heart. I

couldn't go to her place. Her's and Michael's home. Oh, I'd been to Michael's dozens of times over the years. I'd be welcomed in a heartbeat. No, I wouldn't go because I was the one who no longer fit in the trio of buddies.

"You want to talk about this?"

"No." Quicker and sharper. I had to stop reminiscing about the good times. Not that we wouldn't have good times in the future, but things had irrevocably changed today. Because Caressa and Michael might still be my best friends, but they were also romantically involved. Not just involved, but living together. Freaking ready to pick out china patterns. And if the dark circles under their eyes were any indication, fucking like rabbits.

How did this happen?

Shit. Not only had we crossed the Lion's Gate Bridge, but we were now heading south down Burrard Street. I'd lost a good fifteen minutes pouting about a situation in which I had zero power to change things. I could accept what was or sulk for a super-long time and risk losing my best friends. In truth, I owed Donovan something.

Anything.

"Caressa's home."

"Yeah…" A neutral note.

"Well, we got together with Michael on the Drive on Friday night. Long story short, before we were able to have a real conversation, she had to deliver a baby, and then I had to leave because we had an early shoot. If I wasn't so focused on my career, I might not have lost her."

"How did you *lose* her? I mean, how do you *lose* a person?"

"You let your other best friend make the moves, and

suddenly, you're out in the cold." More figuratively than literally, but I'd gotten into my car this afternoon and jacked up the heat because I'd sat outside for almost an hour after they left. Even though I'd worn my leather jacket, the temperature had dropped, and the smell of snow had been in the air. Vancouver didn't get snow very often, once or twice a winter, but the meteorologists predicted more volatile weather than normal this season, including more snow and more rainstorms. Well, my home had a gas fireplace and a generator, so I wasn't worried.

Michael's condo had all the amenities as well, and since the downtown core almost never lost power, he and Caressa would be warm in their place.

Their place.

The thought still boggled my mind.

"You're thinking again." Donovan maneuvered onto West 4th and headed toward Point Grey.

I might not have bought a fancy car, but I'd invested my first year's paychecks and bought a house in one of the most expensive and exclusive neighborhoods in Vancouver. From a kid in poverty in the Downtown Eastside to a property owner in Point Grey with no mortgage. Housing prices in Vancouver were ridiculous, and I'd likely bought near the top of the market, but I didn't care. Certain real estate would prove to be a good investment, and more importantly, I had the house I'd always dreamed of. Two stories with a walk-out basement and an amazing view of the downtown and the North Shore Mountains. I still tucked away a significant portion of my salary because *VJ* could be canceled at any time, and I faced huge property tax bills for as long as I owned the place, but I didn't mind. Living well below my means was just fine with me. My needs were simple, and my desires were mostly unattainable. And money wasn't likely to bring me happiness anyway.

Pulling up to my house, Donovan tapped the garage door opener. It had room for two cars, and we could park four more on the driveway. Alas, my one tiny car lived alone. Hell, I didn't even have much stuff in the garage. A pair of skis I rarely used, a mountain bike I did use, and a few other abandoned items.

"Is that a home gym in those boxes?"

Shit. Should've had Donovan park the car on the driveway. Except the stairs up to the front door would've been hell while the house had none from the garage to the main floor—elevation was not going to be my friend tonight.

Or for the foreseeable future.

Crap.

"It is." Succinct.

"Well, I'll be setting it up tomorrow. I know you prefer cardio, but you're going to need to stay fit while staying off that leg. Weights'll be a great way to do it."

I did not believe weights were going to be a *great way* to do anything because, despite everything, I still preferred martial arts for my workout.

"I'm lean and quick the way I am. If I beef up, fans will notice."

Whine much?

"Pretty boy, bulking up is going to be the least of your worries. We won't be doing any sessions on the mat for a while, and this'll have to suffice. I'll come by tomorrow when the physiotherapist and doctor are here. I'll set it up, and we'll see what you will and will not be able to do."

"Doctor? Why do I need a doctor?" God, was I actually whining?

Yep, I'd sunk that low.

"Precaution and the insurance company's going to insist on it. They may also pull your coverage to do so many stunts on your own."

Shit. That'd never occurred to me. Fuck, just more and more of a mess and an insurmountable mountain to climb. I'd do anything to go back an hour and… What? Put in my best effort? I'd done that—but my mind had been unfocused.

"Look, the physiotherapist is Zoey Morneau. She's been around a while but is up on the latest treatments. Rumor is she's angling for a spot on the team roster for the Whitecaps, so you'd be a feather in her cap and a good line on her resumé. Be nice to her, and she might not wear you down. Be good to her, and she might not knock you around for being such an ass. Give her less than one hundred percent, and I'll be down here riding said ass."

"Don't you have better things to do?"

"Not going to lie—I do. I have a cast who still have lots of stunts to do. I have a schedule to rework. Lucky we've been picked up for the entire season so I can do some work with future episodes. Not how I prefer to work, but I'll take whatever I can get. Plus, Julie's been bugging me to up her training regime, and I've held back because her shooting schedule's always so rigorous and I didn't want to wear her out. I was going to wait until the end of the season, but now'll be the perfect time to teach her a bunch of new tricks. It'll make her more agile and better able to compensate when you do finally drag your sorry ass back to work."

"I'd be there tomorrow if I could."

"I know you would, but since you can't, we'll figure it out. I'm thinking of asking the writers to work in some scenes with Lyric doing training so it won't look out of place if she's got new moves when you come back."

Already planning—that was Donovan. He was one of the best in the business, and *VJ* had been lucky to land him. Of course, me putting in a good word hadn't hurt. Donovan might owe the chance to me, but he'd more than proven himself capable.

Eyeing the distance to the back door, I sighed. Actually sighed. Judging by the pain I felt now, the vastness might as well be all the way to the top of the Grouse Grind instead of ten feet—and the distance to my bedroom might as well be a cycling trip up to Squamish. Would be just as challenging. If not more, were I being honest with myself.

"You have an office chair with wheels, right? I'm going to roll it out and then roll you to the master suite. At least you had the smarts to buy a house with most of the essential things on the main floor."

Except the basement was where all the fun took place. Donovan knew that, and perhaps his comment was a way to goad me—a way to rub in the fact there would be no playing in the near future. A way to remind me that play had always come second to the business at hand. And I'd do well to remember that, even as some hot images flashed through my mind. Six weeks without sex, I could handle.

Wait. Was sex off the table? Missionary style, sure, but other, more creative ways? Who the hell was I supposed to ask? Donovan'd laugh his ass off, and the doctor might make a note in the chart. The insurance company would just love to know I was more concerned about when I could resume my sex life versus how quickly I could return to the show. How about the physiotherapist? Zoey, right? Odd name but if the woman was as good as Donovan promised, maybe there might be hope for me yet.

Pushing the thought of how much damage the rolling office chair was going to cause to my hardwood floors, I resignedly accepted my new reality for the next while. I'd prefer crutches, but stability was key, and the one time I used them before, it'd been an unmitigated disaster. Michael and Caressa hadn't laughed too much. But the soon-to-be nurse had continuously admonished me for not doing it the *right* way. Caressa'd been an ass-kicker even back then, and I'd be surprised if anything had changed. Then again, spending years in South Sudan was bound to have changed her, and if I was willing to admit it, I'd seen the change for myself. Even just the decision to move in with Michael was evidence of a monumental internal shift for her.

"I swear to God, buddy, if you don't start focusing, things are not going to get better for you."

Focus. I had to stop losing focus. Had to get my mind in the game. And just in case I forgot, the jostling of my leg against the arm of the chair while Donovan hauled me into it was enough to make my eyes water and to force me to bite back a curse.

"Into the hot tub we go with some good anti-inflammatories. Then into bed for you and hopefully a good night's rest. Things're going to start early tomorrow."

I had no good arguments to those plans, so I just went along for the ride.

Chapter Fourteen

Michael

For the second night in a row, Caressa awoke struggling and breathing like she'd just run a marathon.

For the second night in a row, I held her, trying to calm and comfort her to the best of my ability.

For the third night in a row, we lay awake long after the tremors passed.

I'd stayed silent the past couple of nights because, uh, not my place to push. She was due to start seeing a counselor, and together they'd work through the issues, right? Well, I was having doubts. Stroking her damp hair away from her brow, I was careful just to soothe and not to do anything that might be misinterpreted.

"Can you…" God, did I really want to go there? Try to be more than a friend? Try to help her tackle her demons?

"Her name was Raqiyah." Caressa's voice was tremulous. "She was thirteen years old when she was raped. A man from another village, I think. She never said, but when she came to me, she was already about four months pregnant." She managed a sniff, a tremble, and an attempt to rein in the pain I felt to my soul. "The men in the village grabbed her from the clinic, dragged her outside, and stoned her to death."

A thirteen-year-old girl? Stoned because she'd been

raped and had gotten pregnant? And how was I supposed to comfort Caressa now? What words could I offer in the face of such horror and violence?

None. I had nothing to offer but a shoulder and meaningless comforting words. Insufficient. Inadequate. Lacking.

"I'm sorry." Her words were quiet, accompanied by an inelegant sniff.

I reached for the tissue box, then offered it, and once she plucked one, I put it back on the nightstand. To my amusement, she was just as inelegant when she blew her nose. I found it reassuring she was comfortable being just Caressa with me and didn't feel the need for artifice. It wouldn't have suited her, and it would've put me on edge. I was grateful she didn't ask for the reason the tissue box was so close at hand. More than a few nights on my own and…well, that didn't matter anymore.

Brushing my knuckle gently down her throat, I was reassured her pulse had returned to normal and the tremors were gone. Pulling her closer, I placed a kiss to her sweat-slicked brow.

As if anticipating the move, she pushed herself up so lips met lips. My surprise had me opening my mouth, and she took advantage. Her tongue entered my mouth and immediately plundered. Demanded reciprocity. As her need ratcheted up for both of us, her hands, previously on my chest, flexed, turning her fingers into claws. None-too-gentle claws either. The desperation to her assault on my senses overwhelmed, and my brain ordered me to stop while my body responded to the stimulation. As I pulled back, she growled and snagged my erection. I hadn't wanted to respond, but my body was in the game while my mind still struggled to catch up. I'd meant to comfort and reassure, not to elicit a sexual reaction.

Also, possibly my action had nothing to do with this onslaught. The last two nights we'd resettled after the nightmare and she'd gone back to sleep—less fitful than before but not the deep restorative sleep she desperately needed. Tonight's aggression was different.

"Stop thinking, Michael, and just fuck me."

Well, when put like that, how was I supposed to respond?

With logic, of course.

"Caressa, sweetheart, maybe this isn't the best time, you know? You've been through a trauma and—"

"I don't need fucking platitudes. I need you inside me as soon as possible."

When put like that, how was I supposed to refuse?

As if sensing weakness, she snagged my hand and placed it to her breast. The nipple pebbled immediately—an encouragement for me to increase my ministrations if there ever was one. I tweaked, I tugged, I soothed. Anything to elicit more mewls of need.

She reciprocated by placing her mouth to my nipple and biting. Not hard, but enough to get my full and undivided attention. In response, I trailed my hand down her flank and insinuated it between her thighs. I wasn't certain what I'd find, but her juices soaking my fingers wasn't it. At the first touch of my finger to her clit, her body arched as if she'd been hit by a bolt of lightning.

Quick as a cat, she pushed me onto my back and straddled me. In mere moments, she guided me to her, and I gained entrance, sliding right in. *Coming home.* Each time we did this, I had a feeling of coming home. Like this was where I belonged and where I was most happy. And apparently she did as well, if her moans were anything to judge by.

"Fuck me, Michael. I need it hard."

What the lady wants…

I gripped her thighs and set a punishing rhythm, using my muscles to thrust upward quickly, not giving her enough time to recover between each push. Despite her breaths coming in short gasps, she was right there along with me. Her fingers grasped my abs, flexing and lightly clawing my muscles. Her desperation matched mine as my body wound tighter and tighter, seeking the release promised by our joining.

I wanted to cup her breasts, maybe tweak her nipples, but I needed my hands to hold her tight to maintain the pace she set. And the friction was going to send me over if she didn't go first. And I wanted her to go first. Needed her to. My reputation as a selfless lover demanded it, but as I came closer and closer to the edge, I fought the release my body craved. Then, in a moment of clarity, I slid my hand, pressing my thumb to her clit and rubbing as gently and precisely as I could.

Success.

Her inner muscles clamped around me and, thank God, sent me spiraling upward and then crashing down to the ground. She'd arched backward upon the beginning of the orgasm, but now she collapsed on me as if seeking something. Comfort? Love? Compassion? All things I could offer in different measures, but none I was sure would be enough.

From the base of her skull, I thrust my hands in her hair, dragging her closer and taking her mouth for a punishing kiss. I was going to take every advantage I had, but I also recognized I was going to need help.

I was going to have to call in the big guns.
I was going to have to talk to Cole.

Chapter Fifteen

Cole

No two ways about it, Zoey Morneau was a taskmaster, pain in the ass, and all-around bitch.

And fucking good at her job.

So good that by the end of the first hour, I was ready to surrender. Even in my toughest training sessions with Donovan, I'd never felt so…inadequate. Incapable. Not up to the task.

"That's good, Hamilton. Give me ten more reps, and we'll move to your ankles."

Ankles? I had muscles in the ankles that could be strengthened? On second thought, better not to ask. I'd made a few comments near the beginning only to quickly discover that although Zoey likely had a wicked sense of humor, it wasn't going to come out of the closet as long as we had serious work to be done. Maybe once the session was over?

If it ever ended. I had no illusions I might expire before she called it a day.

Zoey's fortitude was unrivaled in my experience. Except, perhaps, by Caressa. Even in her first days of nursing, she'd been confident. Sure, yet perfectly willing to ask questions and admit when she didn't have the answers. Even when confronted with Michael and my objections to her plan to volunteer in South Sudan, she'd never lost her cool. Never wavered. Never backed down—even in the face of anger on Michael's part and desperation on my own.

Then, as if I were able to conjure her by will, she appeared on the threshold between the living room and the main floor den where Donovan'd so kindly set up all the gym equipment he thought I might need. Equipment that had been languishing in the garage but now had a prominent place in the center of the room.

"Caressa—"

"This is a private session, ma'am. You'll need to wait for us to finish."

Completely unperturbed by Zoey's forceful order, Caressa stepped into the room. She took in the entire scene before a little V appeared between her eyebrows. "This isn't just an exercise routine, is it?" Hands on hips, she pivoted to me—those damning pale-blue eyes impaling me. Slaying me in half and demanding I answer her question.

"Minor injury, that's all."

Zoey actually snickered.

Caressa's eyes widened. "What the hell happened?"

"He lost focus." Apparently Zoey'd conferred extensively with Donovan. "And you're giving him another excuse to not do what needs to be done."

Her tone must've caught Caressa's attention because two little spots of pink appeared on her high cheekbones. "Well, I'm not here to cause problems—"

"Don't go."

To hell with Zoey, Donovan, and all the fucking exercises. Caressa'd never come to me before like this, and despite her attitude, I couldn't miss the dark circles under those beautiful stormy eyes.

"I can step out…"

"Zoey, this is Caressa Klein. She's a nurse and will be helping out around here when you and Donovan aren't around." Well, good to know I could still spout total bullshit off the top of my head.

"Oh, I am, am I?" Her arched eyebrow assured me that I might've dodged a bullet, but she still had a sword with my name on it.

Zoey's hands hadn't left her hips. "Nurse specializing in what, precisely?"

Oh, she did not just—

"BCIT grad, four years in emergency medicine, five years in South Sudan doing everything, including maternity and trauma, and now back in the ER at St. Paul's." The daggers Caressa's eyes shot did nothing to fell the other woman.

"Well, glad to hear it. You'd be amazed how many famous people have *nurses* and other professionals. He going to pay you?"

First *nurse* in air quotes and then bringing up money? Obviously, Zoey wasn't worried about being canned. And obviously, she took her job seriously. In fact, if my interests weren't otherwise occupied with the other woman in the room, I'd have likely found her confidence a turn-on. No way, however, would I dip my toe in that pool. Even if Donovan hadn't warned me off, I didn't mix business with pleasure. Plus, the woman might be an inch or two shorter than Caressa, but she outweighed her by a good twenty-five pounds. Sure, I sometimes liked sturdy and built women, but these days I was all about willowy and waifish. Not as tall as myself, but taller than many.

"I wouldn't take Cole's money even if he offered all

of it." Caressa's disgust was plain. "My next shift is tomorrow at St. Paul's, but I can put it off if he needs me."

"He doesn't need full-time care." Zoey, apparently, was not going to back down. "As long as he doesn't do anything stupid, he should be fine. Just…get him to use the crutches, okay?" She glared at me as she methodically wiped down the equipment and tidied up. "He seems to have some weird phobia of them…"

"Because he can't use them worth shit." Caressa's amused contribution. "But this time Michael and I'll run roughshod over him." Some of the stress had vanished, and her eyes twinkled with barely suppressed amusement.

"Is Michael as hard-assed as you?"

Zoey's question was so plainspoken that I actually sputtered—grateful I wasn't guzzling water as I'd been most of the morning.

Caressa raised an eyebrow as she appeared to carefully consider her answer. "No, I'm tougher. Stronger. Less likely to accept bullshit." A corner of her lip curled. "He'd deny it strenuously, but Michael's more of a nurturer. He's the one you go to with a broken heart or a bruised ego. I'll patch you up, and Cole'll kick you in the ass and send you back into the world. Ready to defend you at every turn."

The physiotherapist tossed the towel in the bin. "You three sound inimitable."

"An unbreakable bond." Caressa held out her hand. "Thank you for putting up with him. I suspect he didn't make it easy."

Zoey laughed. "Oh, he puts up a good front, all professional and such, but he's just a big baby. Hates to be felled by a girl."

"You?" Caressa's voice betrayed her surprise.

"Oh, I wish." Zoey shrugged into her winter coat.

At least now Caressa wore one as well.

"No, Julie took out his IT band. I'm just here to pick up the pieces and rehab him until he can get back into action."

"Well, shit, Cole, you never do things by half measures." Her words might be sarcastic, but I recognized the underlying concern. Damn, I'd upset her.

"I'll be back tomorrow." Slinging her bag over her shoulder, Zoey gave a salute. "Later, boss." With that final zinger, she was gone.

Heavy silence remained in the wake of her departure. I sat on a chair with my leg elevated, facing a force of nature in the guise of my best friend. Her long black hair was tamed into a submissive ponytail, leaving my view of her face completely unhindered. I'd seen right through all the bluster with Zoey. And had suspected the fiery storm had yet to be unleashed.

"What the actual fuck, Cole?"

Right on cue.

"Well, you know—"

"No, in fact I don't know."

Ouch. "I was practicing a scene and ducked left when I should have pivoted right."

She waved me off as if my confession was of no consequence.

Well, damn.

"Why did you not call us? Because I'm assuming this didn't happen in the last hour…"

Us? Oh shit, she already considered herself a unit. Caressa and Michael. Michael and Caressa. Before I could respond, she dropped her knapsack on the floor and flounced out of the room. I didn't particularly like the word, but it described exactly what she'd just done. She was pissed.

What's she going to do?

At least she hasn't left.

Within moments, she was back with an ice pack. Without ceremony, she marched over and pressed the pack to my leg. Unerringly hitting the exact spot. "What's the prognosis?"

How was I supposed to think straight when she was that close and glaring at me with those beautiful eyes? Stunning eyes clearly still haunted. Even more than when we'd been children and she'd been living with a neglectful drug addict.

"Why are you here?"

Startled, she nearly dropped the pack. Only my swift reaction saved it from falling to the floor, but the effort flexed my leg, and I cringed.

Fuck.

"Am I not welcome here?"

"Of course you are. I didn't realize you knew my address." A far distance from the place I'd last lived when she'd been in town. Metaphorically, if not literally.

"Michael knew the address, and he was the one who encouraged me to come over." As if having said too much, she retreated. She backed away, dropping her gaze. Then, as if searching for something else to look at, she gazed over to the window and gasped. Not a surprising reaction because I saw the same vista every day.

"It's stunning, Cole. Truly…" She wandered over, then extended her hand across the length of the glass, finally settling it.

Fingerprints.

Oh, for fuck's sake, you have a cleaning service to handle something so mundane.

My best friend was here and appreciating why I'd dropped the big bucks for this place. I might've opted for cheap and reliable for my vehicle, but I'd dropped a pretty penny for the spectacular view. Now, in early winter, the Grouse Mountain was covered in snow. The nearer cityscape of Vancouver contrasted with the majesty of nature. Something soothed in the dichotomy. As if I were witness to a constant battle of man versus nature—but that, because of the mountain, nature would always win.

"Worth every penny, eh?"

She didn't turn, keeping her hand on the pane. "You could feed a village in Africa for years on what I know you must've paid, but I don't begrudge you the choice. If you have to live in the city, pick somewhere you can lose yourself. Here, on English Bay, you have an odd privacy. Point Grey is exclusive enough you don't have the riffraff as your neighbors. Yet you're close enough to the downtown core to get whatever you need."

"And it's just a quick trip across the bridge to get to the North Shore. The studio isn't far from the Upper Levels section of the highway, so it's all terribly convenient." Especially given I could hop in my little compact car and get wherever I needed to go. Only an accident on the bridge ever truly slowed my trips to and from work as I avoided rush hour whenever possible. When that meant going extra early, I'd just work on my lines or practice the choreography. Never was a moment wasted in my life.

Until now.

And as nice as this conversation was, I wasn't getting anywhere. Not where I really needed to be, anyway. "Why did Michael send you here?"

"Not send...exactly." Still she didn't break away from the view.

Several oil tankers were visible in the Straight of Georgia, and one or two insane pleasure boaters were enjoying the beautiful sunshine despite the chilly weather. In another few minutes, the sun was going to angle just right against the water, and it'd sparkle.

"I'm having trouble adjusting. As you predicted."

I didn't miss the wry tone in her voice. Well, I deserved that. "I'm sorry to hear it. You want to talk?"

A shake of her head.

And no words.

"You start back, what, tomorrow? Day or night shift?"

"Night."

"So, throwing you into the deep end and seeing if you can swim."

Now a rueful chuckle. "Every shift is the deep end at St. Paul's. I'll be mainly observing for the first few shifts. Getting the lay of the land, so to speak. I know I'm a little rusty, mostly on drug protocols, and I haven't worked their computer system before but..."

"But you're a swift study, and you'll pick things up quickly. They're lucky to have you, Caressa. So what's really going on?" To be so unsure of herself wasn't like her. So questioning.

"What if I can't handle it?"

"Then you quit." Simple and straightforward. Plain as day.

Finally, she turned. "It's not like I can just walk away—"

"Why not?" I caught her gaze and held it. "There are tons of nursing jobs out there. I know you prefer the public sector, but the private sector is begging for recruits."

"So I can do homecare visits?" Her voice dripped with sarcasm.

"Do people homebound deserve any less than the best care? Invalids like me need help too, you know."

She actually snickered. "Cole, you've never needed anyone."

You. The thought came quick and unbidden. I needed her. I'd always needed her and probably always would. Even if she belonged to Michael, I'd still want her in my life. She was my oxygen—my reason for living. Still, I was losing her—both in this moment and in general. "What about maternity checkups? Don't they send nurses to check in with new mothers? That'd be right up your alley, so to speak."

For my genius idea, I received only pursed lips as a response.

"How's your leg?"

Our conversation had been so intense I'd forgotten. "Very numb."

She nodded, striding over and holding out her hand. Obligingly, I slapped the ice pack into her palm and waited somewhat impatiently as she took it to the kitchen and eventually returned.

Her scowl was back. "You never told me the prognosis."

Because I'm still in denial. "Several weeks. Less if I'm careful. More if I'm not. I'm off for the rest of the week. After New Year's they'll let me back on set, so I can do any and all shots that don't involve standing, walking, or anything else physical."

Sitting on the weight bench, she pointed to my leg. "This is serious, but I suspect you know this. They've given you crutches, right? Well, use them, or you won't get better. Your instinct'll be to push when you really need rest." Her brow furrowed. "When was the last time you took a break? You did a small film between last season and this one, right?"

I shouldn't have been surprised she'd remembered, but I was. Touched as well that during the hell she'd been enduring, she'd taken the time to absorb the contents of the letters I'd sent. Well, short missives. Michael'd done the bulk of the heavy lifting in that regard. I contented myself with knowing Michael was sending plenty of letters, emails, and sunscreen. Maybe if I'd been more forthcoming and taken the time to communicate properly, Caressa wouldn't have been so quick to jump into Michael's bed.

Of course, that line of thinking wasn't going to get me anywhere.

"Yeah, a smaller film. Indie shot by a friend of mine from theater school. He's an amazing director, and if he ever finishes the edits, I think it'll be a good film."

"So what's the hang-up? He need money?" She shot a quick look around my place.

Oh.

"Nah. I mean, I fronted him some of the money, but that's not a concern. He's a perfectionist. He could've been done with this project months ago, but he's just not quite happy with it. Apparently, my stuff is good, but some of his *mood* shots aren't quite right. Now, I work in the business, and I'm not sure what he means. I've offered to screen what he's got, but he won't let me. He claims it'll mess with his creative process."

Caressa's nose twitched. "It's a good thing you're not waiting for revenue. Sounds like it may never see the light of day."

"Or the inside of a theater." I smiled indulgently. "No, I'm not counting on the money. In fact, I've told him to keep the revenue and invest it in his next project."

"You're that confident in his abilities or just don't need the money?"

"Both." There, honesty. And time to change the subject. "What can I do for you, Caressa? I know you're here for something. I totally understand you're struggling with being back in civilization, and you told me you're going for counseling—"

"I am."

"But it's not enough, is it? As much as I enjoy your company, I don't think you're here to shoot the shit." I'd love it if she was, but that wasn't her style. Everything she did had purpose. No wasted energy for my good friend.

Her expressive eyes confirmed my suspicions because the weariness was back. Once in a while she'd pull out of the memories, but most of the time she seemed to be back in Africa. When she finally spoke, she caught me off guard.

"I'm worried about Michael."

Michael? What the... I held myself still, silently willing her to come to me.

Her brow furrowed in concern as she broke eye contact. "I suppose I should explain... I'm the problem. I'm happy, don't get me wrong, but..."

Again, her voice trailed off, and I bit back the desire to demand she be more precise and concise. She didn't normally waffle, and it concerned me greatly.

"I'm not the same person I was when I left."

"None of us are." I was pointing out the obvious— but trying to do it carefully. I had to keep her present with me.

I received a shrug and another long pause for my effort. "I'm not sure Michael has accepted that."

She yanked on her ponytail to tighten it even farther, and I winced. I occasionally wore my hair in a leather thong, and damn, those things could hurt. I marveled at the women who wore them all day long. Would give me a damn headache, I was sure.

"I know five years has passed, but Michael...well, he's as successful as ever. He says he's doing well at work, and he seems happy."

"All those things are true." *Tread carefully.* "But he changed, Caressa. We both did. Worrying will do that."

She used her arms to lever herself off the bench and then wrapped them around her narrow waist. "But he's still worrying, Cole. You both are."

Well, duh. "That's true. But give us time. We're still getting used to you being back in Canada and safe—let alone back in our lives. We both missed you, but..." Was I really going to do this? Was I going to throw my feelings out the window and put Michael in the best light possible? Of course I was. Michael was also my best friend. "I think Michael missed you more than I did. I had an incredibly busy career to distract me, and even when I came home at night, I had to go straight to bed because we'd be back at it first thing in the morning. Michael had more downtime. And I think his propensity for worrying made him more…obsessed."

"Really?" I caught the true skepticism in her voice. "That he worried? Of course—"

"No, I mean that he worried more. I mean, it doesn't matter because it's not a contest." She waved away the objection even as she made it. Typical Caressa—to call me on my bullshit and then offer me a way out.

So was I going to hide and slough it off or be honest and lay things on the line?

Man up.

"No, you're right. I did worry. I worried a lot, especially this last time. I couldn't figure out why you refused to come back to Canada between deployments. Didn't want to believe Michael and I were such horrible people that you couldn't trust us to respect your decision."

"Did you?"

Damn. "We tried to. I mean, you're an adult and capable of making your own decisions. We just worried you were being swayed by emotions rather than logic." *Well, fuck it.* "I know you want to go back. I can see the guilt eating away at you, and I desperately want to order you to stay put, but I can't do that. I can only encourage you to get counseling and to open up to Michael. I have to trust he'll say the right things, do the right things, to keep you here in Vancouver. Here where we can keep an eye on you and make sure you have everything you need. Do I want you working with the drug addicts from the Downtown Eastside? Probably not. Would I prefer you do checkups on healthy babies and moms? Of course. Both jobs risk your heart if something goes wrong, but only one risks your personal safety."

"I don't have my sea legs, Cole."

Her words tore at me, but I waited for her to continue.

"I thought if I just got back to nursing, it'd be okay. And maybe it will." Those words were uttered in a rush. "What if I'm wrong?"

Her indecision concerned me. "We all have doubts, Caressa. I have them, for sure. I may seem like I have my shit together, but I don't. Every day I worry about being the best. The best at knowing my lines. The best at nailing choreography. The best at acting. Now, how unrealistic is that? I play the equivalent of a superhero, and I worry that my Shakespearean professor will feel embarrassed at having been my instructor. I worry about my looks even though there are legions of fans who assure me I'm hot shit. And I'm terrified the higher-ups are going to decide I'm not worth the effort now that I'm injured. How hard would it be to kill off my character and turn Lyric into the superhero? A woman can do it these days, you know?"

"I've seen *Wonder Woman*, if that's what you mean. And several other movies where the women dominated." Caressa's nose wrinkled. "Lyric is a great character, but she's an antihero. I suppose they could give her a series, but replacing you with her as the lead of *Vigilante Justice* misses the point. Unless they turn her into the good guy—"

"You're not helping." The words came out as a grouse, but I didn't care because she was just putting words to the doubts that'd plagued me for the last dozen or so hours.

Her expression morphed into concern, the little V of worry back between her brows. "Have they said anything? About replacing you?"

"No." And they weren't likely to as long as I recovered as quickly as possible. I didn't want to dwell on this topic, but I couldn't seem to move on to another topic. Any topic. Still, I tried. "So aside from doubts about work, how are you?" The haunted look ghosting her face told me that I'd picked the wrong topic. *Damn.*

"I…" Her hesitancy was clear. Again.

Something was going on, and I had no idea how to break through her walls. My temptation was to use a sledgehammer because knocking on the door wasn't gaining me the entrance I so dearly wanted.

"You want food? I can whip something up…"

On cue, my stomach rumbled. The protein shake I'd consumed for breakfast had been hours ago. "I'd offer to help, but I think that'd be a disaster."

Finally, for the first time in what felt like forever, she smiled. A true, genuine grin. "Cole, you're much more talented in the kitchen than I am." She pointed to the crutches. "You willing to try again?"

"Well, I'm still not proficient, if that's what you're asking. If you don't mind, I could use a spotter." But first I needed to deal with an indelicate issue. "And if we could stop by the little boys' room first, that'd be amazing."

Another grin. "Okay, but I'm not holding it while you piss. You hit the toilet seat, and that's on you."

"Hey, I always lift the lid and then put it back down." She'd been the one to teach me that little trick. Staying in the ladies' good books or so she'd intimated. I'd never had any complaints.

And there'd been a few women over the years. And a few guys as well, although I never got the sense they cared about toilet seats. A few of my guests came back more than once. They wanted what I had to offer, and we found mutual satisfaction. But there'd never been anyone special. Anyone who captured my imagination. Anyone who made me want to settle down.

The reason stood before me. Now, in the harsh light of day, I could see what never dawned on me during those nocturnal encounters—none of the women had been Caressa. None could hold a torch to her. Some had been beautiful. Some had been whip-smart. Some shared my proclivities. And that made us a good match. But none held a candle to my best friend.

So none had stayed long. When had this started?

Shit.

Since she'd left for Africa, or just shortly after. I'd had those short-term relationships, mostly with women in the business. Was this why I was so angry with Michael? He'd swooped in and swept Caressa off her feet when I'd been intending to do the same thing? I'd told myself getting her to stay here was just about making sure she was safe, but now I needed to admit to myself it'd been more than that.

"Cole!" She snapped her fingers in front of my face.

Double shit. "Sorry, just trying to remember what food is in the fridge."

"Bullshit."

What? How could she possibly know?

"You're as sharp as a tack. Or you always have been in the past. You were thinking about something far more absorbing." Her eyes shone with concern. "What's really going on?"

"Do you love Michael? Really love him?"

If she was surprised, she hid it well. She moved swiftly to my side, then dropped to her haunches before me. She placed a hand against my cheek, and I resisted the urge to rub against it.

"I'm sorry we hurt you. This was never our intention, and I can see now that we went about it the wrong way."

"Why the rush, Caressa? I know you intimated it just happened, but did you really have to fall into his bed? Into his life?" I didn't mean to press and question, but the compulsion overtook me. "Was there really nothing going on before? Or while you were away?"

She rocked back onto her heels, withdrawing her hand quickly. Instantly, I missed the contact and regretted my ill-considered words. She'd been close, closer than she had been since she'd gotten home, and I'd pushed her away. *Bright move, asshole.*

"You said you needed to urinate." Her words were professional and detached.

They left me cold. "If you hand me my crutches, I can make do. I'd ask you to lock up when you leave—"

Her look of hurt nearly gutted me.

"You want me to leave."

"No." God, how could I make this right? "I'm just trying to understand, but I seem to be making a mess of it. Please stay, okay? You don't have to cook or anything, but if you could stay, I'd like it. No more interrogating, I promise."

She didn't look convinced, but she grabbed my crutches and handed them to me. "I'll stay close." Her lips curled, and her nose twitched. "Unless you've suddenly developed the ability to walk with these properly. Honestly, Cole, for a man who is so graceful, you're a hot mess with crutches."

I wasn't going to argue and was relieved to see her

mood lightening. As I maneuvered to the bathroom, I was tempted to overplay the clumsiness, but the risk of further injuring myself was just too great. I'd already been put in my place and couldn't afford to take any risks. Once I was alone in the bathroom, I got my fly open and my dick out without too much trouble. Donovan had helped me in and out of the whirlpool tub last night, but he couldn't be here all the time. How did people cope with stuff like this? At least I didn't have to worry about a day job and how to get about. Money also wasn't going to be a problem as I had plenty socked away. Good thing because I'd be taking taxis any time I needed to leave this place.

"How's grilled cheese and tomato soup?" Caressa's voice carried through the door.

I tucked myself in, flushed the toilet, and slid over to the sink so I could wash my hands. "Uh, sounds great." And it did.

Of us three, Michael was the best cook, but I held my own. Caressa had never quite mastered the more complicated meals, but she was great with the basics. I opened the door, and she hovered as I made my way over to the couch. She offered assistance, and pushing pride aside, I accepted. Her hands on me did weird things to my gut, but I ruthlessly set aside those feelings as well.

"May I?"

She indicated my left thigh, and I nodded. Her fingers gently probed the painful muscle, and she frowned in what appeared to be consternation. "You did a good job, Hamilton."

Her scent enveloped me, and I was a goner. She didn't wear perfume or even scented products, so the smell was entirely her. Something achingly familiar.

Something I wanted to seize and never let go of. Something I'd never been able to forget.

"I've been given a week to stay off my feet completely, stuck here no less, and then I can gradually return to work."

"Oh, such a hardship to be stuck in this beautiful place."

My living room had the same view as the den on one side of this room and the master bedroom on the other. Downstairs had a party room built to maximize the view, and upstairs three of the guest bedrooms all faced north. Basically, my house was an entire wall of windows at the back. The front was more circumspect so gawkers who found the place couldn't get a good look. One enterprising young photographer had rented a boat and had snapped a pic of me on my back deck by the infinity pool. In Speedos, thank God. The studio lawyers had issued a threat to sue because of breach of privacy. No one had come around that way since, but I'd never take the chance. Not that I'd been known for my nude sunbathing before becoming famous.

"Even the most beautiful home can be a prison. You know that."

She frowned. "I'm pretty sure I've never lived in the lap of luxury and been forced to endure captivity."

"You should try it. Come stay with me."

The stricken look on her face informed me, in a way that no words could, that I'd stepped into something. Something more than just a *hey come stay with me*. "I was—"

She held up her hand. "I know you didn't mean it like it sounded, Cole. I'm just…" She released my leg and moved into the kitchen, turning her back on me.

I expected her to leave, but she began opening and closing cupboards—obviously searching for the necessary props to make soup and sandwiches. I could try to tell her, but I was likely to fuck that up too. When was the last time I'd used a pot anyway? Besides, she apparently needed something to do with her hands and her mind. I hadn't been serious she move in, right? She was with Michael now, and that precluded getting involved with me, right? I really needed to get my head on straight.

"I'm going to use tomato soup, okay?"

"Sounds amazing. I didn't realize how hungry I am." For more than food but I wasn't going to say that.

Chapter Sixteen

Caressa

"I went to see Cole today." I'd specifically waited until dinner was over and we were loading the dishes into the dishwasher. This way I didn't have to look Michael in the eyes because I didn't want to know how he felt about this development. Or maybe I did because if I *really* didn't want to know, I wouldn't have mentioned it at all.

Michael stilled, dinner plate in his hand, bent over the machine. "Oh, well, yeah, I figured you might. I mean, I gave you the address, eh?"

He had and wouldn't have asked if I'd used it because he respected my privacy. This was too important not to share. "He's injured himself."

The last plate put in the dishwasher, Michael straightened and closed the door. We hadn't dirtied enough dishes in it to justify running the machine, but we'd do it sometime tomorrow. He nodded toward the living room.

I settled on one end of the couch, turning so my back was against the armrest. I pulled my knees up to my chin, then rested my head on them. A protective and defensive stance—and most likely completely unnecessary, but something I felt compelled to do. Michael mimicked my pose, although his legs were bent sideways and crossed, feet still touching the ground. His arm rested on the back of the couch, and he angled himself toward me. His posture was in direct contrast to mine—completely open, nothing to hide.

I gulped. *Should've brought a glass of water.* My mouth was dry.

Michael's gaze never wavered as he waited for me to speak.

Finally, I broke eye contact. "His IT band. He didn't pivot correctly, and Lyric, sorry, Julie hit him square in the leg."

"That simple?"

Shrugging, I wiped at lint on my jeans. "Well, he lost focus, and she got him just at the right angle. Not an easy injury to sustain, but painful with a longer recovery time than most people appreciate. Usually runners get the injury—but at just the correct angle…"

"So what's involved?"

"Weeks of physical therapy and a slow recovery. He said he'll be back on set in a couple of weeks to shoot scenes that don't involve anything physical." Another brush and still not looking up. "He's frustrated, and a small part of him worries they'll replace him even though that's ridiculous. He is *Vigilante Justice*. Julie's going to take on a bigger role, but I think they'd been moving in that direction anyway."

"Do you think she and Cole are an item?"

My gaze shot to his. "Even if they were, it's none of our business."

He bobbed his head in an odd side-to-side motion. "I know, but I'm not speculating as a fan. I'm asking as a friend of his. But you're right, none of my business."

I huffed. "I think he's tired of all the speculation.

She's single, he's single, so everyone assumes they'll get together."

"Well, they do have chemistry…"

"On screen. Sheesh, Michael, I expected better from you than pure speculation."

"So you talked to him about it." His gaze darted away. Just for an instant—but I knew his tell.

"It doesn't matter if he's with Julie or not. I'm with you—"

"I didn't—"

"You didn't have to." I clucked my tongue. "We haven't been together a week, Michael—I'm not going to cheat on you. You need to trust me."

"I do." His gaze was unwavering, his words strong.

"Then why…" *Ah, shit.* "Cole isn't going to make a move on me. That's not his style, and you know it. He doesn't poach in other people's territory. He's respectful of what we have. What decisions we've made."

Michael's lips pursed.

"Spit it out. Prevarication doesn't suit you."

"We really hurt him, Caressa. A lot. Even when you were talking to him on the bench, I don't think he was as honest with you as he was with me. I think he wanted something more with you. He'd planned to ask you to move in."

Well, isn't this interesting? "Like you asked me to move in or like as a friend?"

"I'm pretty sure he planned platonically. He didn't want to spook you. But if things had progressed to more, I don't think he'd have been disappointed. I think he'd have been fucking thrilled."

"Like you were."

He opened his mouth to speak, hesitated, then closed

141

it. A frown marred his beautiful face. "I didn't plan this."

"But you think he did."

"I don't know."

Well, at least he was being honest. "To what end, Michael? Cole has access to the most beautiful and sophisticated women. Both here and down in LA. And I'm sure in New York and anywhere else he wants. There is no shortage of women throwing themselves at him."

"But not you, Caressa. Don't you see?" He ran his hand through his hair in evident frustration. "Guys, and women as well, often want what they can't have. Forbidden fruit and all that."

"So you wanted me because you couldn't have me? Because you perceived me as unavailable?" *Am I honored or hurt?* Probably a bit of both.

"I didn't see you as a conquest, if that's what you're thinking. That night, as you stood in my room, I realized I couldn't live without you—and that the love I'd always felt for you had morphed from friends caring for each other into something more serious. Something romantic."

He was in earnest, and my heart took a knock. I was so desperately confused because several times today I'd gotten signals from Cole. Signs he wanted more. But he'd accepted things the way they were, right? "And if I hadn't come home with you that night? If I had moved in with Cole and he'd eventually persuaded me to come to his bed?"

Stricken. Michael's face blanched white, and his lips pursed. "I don't know. And that's the God's honest truth. Did I just suppress feelings that were always there because I didn't want to lose your friendship? Possibly. Did I refuse to see what was so clear in retrospect because I didn't want to upset what we had? Probably. Did I ignore the pain and panic while you were away and then give in to the sheer relief when you were back in my presence? Undoubtedly. Will it kill me to lose you? Whether if you go back to Africa or if you choose to leave me for Cole? Absolutely." His eyes blazed with passion, and the flecks of gold in his hazel orbs sparked with fervor.

He stole my breath. Michael'd always been the dispassionate one. The logical and methodical one. The one who mapped out our path to get out of poverty and had pushed us to succeed. He'd been determined, and maybe that had been his way of showing passion. But the man before me? I barely recognized him and had no chance to react before he moved. I wasn't scared—but when he dropped to his haunches by my side, I was surprised. Shocked was an even better word.

He enveloped my chilly hands in his warm ones. "I'll support you no matter what, sweetheart. I'm just hoping you'll give this a real shot. Will I hold you to forever? Absolutely not."

My heart slowed to a leaden thud in my chest.

"I'm not saying I won't fight like the devil to keep you, but I'm not going to hold you back. I want you, Caressa. You know that. And I need you to cling to that. But if you met someone else, would I prevent you from being happy? It'd kill me, but I'd let you go. If that's what you really wanted. I might fight—but not dirty."

"Are you saying this is a lark for you?"

His eyes widened. "No." Sharp and quick. "This is a forever kind of thing for me, but I understand that it's new for you. I understand I've pushed you into something you might not have agreed to otherwise. That

Gabbi Grey

this wasn't the course you'd planned for your life. Am I a selfish man in wanting you to myself? You bet. Will I hold you back if you want to move on? Never."

Confusion assailed me. So he wanted me in a forever kind of way but wouldn't hold on to me if I met someone else or chose to leave him? Why did that hurt my heart? On its face, he offered a simple proposition. And understandable, given his upbringing. His parents should've divorced years ago instead of making each other miserable and, by extension, abusing their young son. They'd blamed him for everything from their poverty to their excessive alcohol abuse. As if a child of five could influence anything about an adult's life.

"I don't want Cole, Michael—I want you." And I meant it. In this moment, I was certain I'd made the right choice to move in and share my life with him.

He dropped my hands and raised his to cup my cheeks. He pulled me in for a kiss, and I tasted desperation as he thrust his tongue in my mouth. Or maybe my own panic drove us. Mutual fear of losing something so new. So tenuous. So nebulous. His hands dove into my thick locks as he tugged me closer. He pulled back only far enough to whisper, "I want to make love to you."

If we hadn't been sitting on a leather couch, I'd have yanked him over me, but practicality won out. "Let's go to bed, Michael."

Chapter Seventeen

Michael

Two days.

Caressa'd started working two days ago, and each night I'd lain alone. And worried. She was on a three-on, three-off shift series, so she had one more night before her days off. Then she'd have to switch over the day shifts. I'd read the statistics about the health of shift workers, and it ate away at me. If I could just convince her to take a job that only required days. Better yet, just weekdays. Then we could spend every spare waking moment together.

Gross.

I'd become one of *those* men. A man who obsessed about his girlfriend—always wondering what she was doing and who she was doing it with. Oh, I knew she was at work dealing with drug addicts and heart attack victims, but something was always nebulous about that work. What if a cute guy came in requiring stitches and he hit on her? What if there was an attractive doctor who talked her up, allowing her to show her knowledge and skills, rather than relegating her to just an assistant? Those were the guys I worried about the most. The slick-talking ones who professed a love of equality but really only wanted to subjugate their women once they had them.

And wasn't I just going off the deep end?

This wasn't like me. Normally, I was an even-tempered and rational man. I logically thought out each scenario and was able to reject the ridiculous ones out of hand.

Not this time. Not when it had to do with Caressa. My primal instincts kicked in every time I thought of her. I wanted to storm down to the hospital, throw her over my shoulder, and drag her home. Then I'd lock her up until she agreed to marry me, wear my ring, and be mine forever.

Forget that I hadn't even proposed marriage or that I'd promised her freedom if she ever requested it.

Get a grip.

I'd only been in bed for an hour. The witching hour hadn't even come and gone yet. In desperation, I grabbed my phone to check for any missed texts. And since Caressa'd made it clear she'd never call during a shift, I found nothing but an empty screen.

Fuck.

Then, as if by summoning, the screen lit.

—Are you awake?—

Damn, not who I hoped for. The opposite in fact. Cole.

—Yes, I am.—

I wanted to ask what the consequences would've been if he'd woken me, but I was too far down the rabbit hole to care.

—Caressa's at work?—

—Yes.—

—Come for breakfast. The two of you, if you can convince her.—

I wanted to point out we might have other plans, but

I wasn't up for any potential discussion.

—I'll ask her. No guarantees.—

—All I can ask for.—

Nothing more came for several minutes, so I assumed we'd concluded our discussion.

—I have a proposition.—

Okay that sounded ominous. Especially given I'd issued the challenge that he could go after Caressa if he chose.

—I'll do my best to convince her because I assume you're not going to share details with me.—

—Correct. Good night, Michael.—

I popped off a text to Caressa with the invitation, then one to my admin assistant's work phone, letting her know I'd be late into the office. I never took time off so was owed a pile of it. I didn't have anything pressing, so a few hours wouldn't make a difference one way or another.

Believing sleep would prove elusive, I grabbed my e-reader with the intention of perusing the latest engineering trade magazine that had arrived.

Within moments, I was out.

My phone alarm blared me into consciousness, and as soon as I turned it off, Caressa's text appeared, asking me to pick her up after work so we could go to Cole's together. Since that had been my plan, I'd set the alarm accordingly. I showered quickly and hustled out the door without even stopping for coffee.

Cole'd have some.

I pulled in to the back of St. Paul's with thirty seconds to spare and watched as the clock on the dash flipped to seven.

Caressa didn't emerge for another twenty minutes,

and I seriously regretted not having snagged some form of caffeine. She slid into the SUV and leaned over to kiss me. She appeared haggard.

"We don't *have* to go to Cole's. He'll understand."

She shook her head. "No, I want to go. To hear what he has to say. I mean, what if he needs something?"

"He could've asked last night. He had to have known I'd have done whatever he needed."

"Might be easier for him to ask with me there."

I wasn't convinced of this, but I drove us up north on Thurlow Street toward the Burrard Street Bridge. The sun barely crested the eastern sky as I turned right onto Cornwall Avenue and what would eventually become Point Grey Road, one of the most exclusive streets in all of Vancouver.

Cole'd made it. Of that, I had no doubt.

Caressa yawned.

"I'm sure Cole will have coffee. Oh, but you probably shouldn't drink any since you need to go to bed soon."

"Don't tell me what I need." She snapped the words. Then immediately sighed. "Sorry."

"Rough night?"

"Yeah, but I don't want to talk about it." She tapped her window. "Did Cole give you any clue what this is about?"

"Nope." I pulled in to his driveway but was slow to cut the engine.

Caressa turned to me.

I met her gaze.

She reached over to turn the engine off. "Nothing is going to change between us. Frankly, I find your lack of faith unsettling." Without another word, she got out of the car.

Damn the woman—always able to read my mind. I *was* worried. The promise to not fight if Caressa wanted to leave me taunted me at every turn.

You're an idiot.

Something I told myself multiple times a day. I slid from the SUV, and after I closed the door, I locked it. To my surprise, Caressa yanked out a key and inserted it into the lock. The mechanism gave, and she entered the house, repocketing the key. Hell, I didn't own a key.

I followed her and shut the door behind me, then I engaged the lock.

We removed our shoes and hung our coats in the front hall closet.

I snagged her hand as we walked farther into the house.

The kitchen appeared pristine. Had the cleaner come yesterday? Oh no. Likely Cole wasn't doing anything in there. Not that he did much cooking anyway. Although he'd cooked a few meals for me over the past few years. Always while on hiatus. To keep himself occupied, or so he claimed. He liked to keep moving and so resented the forced downtime. That was the reason he took so many movies and minor roles in other shows during his time away from *VJ*.

We discovered him sitting on his sectional, facing out toward the water. The morning sun sparkled on the water, and the imposing snow-capped mountains in the background stunned.

The million-dollar view.

Closer to ten, these days, but I held my tongue.

Cole set his tablet aside and grinned. The amiable smile I was accustomed to.

But the shadows under his eyes were unmissable.

"Have you had breakfast?" Caressa advanced toward Cole.

He shook his head. "The delivery service should be here any minute."

God, I'd never considered having breakfast delivered. Maybe if I was incapacitated? This concept of food at the drop of a hat delivered to my door was something I still grappled with. All these ultimate conveniences. That meant someone else had to do the heavy lifting. And this level of consumerism wasn't good for the planet.

Seriously?

"I'll make coffee." Caressa headed toward the kitchen.

I made to follow.

She placed a hand on my arm and gestured her head toward Cole.

Fair enough. I remained in place while she headed out of the room. I wandered over to the windows to get another look. My downtown view was of other condos. Nothing like this spectacular scenery.

Cole cleared his throat, and I pivoted.

"You could enjoy that view more often."

I cocked my head.

"I…" He cleared his throat again. "I'd like if you were here more often."

Me or Caressa? Because he'd never given any indication he wanted more than our irregular dinners. Had certainly never hinted at wanting anything else.

"What are you trying to say?"

He glanced over his shoulder.

"She's in the kitchen." I'd keep a sharp eye on the

doorway, and as long as we pitched our voices low, she shouldn't be able to hear.

"I'm saying it'd be nice if you moved in. Both of you. Like old times."

Only I'd be sharing a bedroom with Caressa instead of with him.

My mind immediately rejected the idea. Caressa being around Cole all the time, in this house, would show her all she was missing while being with me. He could give her things that'd never be within my grasp. We hadn't discussed having children, which we probably should've done before now, but we couldn't have them in my condo. We'd need to look for a bigger place. But buying a house for under a million and a half in Vancouver was virtually impossible. We faced moving out to the suburbs. Which meant huge commutes for both of us. Well, I might be able to work from home a couple of days a week. And perhaps Caressa'd consider a hospital out where we could afford to live…

Likely not. She wanted to be near where we'd grown up. In a hospital that served marginalized communities, the addicted, and the poor. And sure, all those things existed in the suburbs, but the need wasn't as great.

"What are you thinking?"

I met Cole's gaze.

Caressa entered the room, carrying a tray. She set it on the coffee table. She handed one mug to me and one to Cole. Then she took the third, sat on the couch next to Cole, and tucked her legs under her.

After a moment, I sat next to her, angling myself so I could see both of them. I peeked and saw a string for a teabag hanging out of Caressa's mug.

She caught me snooping and scowled.

"Decaffeinated."

I shrugged. Yeah, I was concerned. I had the right to be.

Or so you tell yourself.

She turned to Cole. "So what's up?"

The doorbell rang.

I rose and reluctantly left the room. I hustled to the front door and opened it to find a young woman with a bicycle helmet on, holding a large insulated bag.

She removed a large paper bag of fragrant food bearing a local chain restaurant logo, handed it to me, pivoted, and headed back to her bike.

Struggling for my wallet, I nearly dropped the food. "Uh, tip."

Already on her bike, she waved me off. "He always tips big." She shoved off and was on her way.

Of course Cole did. How ridiculous of me to think otherwise.

I shut the front door, locked it, and headed to the kitchen. Organizing three plates of food took little time as my friend had ordered all our favorites. I entered the great room with Caressa and Cole's food. I tried not to read anything into their relaxed posture as I hotfooted it back to the kitchen to grab my own plate. Upon my return, I retook my seat.

Both Caressa and Cole devoured their food. No words were spoken as they ate.

I nibbled but found my appetite had fled.

Caressa snagged Cole's empty plate and turned toward me. She arched an eyebrow when she found I'd barely eaten.

"Not really hungry."

She glared.

Ouch.

"I'll wrap it up for later." She snagged the plate and headed to the kitchen.

Cole met my gaze. "I haven't asked her yet."

Oh, so I could've eaten my breakfast sandwich without the impending sense of dread. I pondered that thought for a moment. Nope, still would've felt queasy knowing the conversation was still to come.

Caressa returned with a carafe of coffee. She topped up my mug and poured more for Cole as well. Then she took it back to the kitchen.

"Do I have your support?"

I met Cole's gaze. Saying *no* would be so easy. Especially given that was how I felt. And the competition I'd initiated. But the decision had to be Caressa's. In my heart, this truth resonated. She was a grown woman. Able to make her own decisions.

She returned with her mug of steaming tea, but this time she sat in a chair facing Cole and myself. The windows backlit her, and her hair shone. Despite the evident exhaustion, she took my breath away.

"Spit it out, Hamilton."

Cole acknowledged her command. "I want you guys to move in. I have four spare bedrooms, so you could have as much space as you needed."

She squinted. "For how long? Until you're healed? Because I'm pretty sure you could hire someone to come and take care of you. Not that I'm not happy to do it, but my shifts are pretty crazy right now. And they've asked me to work some extra shifts over the holidays."

"No."

"Absolutely not."

Cole and I met each other's gaze. Yep—on this we

were united.

Caressa stuck out her chin. "I can damn well do whatever I please. The extra money'll come in handy—"

"I'll hire you." Cole slashed the air with his hand. "Whatever you want to charge. Double what you're currently making."

She rolled her eyes. "Plenty of care aides would love to come work here, Cole. At a fraction of what you'd pay an RN. You don't need a nurse."

"I need someone who cares."

"Plenty of personal aides care about their patients. You need to find one who isn't starstruck, though. I mean, there must be people in Vancouver who've never heard of you."

"Of course there are." He snapped the words. "But I want you."

"Well, you're not going to get me. I need to be needed. And you don't *need* me."

Cole glanced at me.

I held up my hands. No way was I getting involved in this mess. I took another sip of coffee and waited to see what would happen next.

Chapter Eighteen

Cole

I'm losing her.
Did I ever really have her?
Yeah, valid point. I'd hoped to have them move in, and I planned to convince Caressa that I needed her—that she could quit her job at St. Paul's. Then, when I recovered, she could consider taking something easy. Something that didn't require these insane hours.

More fool me.

"You need to apply heat." Caressa rose and headed into the kitchen.

I met Michael's gaze for the dozenth time this morning.

"Dude, you know her as well as I do. At this point, if she didn't have the contract with St. Paul's, I'm not sure she wouldn't be headed back to Africa."

Interesting that he didn't think their relationship was enough to tether her to Vancouver.

Caressa returned with a hot pack.

Obediently, I took it from her and placed it against my leg.

The muscle seized in protest.

Fuck.

Fuck it all.

Caressa eyed me. "Is Zoey coming today?"

I nodded.

"And you're going to do your exercises."

"Yes, Mom."

She glared.

I winced. "Sorry, that came out wrong."

"Why are we really here, Cole? I mean, breakfast was nice, but I have to get up in nine hours, and Michael needs to go to work. You said you needed us. We're here. What now?"

"He's worried about you, and he's hoping to manipulate you."

Jesus Fucking Christ.

Caressa held my gaze even as Michael's words settled.

"I'm not manipulatable. I'm not gullible. I'm not a child looking for love and approval."

Ouch.

"I just want things to go back to the way they were. For a few weeks, at least. I've missed you. I've missed Michael too. Can't we just hang out? For the holidays, at least?"

"You don't even have a tree."

Point Caressa. "Well, that's something you can rectify. I've got boxes of decorations. I can't help…"

"But you can supervise." No missing the dripping sarcasm.

"Okay, so maybe this was a bad idea." My gut churned as I thought about them walking out of my house—together. Possibly forever, if I didn't turn this around. "Except…"

Caressa crossed her legs. "Except…"

"The studio is threatening to withdraw permission for me to do many of my stunts. I need to recover quickly in order to prove to them this was an aberration."

"Hire a nurse, Cole, if it's so goddamn important. You know what you should be doing. You certainly don't need us around nagging you. If you don't take this seriously, that's on you—not us."

I didn't like how her language so easily included Michael.

Jealousy is a wasted emotion.
Tell that to my heart.

"And is withdrawal of permission for you to do dangerous stunts really a bad thing?" Michael indicated my leg, propped on the long end of the sectional.

I winced. "For me, it would be."

"You think your only worth to the studio is your ability to do stunts." Caressa glared. "Jesus, after four years you're still thinking they're going to fire you? We had this discussion. You are *Vigilante Justice*. No one else can do that role."

I'd learned, over the more than ten years in the business, the notion was quaint. Everyone was replaceable. Okay, maybe not some of the big action superstars in the franchises, but I wouldn't put it past a studio executive if the actor became too much trouble.

Caressa leaned forward, then placed her hand on my foot.

Fire lit through me.

"What's really going on?"

"I'm lonely. I can't bear the thought of another Christmas alone."

Although this wasn't the bald-faced lie about the studio, the words were just as manipulative.

Caressa's gaze shot to Michael.

I surreptitiously glanced back and forth between the

two of them—watching the byplay with interest. We'd always had the ability to read each other's thoughts. But to my distress, I couldn't figure out what they were saying to each other.

"Today's the twentieth…" Michael rolled his eyes to the ceiling. A sure sign he was doing those mental calculations he was known for.

"I'm off tomorrow morning for three days." Caressa fiddled with her fingers. "I'm back on days for the twenty-fourth through to the twenty-sixth, but they've asked me to work the twenty-seventh and eighth. Then I have the twenty-ninth off before I start back on the night shift on the thirtieth."

Michael grunted. "You realize you're working Christmas Eve, Christmas Day, Boxing Day, New Year's Eve, and New Year's Day."

She shrugged. "Low person on the totem pole. Plus, I don't have a family."

Even I objected to that. I raised my hand, but she swatted me off.

"I don't have kids, guys. Or a husband or parents or in-laws. Yes, I have you two, and yes, you're important to me, but let's be honest—it's not the same thing."

Michael and I exchanged glances. Yeah, point Caressa.

"You'll move in tomorrow morning?"

She pressed a hand to her forehead. "If it means that much to you…yeah, I guess so."

Such enthusiasm.

"I'll pack tonight before I go to work. Michael can move our stuff. He can either come tonight or tomorrow morning." She met his gaze. "You don't mind picking me up from work again?"

"I never mind picking you up from work."

Her smile softened, and her eyes got a dreamy quality to them.

Was I doing the right thing? I just didn't know anymore.

Their departure, about ten minutes later, coincided with Zoey's arrival. She and Caressa exchanged small talk while Michael held my gaze.

He knew. And he didn't like being manipulated.

But of the two of us, I was worldlier. I'd done more, seen more, endured more. Maybe endured wasn't the right word…just that I'd fought harder to get where I was. School had been easy for him, and he'd found a job right away. Eventually, his condo had followed. My path had been rockier. And now I threatened his happiness.

I was a bastard.

And as Zoey took me through my paces, I felt every pound of that emotional baggage. I didn't want to be alone. I did need help in sticking to the rehab regime. I needed the support I could only get from my two best friends.

"Goddamn it, Hamilton, you're not focusing."

Oh God, the constant refrain in my life. "I am. I swear."

Zoey stood before me, hands on her hips. She didn't look impressed. "Well, I need to report back today. Your boss is itching for a progress report."

I had several *bosses*, so I tilted my head in question.

"Valentino Langston. Although I've heard Lisette Grenier is champing at the bit and Donovan Riggs wants to throttle you."

"Val." I swore under my breath. He'd recently been added to the show as an executive producer—his background in Hollywood blockbuster action films was slowly seeping into *VJ* as our production was stepping up—more stunts, bigger action sequences, and more daring plotlines. I liked his influence as our ratings jumped, but I didn't like the idea of him breathing down my neck. "I'll talk to them."

"And they'll get my report." Zoey wiped down the equipment. "I'll omit the lack of attention because I can see you're doing the work, but I understand lack of focus got you into this mess in the first place. Wouldn't have anything to do with that lovely young woman, would it?"

Since Caressa was less than half-a-dozen years younger than Zoey, I snickered. "I have to take a piss."

"Well, I'm not holding it for you."

Jesus.

"Could you hand me the crutches?"

She huffed but handed them over.

"You can see yourself out. And tell Val I'm doing my best."

Her brown eyes softened a bit—reminding me of how Caressa could turn gentle when she wanted to.

Wrong thought.

"Yes, I'll tell him you're putting in the effort. And I'll see myself out." She departed as I maneuvered my way down the hall to the bathroom.

I had to find a way out of this situation, but nothing came to me. And I thought Donovan might pop in today, which I would've appreciated for the distraction it would've provided, but he didn't, and by dinnertime, I was at my wit's end. I wanted to prowl. I wanted to stalk. I wanted to go upstairs and make certain the bedrooms were ready for guests—yet I could do none of those things.

Well, the bedrooms didn't really need to be checked. My cleaning service had visited two days ago, and on a whim, I'd asked them to go over all the bedrooms. Occasionally, I considered hiring a housekeeper, but I didn't create enough mess to warrant hiring someone. Coming home to a hot meal would be nice, but I was just as capable of picking up fast food or ordering in if I was home early enough. I even managed to track down healthier options.

A key in the lock drew my attention.

Moments later, the sound of rolling suitcases hit me.

Seconds after that, Michael appeared in the hallway entry. He flipped the keys in his hand. "Caressa ordered me to make a copy for myself. And then she insisted I come tonight to ensure you weren't lonely." He eyed me. "That was total bullshit you shoveled. Well played."

In that moment, as my heart leapt into my throat, I realized I hadn't been shoveling bullshit. I was lonely. I did want company. I didn't want to be alone over Christmas. "I'm glad you're here."

Chapter Nineteen

Caressa

Lethargic toddlers were always a concern. As I recorded the vitals of the little girl, I peppered her parents with questions.

They maintained they had no idea why I couldn't rouse their daughter. I couldn't find any signs of viruses or obvious infections. I was about to call the doctor when he breezed in.

Only he wasn't who I was expecting. My stomach twisted into knots, and bile rose in my throat. "Dr. Caruso. Uh, where's Dr. Lipschitz?"

"She's had to leave. Looks like it might be food poisoning. When her condition worsened, the administrator called me. I'm on call for the ER here. Didn't you know? Oh, or are you just back from Africa?"

I should've been prepared to see Franklin again, but I wasn't. It disconcerted me that he'd followed me so closely that he knew I'd been in Africa. Or he'd made an educated guess. And Evelyn Lipschitz had looked ill earlier, but she'd sworn she was fine. We had another doctor working, so I assumed we'd survive. The waiting room was packed, but that was nothing new.

"This two-year-old has presented with extreme lethargy. I cannot rouse her, but she doesn't appear to be in a coma. Her pain response is average, and I can't find any sign of illness. I recommend—"

"Yes, full blood panel, urinalysis, and…" He consulted his tablet. "That'll do for now. I see you've hooked her up to a monitor. Uh, good work." He pivoted to the parents.

The mother wore an impeccable navy-blue suit with high heels and pearls. The father's tailored suit must've cost a fortune. They'd said something about attending a Christmas party and coming home to find their daughter ill.

I didn't like to judge, but something didn't feel right.

Franklin tapped the stylus on the tablet. "We're going to run some tests on your daughter. Hopefully, we'll get some answers shortly." Without even asking if they had questions, he left the curtained area.

They turned to me.

"I'll have someone here in a few minutes to take blood. We're going to take care of your daughter."

And then all hell broke loose.

The girl's heart rate, which had been slow, stopped. Just…stopped.

Alarms blared, and within moments, several nurses and Franklin appeared.

I lowered the head of the gurney and prepared to do CPR.

The parents backed away.

Franklin took over, and the next thirty minutes were pure panicked chaos. Orderly chaos, but chaos nonetheless. In the end, the CPR failed. We never were able to restart her heart.

She was gone.

And I still had no idea why.

Franklin, finally having called time of death,

whirled on the shell-shocked parents. "Did she ingest anything?"

The mother shook her head, but the father slowly nodded.

"Well?" Franklin prompted. Well, bellowed.

"She ate some brownies. I mean, not that many and we thought…"

Jesus.

"Pot-laced brownies?" His voice carried the incredulity I felt.

I'd repeatedly asked if she might've gotten into something, and they'd maintained she hadn't. We would've run a tox screen to include drugs, but she'd crashed.

And now it was too late. If I'd known when she came in. If we'd known at the beginning of the resuscitation. If…

Franklin turned on me. "You were responsible for taking an accurate history."

"I asked." Questioning me in front of grieving parents was completely unacceptable. We could have this discussion in private. He could blame me all he wanted, part of me blamed myself, but I'd repeatedly asked. And Franklin hadn't asked them a single question at all. Maybe if he'd taken more time with them… People reacted differently to doctors, and maybe the father would've been more forthcoming.

Except the man hadn't said anything the entire time we worked to save his daughter's life. At any point he could've spoken up. Yet he hadn't.

"The police are going to want to speak to you." I met the husband's gaze. I wanted to suggest the guy get a lawyer, but frankly, I couldn't bring myself to care.

164

An orderly arrived to remove the gurney, with the toddler, and her parents made no move to stop her. Like they didn't even care. And probably they were in shock, but I'd witnessed incredible grief from parents, and their absolute lack of caring struck me.

On cue, a police officer poked her head in. She must've been here for another reason. She turned to the parents. "I have a room where we can talk."

The woman straightened. "I want a lawyer."

The cop appeared unsurprised. "Sure. Let's head down to the station. You can ride with me."

"Our car—"

A slashing motion from the cop stopped the woman before she could go any further. "We'll make arrangements. Now, if you'd come with me, I'd appreciate it."

I thought her brave to take on a couple, but another cop poked his head around the curtain—and I spotted our security guard off to the side.

The mother, who still appeared unperturbed, nodded. Then she allowed the police to guide her away.

The father met my gaze.

I saw pure, naked grief. Maybe I should've felt empathy…but I didn't.

As the group passed, the second cop handed me a business card. "We'll talk."

Detective Tyson McGillvary.

I nodded and watched the group leave.

Jeff, our security guard, met my gaze. "You okay?"

"This patient's seizing. Can I get a hand?" Another nurse's voice rang out.

I took one moment to acknowledge Jeff's question before I jogged away.

Five hours later, as I stood waiting for Michael, I scrolled through my phone to search. Pediatric deaths after known cannabis exposure were incredibly rare. The acute toxicity could lead to myocarditis…heart problems. Was that what had occurred? An autopsy would be determinative, but I struggled to understand. Depending on the length of time between exposure and presentation at our hospital, the THC, the active ingredient, might not have turned up on tests. Marijuana had been legal in Canada for more than five years. Became legal just before I went overseas. In my ten years of nursing, I'd never seen an acute case. Despite its prevalence in the drug-using population, it hadn't been nearly as popular as the more lethal drugs. I'd worried about the lacing of fentanyl into street drugs, not pot smokers.

A baby lay in the morgue.

I couldn't fathom it.

Had there been something I could've done? I remembered the woman's face—so callous and uncaring. Clearly more concerned about her car than her daughter. Or did grief look different on her? Everyone coped in their own way, right? What caused outward anguish in one person pushed another soul to go deep within themselves. Hell, I wouldn't have even pegged those two as consumers of cannabis. Which perhaps showed a naïveté I'd better rid myself of quickly.

Michael pulled up, and I hopped in. He tilted his head in question.

"Oh." I leaned over to kiss him.

"What's wrong?"

As if I'd ever had a hope of hiding this. "I'll tell you and Cole at the same time." A reprieve—if only for half an hour while we got settled.

"I'm planning on making pancakes this morning. Do you want to try to stay up all day, or do you need to crash now? You need to get back on regular time, right?"

I did. And since today was the twenty-first and I hadn't done any Christmas shopping, I had other stuff to do as well. "I, uh, need to do some shopping."

Michael cut me a glance as he drove over the bridge. "If you're thinking you need to get something for Cole or myself, you know that's ridiculous. All we've ever wanted is you. Home safe. And we sort of have that."

"Michael." I hoped my admonishment hit. I didn't want to be defending my job again. "If you can't keep your thoughts to yourself—or better yet, adjust them—then I won't tell you what happened today."

He sniffed. "Of course I want to hear what happened. I just…well, anyway…" He angled the car to the right. "And you can buy anything you might need online. Most stores will deliver by the twenty-fourth."

"But the pollution from the delivery vans…"

A sigh escaped. "Chances are they'll be delivering something to the neighbors anyway. I get that you're concerned about the planet, but for once maybe worry about yourself as well."

"African countries don't have the luxury for me to care about myself. The effects of climate change are far worse for them—and they don't have the resources to deal with what's happening. The West has the money…"

Michael drove an electric SUV powered by electricity from the province's hydropower system. So clean energy. But even that had come at a cost— Indigenous Canadians had been forced from their lands when they were flooded to create the dams that powered our cities.

After a bit, he turned into Cole's driveway and this time activated the garage door. He pulled in, and I noticed a charging station. Something I hadn't even considered.

"Did he get this installed last night?"

Michael shook his head. "He always had two."

"Oh." I slowly eased myself from the SUV and headed around to the trunk.

"What's up?" Michael came to join me.

"Don't we have suitcases?"

He shook his head, snagged my hand, and guided me toward the back door as he hit the button to close the garage door. "After I dropped you off last night, I grabbed the bags we packed and came here." He cleared his throat. "Didn't figure leaving Hamilton alone for the night was a good thing. I've, uh, got us set up in one of the bedrooms. I unpacked our stuff, but if you don't like my choice—"

I silenced him with a finger to the lips. "I'm sure whichever bedroom you chose was the perfect one. I'm glad you kept Cole company last night, although I'm more than curious what mischief you got up to, and I'm looking forward to crawling into bed after breakfast for a quick nap. Then I'm heading out to do some shopping. I may need to borrow your SUV, or I may just walk up to Broadway and see what I find."

"Uh, sure. Can I keep you company?"

"Nah. I need some time to process all this, okay? And it'll be busy—last Saturday before Christmas and all that." I pressed a kiss to his cheek.

He unlocked the door to the house from the garage and ushered me in.

I did as bade and removed my boots, jacket, and hat. "Smells like snow." I met his gaze. "I've missed snow."

"Yes, I'll bet you have. Maybe we can do a run up to Grouse? Only after the holidays—it'll be nuts between Christmas and New Year's. Well, at least until the kids go back to school."

Even the thought of skiing made me want to weep, showing just how tired I was. I'd worked tons of long shifts in South Sudan, but I couldn't ever remember feeling this exhausted. I should've planned to try to stay awake until tonight, but my eyelids refused to stay open. A huge adrenaline drop. Still, Michael always made the best pancakes, so I could keep up the struggle a bit longer.

"No to Grouse. At least until I'm settled into my job and can stay awake long enough to do a ski run down that mountain." I rested my hand on his chest. "You said something about breakfast?"

He met my gaze and held it for a long time. His pupils were dark in the dim light. "What's wrong?"

"Nothing's wrong." I could brazen it out.

He cupped my chin. "I want to call bullshit, but you have the right to privacy." He scowled, as if the thought was distasteful. "Yes, I'll make pancakes. Chocolate chips?"

"Brilliant."

He stared at me for a moment longer before heading to the kitchen.

After a long moment, I headed to the great room.

Cole sat on his favorite seat on the couch, looking out over the gray morning.

"It might snow."

He turned his gaze toward me. "Is it cold enough?"

"Hovering around the freezing mark. Dipping lower at night, so yeah, we might just get some. Definitely precipitation in the forecast."

"This weather is very different from what you've become accustomed to."

"South Sudan has rain. It's not desert." I was sure I'd written about the rainy season. About the savannah. About the vegetation and wildlife.

"I meant the cold. I paid attention to your letters."

"Oh." Why was I feeling so defensive?

"Are you going to tell me what happened?"

He asked the question so casually I startled. "It doesn't matter."

"You know I'm calling bullshit on that one."

I dropped into the chair across from him and sighed. "Yeah, Michael said the same thing."

"Maybe because you can't hide anything from us. We see you. All of you. Pain, joy, sorrow, and elation—they're part of you, and we see you."

"So you said."

"Caressa—"

"A baby died, and I saw Franklin, and I couldn't do anything about any of it…" I pressed fingers to my lips. Why? Why had I just blurted all that out? He didn't need to know any of that. He certainly didn't need to know my shit. He had enough to deal with. And wasn't I supposed to share this stuff with Michael first? I was living with him, so that meant pouring my heart out to him first.

Right?

I had no idea. I didn't *do* relationships. Out of my depth of experience.

Cole held out his hand.

Clearly, he was asking me to move toward him.

Why? What did he want from me? Or to give to me?

Undaunted, he continued to hold his hand out.

Slowly, I rose.

He patted the seat next to him.

With reluctance, I sat, tucking my legs under me.

He reached out his hand.

I took it. Then I let him tug me toward him. As I did, he wrapped his arm around me and pulled me close. I shuddered as I let him enfold me into an awkward one-arm embrace. I was sure, if he could, that he'd turn his body to pull me in tighter, but I was glad he respected his injury and didn't put my pathetic need for solace ahead of his own recovery.

"We can talk about all this later, and we will, make no mistake, but for now let me just hold you, okay? I think it's been a long time since anyone's held you."

"Michael does it all the time."

He stiffened.

What?

"Well, as a friend, then."

"Michael is my friend."

"Fuck Michael, okay?"

I attempted to pull back, but he held tight. I could've pulled away, but I might've injured him. Which would've been directly defeating the purpose of our visit. That and to alleviate his loneliness over Christmas. A claim that had the distinct smell of bullshit. Cole could've snapped his fingers and had dozens of people here, paid or unpaid. I still didn't have a good grasp on why he felt he needed Michael and me so badly.

He kissed my temple. "I'm sorry. You...you mean so much to me, and you were gone for so long. I don't feel like I've had my chance to hold you."

Okay, he had a point. Michael'd done most of the holding. Most of the comforting. I was ashamed that I'd been so needy since returning. And it didn't look like things were looking up in that department.

"I love you, Caressa."

"I love you too, you big lug."

"No, I don't think you get it. I *love* you."

No missing the emphasis.

This time, when I pulled back, he let me.

Our gazes clashed.

I saw depth in his eyes—something I'd witnessed many times as we grew up, but hadn't seen lately. In retrospect, I should've noted the absence. "You've been holding back on me."

He held the stare.

An uncomfortable feeling settled within me. This was Cole...*my* Cole. We used to know everything about each other. "Michael said you got drunk when I didn't come back."

After his life with an abusive father, he'd sworn he'd never get out of control. In all our time together, I'd never seen him drunk. We'd always had work to get done, so relaxing and getting drunk had never been in the plan. Even when he went out with friends, he'd always come home sober.

"I did." He blinked several times. "Michael had a harder time, I think, but I didn't take the news well either. Five fucking years, Caressa. Those stints are supposed to last six months. You're supposed to come back."

Yeah. Was now a good time to tell him the whole truth? I winced. "I alternated agencies."

His eyebrow arched. "So each thought you were on a break while you worked for the other? And no one figured it out?"

"They were just glad to have me. I was needed, Cole. Surely, you understand that."

"No one needs me."

"I need you." God, the man could be stubborn. "Growing up? I needed you. And your friends? They need you. And I know for a fact that your show needs you. So don't give me some cock-and-bull story about how no one needs you. That's just not true."

He cocked his head. "You've never said that."

I slashed my hand through the air. "Of course I've said it. Jesus, you just haven't been listening. And that's on you." I held his stare. "Sometimes you're the little boy needing love—not able to see what's right before him. Yes, your father didn't love you. Why you reconciled with him at the end, I'll never understand. But you did."

He broke the stare to look out toward the window. "It's not that simple."

"It never is. Human beings are complicated. I'd be back in Africa tomorrow if they'd let me—"

Shit.

He swiveled his head, and his eyes narrowed. "What?"

"Pancakes." Michael breezed into the room, carrying two plates. He halted when he spotted me in Cole's embrace.

I should've pushed away, but some perverse part of me wanted him to see me like this. To see that I was still close to Cole, despite everything.

Michael blinked. "Do we want to try to eat at the table or just plates on our laps?"

"Why don't we do the table, like civilized adults?" Cole shifted.

I pulled back and out of his arms. That disconcerted me. Left me feeling adrift. Unmoored.

Michael strode over to the table to drop the plates, then was back within moments to help Cole rise and get on his crutches.

Fortunately, his ability to manipulate them had improved, and he headed over to the dining room table with ease.

I was slower to rise.

Within an instant, Michael was by my side, helping me up. I suppose he thought my leg had cramped or something, but the truth was much tougher. Doubts were creeping in. Doubts about whether coming here was the right decision. Doubts about my hasty relationship with Michael.

Doubts about whether Cole and I would remain platonic friends.

That thought unsettled the most as I sat across from Cole.

Only when Michael returned with syrup and butter did I realize I should've offered to help.

I attempted to rise, but he waved me back down. He took off and moments later was back with two glasses of orange juice. Another trip and he placed two steaming mugs of coffee. Prepared just the way we liked it.

The last thing I needed was caffeine, but I held my tongue. "What about you?"

"Mine is almost done, and I have bacon frying up as well." He left again.

Ah, I almost didn't recognize the smell.

"You used to love bacon." Cole spread butter on his large pancake and dumped a pile of maple syrup.

I held my tongue with the admonishment I wanted

to make. He was a grown boy, and a few extra calories weren't going to affect him. "I love bacon. Is Zoey coming by today?"

He shook his head as he cut a slice. "I gave her today off. She wasn't happy, but I told her you'd be here, and she said as long as you didn't cut me any slack, she was okay with it." He held the piece aloft. "So are you going to cut me slack?"

No missing the mischief in those sparkling eyes. Whatever had happened on the couch, we'd clearly moved on.

Phew.

Michael returned with a plate of bacon and a juice for himself. After one last run to the kitchen to bring his pancakes and coffee, he sat. "I'm glad you didn't wait."

Well, Cole had dug in. I'd managed to spread butter, add a touch of syrup, and was cutting my pancake into exact-size bites.

Cole swallowed some pancake, took a swig of juice, and smiled. "This is delicious."

Michael pinkened under the praise. "It's just pancakes."

"I never have time to make them myself. And although I love the diner that delivers them occasionally, it's nice sometimes to have someone cook for me."

"I'm sure you could have plenty of women happily cooking for you." I eyed my pancake as my stomach revolted.

"And men," Cole piped up.

Michael stilled.

I'd always wondered but had never gone there. What Cole did in the bedroom was his own business. Whatever it might be, he kept a lid on it.

Then, as if Cole's whole proclamation had never occurred, Michael turned to me. "Are we going to talk now?"

Oh shit. About Cole? About how he claims he loves me?

I blinked.

"About what happened at work."

He'd finished eating.

So had Cole.

I'd barely managed five bites, and I hadn't touched the bacon. "It's not—"

"Don't fucking say it's not a big deal." Michael toyed with his coffee mug. "I promised I'd give you time, but you need to share before you even try to get some sleep."

Because of the nightmares. He didn't say the words—but he might as well have.

"A baby died." I bit into a piece of bacon, savoring the crispiness. Just the way I liked it.

Cole dropped his cutlery. "Say what?"

I shrugged, already feeling the distancing process settling in. "Parents left laced brownies where their toddler could find them. She ate some. I don't know how much, but it must've been a lot. Her heart gave out."

"Jesus."

Cole's rage was incandescent.

Michael's face was blanch-white.

I took another bite of bacon.

After a moment, Cole reached out to place his hand over mine.

He squeezed.

The contact left me queasy. Should I be accepting this comfort? I hadn't saved the child. And shouldn't I be turning to Michael? Wasn't he the man in my life?

Except I'd never differentiated between the two men. This shifting of relationships had my nerves on edge.

"I need to go to bed." I dropped the bacon, snagged a napkin, and wiped my fingers.

"I'll come with you." Michael made to rise when I did.

"No."

He plopped back down.

"Sorry, that came out sharper than I meant. I'm good." I glanced between the two men. "Well, not *good*. But I'll survive. I've watched plenty of children die before." Which was in and of itself a whole other tragedy. But something about a child dying in such preventable circumstances. Well, many of the deaths in Africa were preventable too. If people would just get up off their asses and fix the poverty problem.

But I wasn't going to solve world hunger, lack of clean drinking water, and the state of geopolitics in one breath. People much smarter than me had tried…and failed. I managed to slice my hand through the air, but it took all my strength. "I'll be better after a nap. Good night. Or good day. Or…"

I couldn't do it. I bit back a cry as I fled the table.

No one followed.

Thank God.

Chapter Twenty

Michael

Apparently, the quality of my chocolate chip pancakes hadn't been enough to comfort Caressa.

Duh.

I'd known something was wrong. From the moment I collected her at the hospital, I'd known. And I'd felt relieved when I found Cole comforting her. There had always been times when she turned to him and not me. It'd stung, for sure, but I respected they had a unique relationship. Sure, she saw me as dependable. But Cole was the rock. Solid. Immovable. Impenetrable. In fact, the weakness he'd shown me earlier almost didn't fit with the persona he worked too hard to maintain.

Almost.

I sipped my juice and eyed the coffee. Half a cup remained, but it'd gone cold.

A baby died.

Well, an older child—since clearly they'd been able to eat the brownies. And what kind of parent left pot-laced brownies out where a child could find them? Caressa hadn't shared details, but I wanted to know more. Would my curiosity ever be satisfied? Would she say more?

"I told her that I love her."

My gaze shot to Cole's.

His blue eyes held more shadows. Matching the ones I'd seen in Caressa.

"She knows you love her." See? I could be nonchalant.

"No, Michael, I told her I *love* her."

Damn. I'd been pretty sure that was what he meant, but I'd hoped otherwise. "What did she say?"

"I'd say she was surprised."

Which was not all that helpful.

"Are you still hoping she'll break up with me and start seeing you?" *And why does that thought scare me so much?* Before Cole told me, I'd believed my relationship with Caressa was solid. Or would be once some time passed and we settled into our new lives. Maybe I meant adapting. Because our lives hadn't changed so much as the direction had. We were still us.

Right?

"I'm hoping…" He sighed and rubbed his jaw. "What if…she saw both of us? What if…" His gaze raked over me.

A sense of disquiet enveloped me. In all the years I'd known him, I'd never contemplated Cole being gay. He didn't step out with a lot of women, but I knew of several. Well, more than several. But he kept his private life private, for obvious reasons. He didn't want to be a topic in the tabloids.

I couldn't blame him. His life was complicated enough.

"Spit it out, Hamilton."

He reached out his hand and rested it against the table. About an inch away from mine.

Huh. He wants me to touch him. I had hundreds of times over the years. Cole gave amazing hugs, and from a young age, he'd impressed upon Caressa and myself the need for that human connection between the three of us. More than a few times, I'd startled myself by realizing how close we truly were. I didn't have anyone else in my life who I was this intimate with. I'd enjoyed the company of a few women, but none had reached my soul the way Caressa and Cole could with so little effort.

I placed my hand in his.

He grasped it.

Something inside me shifted. Settled. This was Cole. *My* Cole. He'd never hurt me. He'd never do anything to damage our relationship.

Slowly, he drew lazy circles around my knuckles.

Something inside me stirred. Ignited.

I met his gaze.

What did I see? In return, what did he see? I was straight. Had always been. I'd never looked at guys in *that* way. I could objectively say some men were more attractive—but that was by applying society's beauty standards. The world thought Cole Hamilton was sexy. Logically, I could say the same thing. But the way he was looking at me felt...predatory. I should've been creeped out. I wasn't, though. Fascinated was a better word. Intrigued. Questioning. "I..." Nope. No words.

His smile was slow and, dare I say, sweet?

"We don't have to do anything, Michael. I would never ask you to be anyone other than who you are."

That should've brought relief. But it didn't. In fact, disappointment washed over me.

"But if you wanted more, I'd be happy to show you."

"Show me?" My voice was barely a whisper.

"How it can be. Between men. Men who care for

each other. Men who love each other."

And I was pretty sure he could show me how it might be with guys who didn't dig each other in that way either. His eyes betrayed experience. I doubted there had been any one special person.

Or maybe I was wrong. Maybe there had been. Some guy he'd loved. Maybe some guy who'd broken his heart.

I turned my hand so our palms touched.

He curled his fingers and lightly scratched.

My insides tingled. Yet I withdrew. I pushed back from the table and rose. "I'll do the dishes, and you should do your exercises. Caressa will be disappointed if you don't."

"So will Zoey." He held my gaze. "And how would you feel?"

"Well, you asked us to come here to support you. I'd be a pretty shitty friend if I didn't encourage you to get better." *The sooner you're better, the sooner we can leave.*

Except that idea left me feeling hollow. Left a void in my soul. I didn't want to just leave. Not before I was sure Cole'd be okay. Not before we'd figured out this relationship shift between the three of us.

I dallied as I cleaned the kitchen. What was the rush? I might've also spent some time wiping down the containers in the pantry and organizing them. And perhaps tossing a couple that had expired two years ago. Yes, expiry dates might be arbitrary, but I couldn't risk foods that were this far gone.

Once everything was perfect, I meandered into the den where Cole was diligently doing his exercises. He'd pulled his hair back into a leather thong, and sweat glistened on his face as he did his reps. His T-shirt was damp as well.

Well, I couldn't say he wasn't doing as instructed.

"Do you need me?" As soon as the words left my mouth, I knew I'd made a mistake.

His grin was sharp and quick. "I'll always need you, Michael. But if you're asking if I can make it to the shower to clean myself off alone, then we're good." He pointed to his tablet. "And I have three scripts I've promised to look over."

I cocked my head.

"Upcoming movie projects."

"Ah, well, then I'll leave you to it."

"What are you going to do?"

"I have some drawings to review. I can do it on my computer."

"You can set up in my office."

"Thanks...but I think I'll just use the desk in the bedroom."

He cocked an eyebrow.

Damn.

"She has nightmares, Cole. They've been pretty consistent since she came back. I promise I won't wake her, but if she has one, I want to be there."

He pursed his lips. I could see the argument forming.

But he also likely saw the impossibility of him being there as well. No way could he sneak into the room quietly with his crutches.

I felt badly for him that he was being excluded. I also felt relief this was something I could share with Caressa that we could keep between the two of us—for now, at least.

After holding my gaze a moment longer, he licked

his lips.

Something inside me stirred again.

"I'm a patient man, Michael." Then he turned back to the windows and resumed his reps.

All evidence to the contrary. He'd been impatient for us to move in. He hadn't waited to declare his love to Caressa. And he wasn't being very subtle about his interest in me. I wasn't sure how I felt. About any of it.

I made my way upstairs and crept into our bedroom.

For all her nightmares, Caressa slept like the dead. Now she lay on her stomach, her arm curled around the pillow I'd used last night. Clutching it tight.

Somehow, that little action brought a modicum of relief.

I slid my laptop from my briefcase and settled in the chair, which fortunately didn't squeak.

The blinds kept the room dark, but I was able to work away quietly at the drawings they'd sent me. I'd gone over these calculations many times, but getting everything perfect was critical. I worked on skyscrapers—lives depended on me not making errors. And my supervisor would also check them. I trusted her implicitly, but I still never could shake the feeling of responsibility. The weight. I'd wanted to be an engineer since I was old enough to understand the job. I'd researched every imaginable type of engineer and had eventually settled on civil. Mechanical had been a close second, but I liked the idea of building things. We'd been surrounded by decay during our childhoods—the thought of creating instead of destroying held great sway with me. Since graduating, I'd worked on several large construction projects in the downtown core. Buildings I could never afford to live in, that was for sure.

And what have you done for those living in poverty?
Huh.

Well, frankly, not a whole lot. I donated to a couple of organizations who did good work down there, but I didn't ever go east of Cambie Street, and I certainly didn't go near the intersection of Main and Hastings Streets. I kept away from our old neighborhood and tried to push the poverty and deprivation out of my mind.

And now Caressa worked in the hospital that served this population. St. Paul's, in its current location, wasn't long for this earth. A new massive complex was being built to replace the old decrepit structure that had stood for more than a century. Although Caressa could currently walk from my place, it would be too far for her to walk to the new, modern complex. That wouldn't be finished for at least another couple of years, so I had time to worry about that at some later point.

If she stays there. If she doesn't go back to Africa.
Another wince.

"Michael?"

Without thought, I shut the laptop. As if I'd been caught doing something illicit. I turned in the chair. "Yeah?"

Her hair lay in a riot of curls around her face. Even in the dim light, the circles under her eyes were clear.

I rose from the chair and moved toward the bed.

"Can we cuddle?"

Her words startled me. "Of course." I yanked off my sweater, unbuckled my jeans, and pulled them down. In just my boxer shorts and a T-shirt, I slid into bed with her. Well, I also still wore my socks, which was possibly the least sexy thing ever, but I didn't figure she'd care. I propped myself against the headboard with a pillow behind me and opened my arms.

She came willingly, tucking herself into my side.

I pressed a kiss to the crown of her head and wrapped my arms around her. As always, this felt incredibly right. Like this was the way things were meant to be.

And Cole?

Thrusting the guilt aside, I yanked the blankets up so she was covered completely. Still, she shivered.

"Do you want me to turn up the heat?" Maybe after all that time in Africa, she'd yet to adapt back to cold and damp Vancouver.

"No." She gripped my T-shirt. "Please stay."

"Okay." My body reacted to her nearness, as it always did, but I tamped down any feelings other than comforting.

In her every action, she indicated she needed gentleness and consideration.

"You didn't sleep very long."

"I want to sleep properly tonight, so this was only to be a nap. I just couldn't keep my eyes open, you know?"

"Yeah, I know."

"And I needed time to think."

I stilled.

She didn't say anything.

Time stretched out.

Finally, I couldn't take the silence. "Did you figure anything out?"

"Cole."

Said with an indiscernible intonation. Still, I had no clue where her mind was.

"He said he loves me."

"He told me the same thing."

She gripped my T-shirt in her hand. "A week ago my life was simple. Well, as simple as it could get. I had a job. I had two best friends. I knew where I was going in life."

"Caressa." I stroked her hair. "You still have a job—if you want to keep working there. And you still have two best friends. Nothing's changed. And I think you still know where you're going in life." I swallowed. "This doesn't have to be a big deal."

Finally, she turned so she faced me. Her blue eyes were dull in the diffuse light, her chin rested against my sternum, and her neck was at an angle that couldn't have been comfortable.

I held her gaze.

"I love you, Michael."

"I know."

"And I love Cole too."

"I know." I did. Had always known. But whether she meant in the romantic sense, I wasn't certain.

And I wasn't going to ask for clarification.

"It's just…" She closed her eyes for a long moment. Then she opened them. "I don't want to lose what we have."

I read the doubt. The fear. "You won't." Said with way more confidence than I had the right to feel.

"But…" She swallowed. "If I explore this thing with Cole…"

"Then you explore." I blinked several times. "I'd never hold you back, Caressa—you know that. If you feel more for Cole than sisterly affection and you want to see where that'll lead, then I'm okay with that. If you want us to cool our relationship—"

She shook her head vehemently. "No, that's the

opposite of what I want."

Okay, well, that was something. We had a starting place.

I tamped down the instinctive jealousy. I drew in a long breath, then let it out. "How do you want to explore? Do you want to go out on dates with him? Do you—" I swallowed. "—want to have sex with him?"

"Yes. No. Maybe." Her brow knit. "All of the above. But Cole Hamilton can't just go on a date."

"You guys could go out, surely. Somewhere intimate. Somewhere discreet. Even rich and famous people go out. I'm sure he can ask Peter Erickson. I mean, they're friends, right? And Peter's one of the biggest action stars on the planet. Everyone recognizes him. I'm sure he goes out to dinner with his husband and their kids." I wasn't positive, but I couldn't imagine the couple never stepping outside their home.

Her brow didn't unknit. "It's not that simple."

"It's as simple as you want it to be. Or I can go out for the night, and you can have a quiet, intimate dinner here."

And head off to his humungous bed in his massive bedroom.

"Are you okay with this? I mean, one minute we're making all kinds of commitments to each other, and the next I'm asking if we can be nonexclusive."

I blinked. "Like, you're thinking of dating people other than myself and Cole?"

"No." Her shock and affront were genuine.

"Oh." My nose itched, but I resisted the urge to scratch it. "If you want to date Cole, I'm fine with it. I mean, if you want to see other people—"

"Uh-huh. No. Not at all." She pressed her hand to

my chest. "Just the three of us. Well, I guess Cole can see other people…"

"I don't get the feeling that's what he wants. He wants you, Caressa."

"And you." Said quietly.

"Did he say something to you?" I couldn't fathom this.

She shrugged. "Educated guess? Now my eyes are open, and I'm seeing things. How he feels about me and, I suspect, how he feels about you."

Her perceptiveness never ceased to amaze me. But if I hadn't seen this coming, how could she have? I didn't have a good answer for that.

"How do you feel about that?"

The million-dollar question. Even as I checked calculations for my building, the notion of being involved in a physical relationship with Cole had swirled in my mind. I'd have to recheck those calculations again before I signed off on them. "I've never looked at him in that way. At any guy that way. But you know I'm not homophobic—live and let live."

"I remember you stuck up for that kid at school."

Kid? *Jesus.* "I'd forgotten all about him. What was his name?"

"Kyle." She rubbed her nose. "I remember you and Cole standing up for them."

We'd even come to fisticuffs one day with an older group of kids who were hellbent on making Kyle's life miserable. "Whatever happened to him?" I had no memory.

"Her. She's now a teaching assistant and living in Kerrisdale with her husband. They've adopted two children, and she goes by Kyla."

I wrinkled my nose. "How could you possibly know that?"

Caressa tilted her head. "We were at BCIT together. She was studying early childhood education, and I was in nursing. She transitioned after she graduated."

Jesus. Again. "And you keep in touch?"

"She sent me a digital Christmas card."

"Well, uh, tell her I say *hi*?"

"I can do that." She smiled. "Kyla's incredibly happy, Michael. She's made a great life for herself and is a mother. Which was all she ever wanted. She goes on and on about her kids and her husband."

"And what did you respond with?"

"Well, I told her about Africa. Not the tough stuff, of course, but that I was there. I mentioned you and Cole. She loved talking about Cole and how famous he was becoming." She blinked. "But we're getting off topic."

Yeah, I figured she'd steer us back. She was nothing if not persistent when she had her mind set to something. "So you think we should invite him to join us?"

"I do, Michael. But only if it's something you're comfortable with. If you say *no*, then things don't change."

But they had. And they'd continue to. Cole wouldn't poach, but he also wouldn't hide his feelings. Something monumental was again shifting—much as it had that night in the pub on Commercial Drive. That had been less than two weeks ago. A thought that brought me up short every single time. I loved Caressa. I loved Cole. We'd always been a unit. How hard could it be to throw romance into the mix?

And sex.

Still she held my gaze.

I wouldn't be selfish. I wouldn't be jealous. If things didn't work out between Caressa and myself but they did for her and Cole, then I'd be happy for them. And I'd remember this short time when I had her all to myself. "Okay."

Her eyes lit. Even in the dim light, I caught the glint of glee.

How could I have ever considered not giving her this? In truth, I hadn't. Not really. But I'd needed to settle things in my mind because the shift was going to be monumental. I felt like we were hurtling toward some unseen and unpredictable future, and I simply had to brace myself for impact.

Chapter Twenty-One

Cole

I was tired and grumpy.
But I was also clean.
So…bonus?
Caressa and Michael'd been upstairs for hours now, and my mind whirled with all the possibilities. Was she still sleeping? God knew she needed her rest. But if she napped too long now, then she wouldn't sleep tonight. Were they making love? None of my fucking business, but I could envision the two of them together. And with that image, my cock stirred.

Oh, good to know it still could. The injury had taken a lot from me. Even though I knew I'd recover, I didn't like being confined. True, I didn't go out a lot. But I liked being able to get in the car and drive. Or hop on my bicycle and trek through Kitsilano. Or just go for a walk and risk being spotted. Most of my neighbors were cool about things. Seeing as many of them were as rich as I was and, in some cases, more notorious.

Footfalls down the stairs pulled me out of my reverie.

Caressa and Michael appeared, holding hands.
Okay, then.
"How are you feeling?"
I could've read Caressa's expression of concern in

any number of different ways, but I chose the simplest. "The workout was great, the shower was even better, I had a snack, and I'm reading a thought-provoking script for a movie that's being shot late next year."

"That sounds interesting." Michael cocked his head. "How busy are you going to be?"

"I'm thinking about either fitting in one big film or two smaller ones during the hiatus for *Vigilante Justice.*"

"To keep you busy." Again, he examined me.

"Yeah."

"You know now that Caressa's home, you don't have to work at such a breakneck pace."

His words stunned me. I'd always worked hard. From the time I was old enough to take a job, I'd worked my ass off. I didn't see how Caressa being back would change that.

Caressa shot Michael an indecipherable look.

He shrugged. "Cole's worked nonstop since you left. I guess I just thought…now that you're back…he might take a break." He again met my gaze. "To spend time with us."

Oh shit. That had never occurred to me. They were here now, but they wouldn't be forever. And with Caressa's crazy shifts and Michael's work and my shooting schedule… No, he was right. We'd never see each other.

"Well, I have to run out to do a few things." He pressed a kiss to Caressa's temple. "I'll be back in a couple of hours."

Then he met my gaze—those hazel eyes flecked with gold that had always intrigued me. I hadn't always wanted him sexually, but I sure did now.

She offered him a shy smile. "Thanks for doing

this."

"It's my pleasure." Then he pulled their joined hands to his mouth and pressed a kiss to her knuckles.

Finally, with one last look at me, he released her hand and headed toward the front door.

After a few minutes, likely the time he needed to put on his boots and coat, the front door shut.

Caressa stood before me with her fingers entwined.

Ah. So…nervous. Not something I saw from her often. She carried herself with assurance. Like she knew what she wanted and what would be required of her to get it. She wasn't easily swayed. Which was why I was certain she'd wanted a relationship with Michael. She wouldn't have just gone along for the heck of it.

"Michael, uh, went to get a few things from the condo that I realized I might need." She twirled a lock of hair through her fingers. "And I had a small shopping list that he's taken."

"Shopping? On December twenty-first? We'll be lucky if he ever gets back."

"I'm sure it won't be *that* bad."

I arched an eyebrow.

"Okay, yeah, probably." She scratched her neck. "He might've also offered to go so we could have some time."

My ears perked.

"And, uh, I think we need to talk."

Slowly, I patted the seat beside me.

Just as slowly, she made her way over to me. She sat beside me on the couch but angled herself toward me. She tucked her legs under her ass and rested her hand at the top of the couch, mere centimeters away from my head. I tried to shift a bit as well, but she put a hand on my arm.

"Just take it easy, okay? I really want you rested up and healthy again."

"Sure, so do I."

"So you won't do anything to jeopardize the recovery?"

"Why would I?" What's she getting at?

"I love you."

My eyes widened, and my gaze shot to her crystalline pale-blue ones. Was she… "I love you too."

Slowly, she crossed the infinitesimal gap and twirled a lock of my hair through her fingers.

My scalp tingled.

"Michael and I talked."

"Uh-huh." My heart wanted to take the leap, but my mind just wasn't ready. "And what did you decide?"

"I don't think we've decided anything." That little V that I adored formed in her forehead. "Well, maybe."

"You're prevaricating—that's not like you." Funny, how I knew that. How I knew everything.

Or I thought I had. I didn't know what had happened to her in Africa, and I didn't know what was in her heart now.

"Fair enough." She continued to twirl my hair. She had no way of knowing, but I loved having my hair pulled. I told people I kept it long for the show, the roguish look, but truly I wanted my sexual partners to be able to grab and tug. That always got my cock to sit up and take notice.

Much like now. I sported a semi that was likely to turn into something far more noticeable if she kept this up. Her nearness always reassured me. That was a given. But lately, her proximity had been more. I wanted her—

physically, emotionally, spiritually—any way I could get her. That scared me more than anything because she belonged to Michael.

Well, she didn't *belong* to anyone. No one could own her. Had she given her heart to our best friend?

Might she give it to me?

"Okay." She swallowed.

Okay what? I needed her to elaborate, but I also wasn't going to push. I also wanted to lean in and bury my face in her neck so I could inhale her fresh scent. Likely, she'd showered when she came home from work. No matter how tired she was, she always needed to wash off work. And while I enjoyed showers to energize me, she used them to relax and to begin to wind down.

And she didn't smell like sex. Not that I could remember a time when she had. She liked to keep her private life exactly that—private. Given half a chance, she'd never have told us about that asshole Franklin.

God, she was killing me. I wanted to demand that she simply spit it out. If she and Michael had decided to leave, if my declaration had been too much, then I just wanted to know.

"Michael and I want to try."

I cocked my head as I still held her gaze. All these thoughts swirled in my head. *Does she see my confusion? Or my need for her?*

"Look, he's told me about what you went through while I was away. And I can tell myself that you both were just worried about me. As a friend. But we've always been honest with each other. I've never looked at you guys *that* way because I despaired of losing what we had." The V intensified, grooving even deeper. "We're so much more than best friends. We're like family. And it seemed weird to me to look at you in a romantic way, in a sexual way, because I saw you as brothers."

Ouch.

I couldn't fault her logic, though. The kind of love we shared transcended so many boundaries. We thought we knew everything about each other. She'd known when I had my first wet dream. I'd known when she had her first period. We'd known when Michael had a crush on our third-grade teacher. No secrets.

Or there hadn't been.

When had the walls gone up?

Fucking Franklin.

Before him, I'd known everything about Caressa and the guys she dated. Michael and I had vetted them all. And he'd brought home the women in his life, and yeah, okay, maybe I'd been a bit more circumspect, especially about the guys in my life and the kink, but the breaking point had been Franklin. He'd manipulated Caressa. Convinced her that Michael and I didn't need to vet him. That should've been a red flag to her, but she'd believed herself in love. Only the existence of a wife and two kids had finally dissuaded her from that notion. Had proved what a vile human being he was.

But we'd never fully recovered from that treachery. Whether she thought Michael and I blamed her for her naiveté—we didn't—or whether she simply wanted to get away from the mess, she'd run to Africa. We three had never found an even keel, and then she'd stayed away for five years.

"What are you thinking, Cole?"

Ah, not so good at hiding.

"That I'm hoping you're going to tell me what's going on before I start sprouting gray hairs."

She snickered. But the smirk was short-lived. "That's not what you're thinking at all, but I'll let it go for now. If we're going to make this work, we need to be honest."

"Make what work, Caressa?"

"The three of us."

I nearly swallowed my tongue. I'd hoped, but… "What are you saying?"

"That Michael and I want to try to make a relationship work with you." A faint blush stole across her cheeks. "We both find you attractive—"

"Both?" I wanted to be certain I'd heard correctly.

She nodded. "Yeah. Michael's never looked at another guy that way. But you know he's not homophobic. Like, at all. You just…" She took a deep breath. "You caught both of us off guard. You've intrigued us." Her gaze flicked to my lips before she looked back into my eyes.

Okay. That's interesting.

"Intrigued how?" *I need you to say it.*

"Well…" She bit her lower lip. Incredibly sexy and also something she rarely did. "We want to try, uh, dating you."

"Dating me?" God, I sounded like a parrot.

"Yeah." She blinked. "I went a long time without any physical contact, and now Michael's offered it to me pretty much on demand and you…"

Ah.

I reached up to thread my hands in her hair. Using them as leverage, I slowly tugged her toward me. Even knowing I needed to be careful, I kept pulling her toward me.

Her eyes fluttered shut just before our lips touched.

Just a light pressing of lips. Just a brush. Just…

Fuck it.

I had her in my arms, and I had no idea how long this would last or if we'd ever do this again. I needed to take full advantage.

Yanking her toward me wasn't difficult as she came willingly.

She let go of my hair and pressed both her hands against my chest. But not to push away. No, her fingers flexed and grasped my T-shirt.

I cursed the fabric. I wanted skin to skin. I wanted to feel every inch of her. I wanted inside her in a way I'd felt with no one else my entire life.

Well, except perhaps Michael. Yeah, I'd love to be in him as well.

With as much finesse as I could manage, I nipped her lower lip.

She opened for me.

I thrust my tongue inside. If I couldn't fuck her with my cock, I could at least fuck her with my mouth. Show her what she'd get if she chose to be with me.

Chose.

Except hadn't she suggested she'd be with both Michael and myself? What did that look like? Her and me as well as him and her? Or all three of us?

My cock stiffened at the thought. The image of the three of us in my massive bed. All the things we could enjoy. All the things we could do to each other.

As if reading my thoughts, her hand slowly meandered down my chest, past my waist, and over the button on my jeans to rest on my crotch.

I pulsed in anticipation.

She squeezed.

I nearly came.

A soft chuckle escaped her as she pulled back. With eyes glazed from passion, she appeared to need to blink me into focus. "In case you're wondering what you get out of this."

"And Michael?" I didn't want to be greedy, but I also wanted to understand the parameters of the relationship. Which lines could be crossed and which were protected by barbed wire fences.

Her lips curled into a gentle smile. "He trusts me. And he trusts you. And I trust you," she quickly added. "So it's okay if we spend time alone. Or if you hang out with him, like while I'm working or whatever. In fact"— she released her hold on my dick and moved her hand back up my chest—"I'd appreciate if you filled his time with other pursuits. I'm busy, and I won't always have the ability to come home and meet his emotional needs."

"But he can meet yours."

She tilted her head. "Fair point. But you also bring something to the table."

"And what's that?" My hoarse voice barely got out the words.

"You." She cupped my cheek. "I know you don't see it, Cole. And I understand why. But you have more to offer than just a sexy body and a warm bed. But…" She trailed her finger along my cheekbone. "You have to be willing to let us in sometimes."

Fuck.

"Uh…"

"Not today." She leaned in to press a kiss to my lips. When she pulled back, she still had a lovely smile. "But if we're going to make this work, we have to be honest. And I'll honestly say that I'm not too worried about you stealing Michael away from me, but that thought does flit across my mind from time to time."

"I don't want to steal you." *Especially not if I can have you both.*

Shadows flickered across her eyes.

Fucking Franklin.

I just knew. That somehow the fucking miscreant still had power over her. That he could make her hide in a way that was detrimental to all of us. And I still didn't know all her secrets.

"Will you one day tell me? Tell us?"

"Tell…" Her voice trailed off. "Oh."

"Yeah."

She scratched her fingernails down my stubbled jaw. "We'll see, Cole."

In that moment, she conveyed a message so clearly that she might have said the words. *Push me too far, and you risk losing me forever.*

And I'd never do that. So she was safe with me. For now, anyway.

"I feel like baking cookies."

She started to pull back, but I yanked her in for one last hug.

For just a fraction of a moment, she stiffened. Then she yielded and allowed me to hold her in my arms.

I buried my face in her curly hair and inhaled her lemony shampoo.

Michael'd shipped her lots, as well as many of her favorite products, while she'd been overseas. I'd preferred to send money to her. As well as to the aid organizations, lest she consider giving them what I sent her. That being said, she'd probably done it anyway.

She wrapped her arms around my waist and tucked

her head under my chin. "I missed you."

My chest muffled her words, but I heard them clearly enough. "Double for me, darling. Double for me."

We stayed that way for a very long time. Eventually, she rose.

I didn't miss the sheen of tears in her eyes. I tried to rise as well.

She held out her hand. "I can bake on my own. I'll bring some in when they're ready, and Michael might be home soon."

Then she fled, taking part of my heart with her and leaving hope for the future in her wake.

Chapter Twenty-Two

Caressa

Baking a batch each of shortbread and chocolate chip cookies was easy. Forgetting the look of longing in Cole's eyes was much harder.

He and Michael hadn't pushed. And for a few minutes at a time, I could forget that a child had died on my watch last night. I could push the memory aside and not have to deal. But that never held. I'd think about last night, and that would devolve into questioning every decision I made, most especially the decision to start seeing Franklin in the first place, but the unraveling only began there and kept right on going through to my Africa experiences.

What Cole offered, even though he didn't realize it, was respite from the nightmares. Well, the day terrors, perhaps. Michael'd been trying to cope with the night terrors, but they seemed to be a beast in and of themselves. If I'd been stronger, I would've insisted on sleeping alone. On not subjecting him to the disrupted sleep and the neurotic woman he claimed to love.

Did love. Does love.

Michael's love could never be in doubt.

Neither can Cole's.

I checked the temperature of the cooling cookies.

Perfect.

After plating several, I poured a glass of milk and then headed to the living room.

Cole sat, absorbed in his tablet.

I considered just leaving the food and escaping, but that would be the coward's way out. "Cookies." Ugh, my voice was way too high and singsongy.

He glanced up, smiled, and closed the tablet. Then he frowned. "You're joining me, right?"

"I…was going to start dinner."

His frown intensified. "We can order in."

My immediate and knee-jerk reaction was to say that was too expensive and we couldn't do that all the time.

He's kind of rich. You're making a decent salary.

Well, those statements were true.

So were the facts that fame was fleeting and I could lose my job at any moment.

My phone vibrated in my back pocket.

I handed Cole the cookies and milk and left the room without even checking the number. Only a small handful of people had my number, and if any of them were calling, then it wasn't good.

Well, it could be Kendall calling to wish me Merry Christmas, but I wasn't holding out a lot of hope on that score.

VPD.

Okay, so likely the Vancouver Police Department. As much as I wanted to throw the phone in the closet and never look at it again, I figured that wouldn't solve the problem.

I swiped. "Hello?"

"Caressa Klein?"

"Yes."

"This is Detective Tyson McGillvary."

"I remember."

"I apologize for calling. I got your number from the hospital."

Which might or might not break privacy rules, but I didn't question his need to speak to me.

"How can I help?" *Please just leave me alone.*

"I need to take a formal statement about what happened last night."

Last night? Time dragged so slowly that it felt like mere moments ago and not more than twelve hours. "Of course."

"Why don't I come to you? I'd say I'm in the neighborhood, but I have no idea where you are."

"Hospital didn't tell you?" I might have injected just a note of sarcasm.

"Nope. The clerk gave me a nasty glare. Your license says Mission City. Is that correct? It's not in the neighborhood, but I can—"

"I'm in Point Grey. Mission City was temporary and…" I floundered. Was I going to update the address to Michael's condo? What was the protocol? I inhaled deeply and provided Cole's address.

After a brief silence, Tyson said, "I can be there in fifteen minutes."

"Okay." I hesitated. "Should I come to you? Should I get a lawyer?"

"No to both questions. You're not a suspect. I want you to be comfortable. You're always allowed to have a lawyer present when speaking to the police. Again, though, you're not a suspect. If you want a lawyer, then secure one and call me back. You still have my card, right?"

I fingered the card in the back of my other jeans pocket. "I do. But go ahead and come over. I'll be here."

"See you shortly." He hung up.

Tears pricked the backs of my eyes, and I cursed. After a moment, I wandered into the kitchen to see if I could start something for dinner. Dusk was settling. Michael would be home soon—likely exhausted and possibly frustrated. Cookies and milk wouldn't be enough to satisfy Cole.

I started with the freezer, unsure if I was going to find anything other than frozen pizzas. I was pleasantly surprised to find a large selection of labeled food containers. The frozen turkey caught me off guard. Cole planned to do a traditional Christmas turkey? He was the least likely, of all of us, to be sentimental about holidays. Well, in fact none of us were. As often as not, I'd worked. Cole sometimes had restaurant gigs, and invariably, Michael'd studied. When we were in university, at least. That last year, before I left for Africa, both guys'd had the day off. And…

The memory seized me.

They'd made a turkey dinner with all the trimmings.

And I'd been holed up in a hotel room with Franklin after a long and depressing shift at the clinic. I hadn't known about the dinner the guys had made, and I certainly hadn't known about Franklin's wife and children waiting for him at home. He'd always said he lived in the outer suburbs and he didn't want to drag me out that far, and he'd known Michael and Cole were leery of him, so he'd never wanted to come to my place in case they were over. What seemed so innocent now flashed neon red with all the warning signals I'd missed.

Only Franklin's wife showing up at my work and

confronting me had led to the true understanding of what I'd done. Willful blindness, the woman had accused me of.

She hadn't been wrong.

Leaving for Africa had felt like the right decision. And until a month ago, I hadn't regretted that decision.

Jesus Fucking Christ. Get a grip.

The cop was due in moments, and having tears streaking down my face, or even red, puffy eyes, wasn't a good thing. Of course, he might think I was grieving the lost child. And he wouldn't have been entirely wrong.

"Caressa."

Cole's soft entreaty pulled me from my reverie.

Only then did I hear the soft binging of the freezer, letting me know I'd left it open too long. I shut it and turned to face my friend.

He stood, with the aid of his crutches, and he had a deep worry line across his brow.

My first thought was he should never do anything that might mar his perfection. Which surprised me, because I rarely thought of Cole in terms of perfection, or of anything looks based. He was Cole. My best friend. One of only two people on the planet who knew me almost as well as I knew myself.

Almost.

"I was just…figuring out what to make." I glanced at the microwave and did a mental calculation of how long I had until—

A knock sounded at the door.

Fuck. A litany of thoughts thundered through my mind. The most prominent, of course, was a petulant voice demanding to know why I hadn't told Cole everything to begin with.

Before either of us could move, a key scraping the lock sounded, and, within moments, the front door opened.

I moved to greet the person, whom I assumed to be Michael since he had a key, and I came face-to-face with Detective McGillvary. He held several bags, and within moments, Michael came in behind him, followed by a woman I didn't recognize.

"Thanks for the help." Michael toed off his shoes and moved into the dining room. He dropped several parcels, then returned to collect the bags the police officer carried.

The woman unabashedly gazed around the house and then, like an aimed arrow, hit the bullseye with Cole, who stood off to the side, still on his crutches.

Through all this, the detective held my gaze. "We're sorry to intrude. So close to Christmas, and all."

"It's all right." I spoke quietly, unsure of the protocol. "Uh, why don't you come in?"

He nodded and crouched down to untie his shoes.

"Don't worry about that." Cole's voice rang loud and clear. "We don't care about that."

Which was the exact opposite of the truth. We *always* took off our footwear—no matter whose house we visited. Cole might have a cleaner, but he was a stickler. Too many years living in the slovenly conditions with his father. And my mother. Michael, for his part, had been raised in cleanliness. Just abusive, emotional chaos.

"Well, we appreciate that, but we'll remove our boots. They're on the muddy side."

I couldn't see a speck of dirt on either set of boots,

but I respected the detective's consideration.

He had close-cropped steel-gray hair, which contrasted with his line-free face. I wouldn't have pegged him as more than my age. So…premature gray? His brown eyes were as intense now as they had been last night, and I didn't doubt Cole, and perhaps even Michael, knew who our guests were.

The woman had brown curly hair and pretty hazel eyes that were just as assessing. When she and Detective McGillvary straightened, she held out her hand. "Detective Mariah Gleason."

Michael sucked in his breath.

I shook the woman's hand.

"And I'm Tyson McGillvary." He offered a sheepish smile. "But you knew that. Could you introduce me to your friends?"

Does he know who Cole is? Entirely possible that he didn't watch *VJ*. Mariah's keen interest in Cole assured me that even if the woman didn't know who Cole was, she liked what she saw. I judged her to be a few years older than the rest of us.

"Uh, yeah." I moved toward the living room, beckoning them to follow. "This is Cole Hamilton. This is his house." I indicated Michael, who followed close behind. "And this is Michael Dubois. Also a, uh, friend."

"Shall I take your coats?" Michael pointed to the officers. "You might get warm."

Cole didn't keep the heat turned up, but both cops wore heavy coats.

Mariah unzipped hers and, very subtly, shifted so her ample bosom was visible.

Is it a good sign they're not wearing bulletproof vests?

I just didn't know.

"Hopefully, we won't be taking up too much of your time." Detective McGillvary said the words casually while unbuttoning his wool coat.

"Why don't we go into the sitting room?"

Cole's invitation was casual, but I knew better. He never used the formal room. Or at least that's what Michael had said in one of his many letters describing Cole's home. Some rooms had come furnished, and Cole hadn't bothered to update or change things.

I worried the room might reek of disuse, but apparently, Cole's competent staff kept the room guest ready.

As we stepped into the room, Cole stopped for a moment behind me. Awkwardly, he put a hand to the small of my back.

The warmth seeped through my blouse, and I clung to the sensation.

"You take the blue chair."

Ugh. The blue chair was clearly meant for the head of the household. I'd assumed Cole would take it. On either side of it were matching cream highbacked chairs, and a formal royal-blue settee sat across from it.

While I moved to the appointed chair, Cole plopped into one of the cream chairs, and Michael, clearly reading the room, sat in the other.

The cops perched on the settee across from me.

Detective McGillvary pulled out a notepad. "You're obviously comfortable with your friends staying. Did you call a lawyer?"

This time, Cole sucked in a breath. "Does she need a lawyer?"

"Not at all." Detective Gleason eyed him eagerly.

Or maybe I was seeing things that weren't there. Not every woman fawned over Cole. Given all that had transpired today, though, I was feeling a little protective.

A little jealous.

"I'm worried about patient confidentiality." That should've been a top priority, but having my best friends as security felt more critical.

"We don't need to mention the names of the people involved." Detective McGillvary scratched his nose. "I believe there's a chance the names of the parents will leak out. But you're right—the child's privacy is critical."

"If the child died because of the negligence of the parents, how does it protect them to have the parents' names withheld?" Michael's eyes were wide, his face all earnestness.

"Depends how much money they have." Cole deadpanned this, with flat eyes. He knew about neglectful parents.

We all did.

"Money shouldn't factor into it." Detective Gleason offered Cole a smile that I struggled not to think of as coy.

"But it always does."

Detective McGillvary cleared his throat. "Perhaps you can take us through what happened? From the beginning?"

So I did. From the moment I pulled back the curtain to find a lethargic child on a bed through to the pronouncement of death. I winced inwardly when I brought up *Dr. Caruso*.

As expected, both Michael and Cole stiffened. Cole, at least, had heard me mention his name within this context. Michael appeared completely blindsided as his jaw tightened.

To my everlasting gratitude, neither spoke. Franklin, for all his faults, wasn't the subject of this discussion. He'd been seriously negligent, but ultimately that little girl probably would have died anyway. Even if we'd gotten the right meds on board earlier, she was likely too far gone.

By the time the officers finished their questioning, I was wrung out like a rag doll, barely capable of holding my head up. I'd had only a few hours' sleep in the past twenty-four, and that lack was catching up with me fast.

I yawned as we all rose.

Cole struggled a bit, but both Michael and I knew better than to offer.

Detective Gleason stepped toward him. "Anything I can do?"

God, did she just bat her eyelashes?

I struggled to keep my claws sheathed.

"No, but thank you." Cole righted himself on his crutches. "Just a minor injury that'll heal in no time."

"Were you injured on the job? I heard you do all your own stunts."

Swear to Christ, the woman fluttered her hands.

I caught Detective McGillvary's grimace. Funny, I was starting to see him more as Tyson rather than the more formal title. Perhaps because he'd been so kind to me.

Cole cleared his throat. "I prefer to keep what happened under wraps. If I can keep the media out of it, I'd prefer that."

"Oh, I'd never tell the media."

Detective Gleason's expression of shock was

priceless. Her, I could not think of as Mariah.

"Well, I heard about the time you went to Club—"

"We'll be heading out." Tyson spoke right over his partner.

Normally, I'd find it rude for anyone to speak over anyone else, especially a man interrupting a woman, but judging by the look on Cole's face, he hadn't wanted whatever she was about to say to be revealed.

Which, at any other time, might have piqued my curiosity. Today, though, it just made me tired. Made me want her to leave even more. Made me long for my bed.

Michael led the lot of us back through to the front door.

I ensured I was the last one out so I could turn off the lights.

Cole waited for me and mouthed *are you okay?*

My first instinct was to wave him off. To downplay the hell I'd just endured.

But I couldn't do that—to either of us.

Reluctantly, I shook my head.

He balanced so he could rub my arm. Clearly, he wanted to say more, but voices from the front hall beckoned us.

Only polite to bid our guests good night.

As we entered the front foyer, Tyson straightened from having tied his laces.

I still wasn't sure why he hadn't just worn his shoes. Didn't police officers need to worry about their safety? Be ready to chase suspects at any moment? Having to pause to put shoes on would definitely slow them down.

In truth, all of tonight niggled me. Tyson kept giving me looks that I struggled to decipher. Clearly, he was trying to convey something. *Sympathy?*

"I suppose you'll be speaking to Dr. Caruso." Michael held his gaze steady on the officer as he spoke Franklin's name, but I didn't miss the tic in his jaw.

"Already did." Detective Gleason patted at her curly hair, again glancing at Cole.

"And?" Cole met her gaze, but his face remained impassive.

Tyson glared at his partner, who merely shrugged.

"He might've presented a different take on events."

My stomach dropped.

"Trying to cover his own incompetence." Michael growled the words in frustration. "Never was very good at disguising his mistakes."

Tyson stilled. He looked from Cole to Michael to me. "You've dealt with him before? He said this was the first shift you'd shared at the hospital."

I shot Michael a *thanks so much, you fucking idiot* glare.

He winced.

"Uh, Dr. Caruso and I knew each other years ago. Back before I went to Africa."

In our opening discussion, Tyson had asked me to provide my background. To get a sense of where I came from and what my experience was. He'd been particularly interested in what I'd done there while his partner had clearly been bored.

I loved talking about the charity aspect of my work, often glossing over the tough stuff. I'd done that tonight. Wanting the cops gone, I'd given a bare glimpse into the world I'd inhabited for the past five years.

"You must've been quite young…when you worked with Dr. Caruso."

He's not flirting with you. He's ascertaining facts.

213

"Yeah. Not long after I finished obtaining my nursing credentials."

"They're calling for freezing rain tonight." Cole nudged toward the door, forcing the cops to back up a step.

"Right." Tyson held my gaze a few moments longer.

Please don't look too deeply. You won't like what you see.

"Thanks for everything." Detective Gleason snagged the door handle and opened it.

A blast of cold air hit us all.

I shivered. Now the cold on the outside matched the ice around my heart. Accompanied the ache in my chest. Shocked my body into a strange awareness of the aches I'd ignored for too long.

The police officers left, undoubtedly heading back to their car.

Michael couldn't shut the door fast enough.

Cole growled.

I pressed my fingers to my forehead.

Michael gently pulled me into a hug.

As I wrapped my arms around his neck, I hiccupped a sob.

A child is dead.

Intellectually, I understood that I'd done everything possible to save the toddler and that she'd likely have died anyway, even if I had managed to get the parents to admit what had happened. My heart, though, broke for the little girl.

And maybe a bit for the young woman who'd died inside upon learning of her lover's treachery and deceptions.

And now I faced working with him over and over

214

again. That idea was almost enough to have me scurrying back to Africa.

But not yet.

No, things weren't yet resolved, so going back wasn't an option.

Instead, I would put one foot in front of the next and continue to walk this journey I'd begun. I glanced up from Michael's embrace to catch Cole's gaze.

His eyes shimmered.

I was a goner.

Chapter Twenty-Three

Michael

Caressa felt insubstantial in my arms. I wanted to grip tight and never let go, but logic told me I couldn't do that.

The way Cole stared at her, with naked hunger in his eyes, I knew I had stiff competition.

Not competition.

Collaboration.

Whatever that meant.

My stomach rumbled, and I winced.

Caressa pulled back, wiping at her eyes.

Cole guffawed. "Always did have perfect timing."

"Hey, I was the one who braved the crowds and did the last-minute shopping."

Caressa tucked into my side. "And I'm grateful. I couldn't have handled dealing with all those people."

I wasn't convinced of that, but I let it go. She needed me to focus on the here and now, not the past. I wouldn't forget about it, though. I wanted details of what had really happened between her and Franklin. Not the version she'd trotted out for the police. Which still felt surreal. I never interacted with police—that just wasn't a thing for me.

"Let's order in some food." Cole headed back toward the living room.

Is he in pain? If he is, will he tell us?

Within moments, he was settled back on the couch with his tablet in his hands. "Boston Pizza? Then we can order whatever we like."

He was correct, of course, and within minutes, we placed our order.

I excused myself to take a bathroom break.

Caressa did the same thing.

Cole, grumbling, did as well.

We met back at the dining room, and while Caressa sat, holding Cole's hand, I pulled out cutlery, napkins, and got glasses of ice water. I also checked out the kitchen window, relieved not to see any precipitation yet. Guilt would gnaw at me if our delivery person was out in bad weather just so we didn't have to cook.

With Cole having placed the order on his account, I rested assured that he'd leave a generous tip.

Finally, still not ready to sit still, I organized the contents of the bags I'd brought home. Almost all the gifts were already wrapped, so I moved them under the artificial tree Cole'd set up. Or, well, that someone had set up. I took the rest of the stuff up to the room I shared with Caressa. Taking a moment, I made the bed and righted everything.

Then, realizing I'd again left my two best friends alone, I hotfooted it back downstairs.

Still, they remained as a tableau, unspeaking and unmoving, just holding hands.

The doorbell rang.

Cole reached for his crutches.

I waved him off. "It's all good."

He desisted.

I moved to the front foyer, opened the door, and

greeted a disheveled older gentleman.

He shrugged in apology. "Crazy night." He handed me the bags of food, and before I could thank him, he was disappearing back into the night. He hopped into his car and tore out of there.

My gratitude overwhelmed me as I took in the heavenly scents. Belatedly, I realized I hadn't eaten lunch. As always, worry about Caressa pushed food from my mind. She'd asked for help. I'd gladly done it. Whatever she'd said to Cole, I hoped one, or both, enlightened me later.

I moved to the kitchen and quickly unpacked the food. I'd selected a Hawaiian pizza. Caressa had chosen a linguini dish, and Cole had opted for steak, salad, and mashed potatoes.

"Do you need help?"

Caressa came upon me so quietly that I startled.

Or I was so far into my head that I wouldn't have heard a herd of elephants.

"If you can carry out your food and Cole's, that'd be great."

She nodded. Before she grabbed the plates, though, she wrapped her arms around me from the side.

Awkwardly, I turned into the hug.

"I'm sorry."

"For what?" I was genuinely confused. She had nothing to be sorry about. Was she referring to the cops? Her feelings toward Cole? The death of the toddler? I didn't know—and was afraid to ask. When she didn't answer my question but continued to cling, I held her tightly. So desperately, I wanted to take away her pain. Would do anything to shoulder the burden for her. But I couldn't do that. Whatever demons haunted her, and clearly there had been some before today, she had to find a way to cope. Cole and I could stand by her every step of the way, but we couldn't do the work for her.

Finally, she pulled away. She didn't meet my gaze as she snagged the plates. "Cole will wonder where we are."

He might, to be sure. Or he might also understand we needed a moment to ourselves. A moment to recenter our relationship. A moment to comfort one another.

Because I didn't kid myself. I needed the reassurance almost as much as she did.

I snagged the HP steak sauce from the fridge for Cole and headed into the dining room with my steaming plate of food.

Caressa passed me and muttered, "Steak knife," as she headed back to the kitchen.

Ah, something I'd missed. I could plan out everything and still not catch things. That drove me nuts. I wanted to get things correct on the first go-round. The fewer mistakes I made, the less likely someone might get hurt.

I spent my life trying to make certain people didn't get hurt. Whether in my personal or professional life, that was my goal. I could be single-mindedly focused, and sometimes that drove colleagues nuts.

Honestly, I didn't care. Safety first…then the rest could be sorted.

I sat across from Cole with Caressa at the head of the table between us.

Cole caught my gaze and cocked his head.

He thought I knew what was going on? More fool him.

Caressa returned with the knife. She plopped it

down before Cole, sat, and dug into her food.

I took that as a good sign. If Caressa was devouring food, then things might turn out okay.

As hungry as I was, I was slower to attack my meal.

Cole kept stealing glances, which meant I was stealing them back, since our gazes kept meeting.

"Oh, spit it out." Caressa shoved a forkful of pasta in her mouth.

I met Cole's gaze and nodded for him to take the lead.

He cleared his throat. "I wanted to talk to both of you."

Caressa rotated her hand as if to say *yeah, got that…get on with it.*

"Well, you approached me about…changing the dynamic of our relationship."

My ears perked.

"But I wanted the three of us to talk."

Caressa took a sip of water. "Well, duh."

I chanced a glance. I wouldn't have gone as far as to say she was uncomfortable, but she wasn't at ease either. Something was up, and I couldn't put my finger on it.

"Do you both agree that you want to explore a relationship with me?"

Caressa and I both looked at each other, nodded, then turned back to Cole.

"Yes." Since I hadn't been party to their discussion, I felt it incumbent on myself to make the clarification. Or the assurances.

"And you're talking both physical and emotional."

"Sex and romance." Caressa swirled her pasta on her fork, staring at it intently. "Is this going to make things awkward?"

"At first." Cole tipped her chin so she met his gaze. "But the rules we taught you apply—to all of us. This is consensual. If, at any time, any of us wants out, then it ends. That simple. No one is obligated to stay where they're not happy. Or comfortable." He broke her gaze to meet mine. "And if you two decide that it's not working out with me, then you back away. I'm a big boy. I can take it. What I can't stand, though, is you not being honest with me."

Ah, so that's what he was dancing around.

"I want this, Cole. Whatever this is. I'll admit I'm intimidated." I'd been tempted to search for gay porn, but I worried about Cole's internet history ever being breached. I was careful about my own data, but I was triply paranoid about his.

"We can take it slow." His blue eyes flashed darker than usual. Funny. He and Caressa both had blue eyes and black hair, yet they were a study in contrasts.

Caressa snickered. "When have you ever taken anything slow?" She gently removed Cole's fingers from her chin. "You're a *seize the day* kind of guy. Carpe diem and all that."

As always, I flashed to the scene in *Dead Poet's Society* with Robin Williams. A movie that never failed to make me sad and to feel inspired at the same time. We'd found an old copy in a trash bin, along with a few other eighties and nineties classics, and had watched them religiously at Cole's while his father worked.

Did Cole choose acting because of that movie?

Is that really what you're going to focus on right now? In this moment where the rest of your life is being decided?

Perhaps not that dramatically, but pretty damn close.

Cole blinked. "Yeah, okay, fair enough. I see what I want, and I do everything in my power to obtain it."

"So we're just...things?" *God, please have let me misunderstood.*

"Jesus, no." He ran his hand through his overlong hair. Such a contrast to my near buzzcut. "I just..." His hand shook as he laid it on the table. "I've been in love with both of you forever. And not just in the familial way that things were when we were growing up. If you ask me to pick a moment—the moment—then I'd say the day Caressa told us she was leaving for Africa. I nearly died that day from the pain. The thought of losing you." He directed the comment to Caressa.

And part of me wanted to call him out about being overly dramatic. Except, hadn't I felt the same way? Like my heart was being ripped apart? Like my soul was losing its other half? Like I'd never recover from the agony?

Like Cole, had that been the moment when I realized things had changed?

Caressa blinked. "You never said."

"Would you have changed your mind?"

"Well, no."

At least she was being honest—with us and with herself.

She pivoted to me.

I held up my hands.

She put down her fork. "That's a lot to take in." She squinted, looking out to the bay window with the magnificent view of English Bay and the lights of downtown Vancouver flickering in the distance.

We should probably consider closing the blinds. Except who could see in? Who might look, from the

222

water, and question our little domestic scene? Our little domestic drama.

"I told you I went up the Grind and Cole got drunk the last time we found out you weren't coming home." I kept my words quiet. On the one hand, she didn't need our shit. On the other hand, perhaps laying everything out on the table was the only way to resolve this—whatever this was.

She scratched her nose. "I had no idea."

"Because we didn't see any point heaping guilt on you." Cole reached out to take her left hand.

I grabbed for her right.

She tensed under my touch but, after a moment, relaxed into the grip. Her eyes drifted shut. A shudder wracked her body. After a moment, a lone tear fell.

Since it tracked down her left cheek, Cole wiped it away.

She leaned into the touch as he cupped her cheek.

I will not feel jealous. Because this was how things would be going forward—whomever was closest would offer the comfort.

After a moment, she let out a long breath. "I'm tired."

I squeezed her hand. "I'll pack up the leftovers." To my relief, we'd all made a good dent in the food. I'd tucked dessert in the fridge, so we had plenty we could dig into.

"Why don't…" Cole cleared his throat. "Why don't you guys sleep with me tonight?"

My gaze snapped to him.

In my peripheral vision, I saw Caressa's head snap toward him as well.

"Well…" He gave an awkward shrug as he placed

his knife and fork at the five o'clock position.

"We won't exclude you." I said the words quickly. In an attempt to reassure.

His blue eyes flashed. "I know that. And I think we should agree that it's okay for any two of us to do stuff without the third there—as long as we're honest and share afterward."

My breath caught. *You will not be jealous.* Because that didn't only mean Caressa and Cole could do things I wouldn't know about until after the fact or that Caressa and I could be together and tell Cole later. No, this meant Cole and I could be alone and, uh, doing things. That thought fired my blood, and heat rose from my chest, up to my cheeks, and to the tips of my ears.

"Oh, I think Michael loves the idea." Cole grinned.

Caressa swung her gaze to me at his words. She tilted her head.

"I'm..." I cleared my throat. "I'm okay with that. As long as we always share afterward. I mean you don't have to be specific—"

"Oh, I think you want specifics." Caressa's smile was soft.

"Yeah, he'll wank off to whatever he thinks we're doing."

Cole wasn't wrong. Even the idea of the two of them together was doing all kinds of crazy things to my insides that had nothing to do with jealousy.

"I'll clean up while you two get ready for bed." I put my own cutlery on the plate. "Cole, is this going to jeopardize your recovery?"

"I'm sure Caressa will come up with a creative way to ensure I don't further injure myself."

"She will." Her voice was firm. "And you'll do as

you're told. Or tomorrow I tell Zoey you've been a bad boy."

Cole's licentious façade dropped for a moment. "You wouldn't."

Ratting on him to Zoey might endanger his career.

On the other hand, Caressa'd also want to make sure he followed her instructions to the letter. "Whatever's needed for you to take things seriously."

"Oh, I do." Cole reached for his crutches. "I also sleep naked."

If he wanted that to be a mic drop moment, it failed miserably as he had to maneuver to get up and then hobble out of the room.

Caressa eyed me, cocking an eyebrow.

I scrunched my nose. "I always worry about being cold." We'd slept naked together, but usually *after* peeling off clothes to make love.

"Something tells me we're not going to be cold in Cole's bed."

"No, I bet you're right."

Chapter Twenty-Four

Cole

Brazenly inviting my guests to my bed and announcing I slept naked was the easy part.

Realizing my sheets needed changing and not a hope in hell existed for me to do it myself was a humbling experience.

I could try to brazen it out. But I'd jerked off last night, and although I'd wiped up with tissues, I hadn't done a great job of getting everything. The cleaning crew weren't due for another day. If we could've all fit in Michael and Caressa's bed, I might've suggested that. But we wouldn't, at least not without risking injury to me, so here we found ourselves.

Or rather, I found myself. I managed to strip off my sweatpants, shirt, underwear, and socks. The bed, however, remained elusive.

A soft knock sounded at the door.

"Come in."

Caressa poked her head in first.

She's never been in here. Come to it, I'd never given her a full tour. That needed to be rectified tomorrow. I'd given Michael a tour when I moved in.

Well, not a *full* tour.

He hadn't asked about the locked room in the basement, and I hadn't volunteered any information about it.

"You should be in bed." Caressa made the quiet admonishment as she and Michael entered my room.

They wore the matching guest robes I'd left for them.

Adorable.

And hopefully nothing underneath.

"The sheets need to be changed." I sheepishly pointed to the pile of fresh ones on the chaise lounge.

Michael grinned as he closed the bedroom door.

I rarely did. Close the door. As a child I'd spent hours in my cramped bedroom, wishing I could go into the rest of the apartment—yet knowing I'd face my father's wrath. As an adult, I didn't ever want to feel hemmed in again.

For Michael, the opposite was true. That bedroom door had protected him from the chaos of his life. From the abusive people who should've taken care of him but had instead nearly destroyed him.

As Caressa and Michael set about changing the bed, I tried to push all those negative thoughts out of my mind.

I got glimpses of thighs and even a hint of Michael's ass as they remade the bed. They even replaced the pillowcases on the four pillows. Until tonight, I'd wondered if I'd gone a little overboard with those. Because, for all my grandstanding, I'd never had more than two other people in my bed. It'd happened twice, the three of us never spoke of it, and those memories didn't keep me warm on cold winter nights.

The wonderful memories from my childhood, those with Caressa and Michael, did.

Caressa met my gaze once she'd fluffed the last

pillow and as Michael tossed the dirty sheets in the corner.

"I presume you normally sleep in the center?"

Her assumption caught me off guard. "No, actually, I don't." I pointed to the right side of the bed next to my nightstand with my clock radio, my watch, and my telephone plugged into the charger.

And with the box of condoms and a large bottle of lube tucked inside the drawer.

Only now did I notice that neither Caressa nor Michael had brought their phones.

Interesting.

"Okay. You get in, and we'll tuck your crutches away."

I did as bade, knowing she'd keep them close to me so I could escape if I needed to. *Will I? Will they?* I just didn't have an answer to that.

Getting into bed and settling myself was the easy part.

Watching the silent communication between Caressa and Michael as they toyed with their robes was something completely different.

Finally, at length, Caressa pressed a kiss to Michael's cheek, then stood back and unbelted her robe. The white terry towel material eased down her arms until she caught it, then casually tossed it onto the chaise. She gave Michael one final, almost imperceptible nod, then turned to face me.

Truthfully, my breath caught.

I'd known she was beautiful. Her skin, despite five years in Africa, was a pale white. Although she was slender, she also had nice curves around her hips. Her breasts were full with mauve nipples. Finally, her black curly hair cascaded halfway down her back and almost to the tips of her areolas.

After letting my gaze linger just a moment longer, I focused my stare on Michael. Another gorgeous specimen. He was my height, six foot two, and we were half a foot taller than Caressa. In the diffuse light of my bedside lamp, his skin carried a golden glow. His blond hair and hazel eyes belied his native heritage, several generations back, on his mother's side. Too many years had intervened, and too many marriages with European settlers, but he still had some of the warrior in his carriage. He always stood proud and tall. Yet never as comfortable with his height as I was with mine. He'd still try to shrink away if he was amongst strangers.

Tonight, though, he held himself tall and proud. The only betrayal of nerves was the fuzz of blond hair on his arms and legs that stood to attention.

He might be cold.

I held up the blankets in invitation.

Caressa snagged Michael's hand and pulled him around to the left side of the bed.

Curiosity nearly got the best of me as I waited impatiently to see who would slide in next to me.

As Caressa did, she met my gaze. She scooted right beside me, leaving room for Michael. He followed and switched off the lamp after pulling up the covers.

Taking the cue, I switched off mine as well.

"Oh." Caressa's face appeared paler than normal under the barely there light.

"Yeah, I have a nightlight." The base of my lamp lit with the faintest of pale-white glows. I told myself I needed to be able to make my way around my large room in the dark.

Glad to see you can still lie to yourself.

"I can turn it off if it bothers you. I mean, we all know about sleep hygiene." Caressa'd drilled it into us during our post-secondary years when she learned about the sleep rules in her nursing classes. I'd absorbed the rule but had never implemented it successfully.

Gingerly, I slid down the bed until my head rested on the pillow. I longed to turn on my side, but that would take too much work and endanger my leg. I turned my head slightly.

Caressa lay on her left side, facing me.

Michael tucked himself behind her and propped his head on his elbow so he could see over her.

They both gazed at me.

"Is this because of the closet?"

Caressa's words were soft, but they nearly broke me.

She reached up to run her index finger along my cheek and to tilt my chin toward her when I tried to turn away.

The closet.

Several times, Michael's parents had nearly caught Caressa and me in his room. We'd hidden in the closet and had to listen as one parent or the other whaled on our friend.

How often had I dreamed of that dark space? Of the helplessness?

Caressa'd maintained, correctly, that if we'd made our presence known, we'd have lost our access to Michael entirely. Not wanting to risk that, and knowing he needed us as much as we needed him, we'd kept our silence.

Remembering the nightmares fatigued me.

Michael'd known I had problems from when we'd shared a room.

I used to marvel that he could sleep like the dead while I dealt with the trauma of his childhood with my subconscious. Only once had I shared that information with a counselor.

Revealing my secret hadn't helped. In fact, it'd just made me feel vulnerable. And since I hated that feeling, I never shared that part of my past with anyone.

She continued to hold my gaze.

"Yeah, the closet."

Seemingly satisfied, she scooted over so she could press a kiss to my cheek.

Could I turn the light off just for one night? Might my companions chase away the demons?

Caressa snuggled into my side.

Michael pressed closer to her.

Then, as if it were most natural thing in the world, he trailed his hand up my thigh from my knee to my hipbone. He splayed it across my stomach.

Caressa tucked her fingers in around it, closed her eyes, and let out a long sigh.

I held myself still as they both slowly slipped into slumber.

God. Here I was—energized and ready to go—and they'd both drifted off to la-la land.

Apparently, today had been even more emotional than I comprehended.

Well, for Caressa, at least. All that shit at the hospital.

But Michael? Sure, he'd risen early to pick Caressa up from the hospital. And he'd shopped. Which wasn't fun at the best of times. Had he gone through more than

I realized? Did this new arrangement stress him out?

Slowly, their hands slid from my stomach.

Caressa's went slack.

Michael tucked his against her and pulled her in tight.

Even in sleep, they sought each other.

They don't need me. I was wrong to demand capitulation.

They're adults. If they didn't want this, they wouldn't be here.

And, on that note, I drifted off.

For how long I slept, I wasn't sure. Awareness slowly pulled me back into my room and away from the dream I'd had. Not of closets or of naked friends, but of a movie night we'd shared not long after we moved into our own place. On one of my rare nights off, we'd discovered a marathon of the first three Star Wars movies. We'd made popcorn slathered in butter, eaten peanut butter chocolate cups Michael'd made, and drunk way too much soda.

The dream was so clear in a way the memory wasn't when I tried to grasp on to it. That had been one of the best days of my life, yet I rarely remembered it. And I wasn't going to try to analyze why tonight of all nights. Sinking into something pleasant and secure wasn't a surprise.

Waking up with a hand around my cock was.

Caressa's delicate hand encircled me—just holding on. No tugging or jerking—just a secure grip.

Is she asleep? Does she think she's holding Michael?

Will I always ask that question instead of just enjoying myself?

Carefully, I flexed into her grasp.

She tightened her fingers.

And moaned.

I turned my head.

Her closed eyes caught my attention, but so did the flush staining her cheeks.

I noted movement from under the blanket.

Then I glanced beyond her to catch Michael's gaze.

He grinned and nipped Caressa's ear.

She moaned again. And shifted.

Then her hand tightened on me. Not painfully, but not gently either.

I eyed the cover and then looked back at Michael.

He grinned again. Then he shouldered off the covers and flicked them down with his wrist—unveiling the most erotic sight.

Caressa leaned against him with her right leg tucked back, opening her thighs.

Michael's fingers delved deep between those thighs—moving rhythmically.

Playing with her pussy.

She moaned again.

"Make Cole come, sweetheart. If you make Cole come, then I'll let you come." The glint in his eyes was positively wicked.

Okay, hadn't seen this coming. I'd read Michael as the most reluctant—the most modest. Clearly, he was far more clever and creative than I'd given him credit for.

Caressa didn't open her eyes, but she did tighten her grip on me.

Much more, and I'd be pushed beyond pain and into pleasure.

A place I visited often.

She twisted her wrist a little and gave me a good pump.

My cock, which had already been enjoying the attention, hardened further.

She moaned.

"That's it, sweetheart. Give Cole what he wants."

This time, her eyes opened. Lazily. She met my gaze with those fathomlessly pale-blue eyes that were almost completely eclipsed by her dark pupils. The flush ran from the tips of her breasts, all the way up her neck, and into her delicate cheeks. She licked her lips.

I jerked.

Her lazy smile nearly did me in.

She trailed her index finger along my slit and gathered a bit of pre-cum. Then she smeared it down my length. Not nearly enough to mimic the smooth glide of lube, but enough to get my full attention. She tugged.

I thrust.

That began the process in earnest.

She pulled her lower lip between her teeth as she jerked me off. The movements weren't perfectly synchronized, but that made them all the more erotic. Her frantic motions brought me closer and closer to the edge.

"Come, Cole."

Michael's rough voice surprised me. As did the command in his tone. I was supposed to be the alpha in this relationship. The one in charge. Yet here, in our very first encounter, he was calling the shots.

I'd have to do something about this later.

"Cup his balls. I bet he'd like that."

The angle was awkward, and I cursed not being able to turn toward them, but Caressa managed to follow

Michael's command and take my balls into her hand. Her smooth fingers examined them. Weighed them. Took their measure.

And still, she kept up the steady rhythm of tugs of my shaft.

"I said come, Cole."

No missing the hint of steel in Michael's voice.

As if inexorably drawn by his voice, I closed my eyes, thrust my pelvis up, and erupted.

Caressa nursed me through the orgasm, gentling her movements until she was nearly still.

I wasn't going to worry about where all the cum had gone. I had several sets of sheets.

"Now me."

The petulance in her voice made me smile.

I opened my eyes and glanced over as Michael delved his hand between her thighs again.

She hitched her leg back and over his—giving him maximum access.

Tentatively, I pressed my thumb to her cheekbone. I wanted to touch her. *Needed* to touch her. But the first time felt reverential. Like I was breaking a sacred pact between the two of them.

"Play with her nipples, Cole. She has the most fucking sensitive nipples."

Caressa's gaze shot to mine.

Was that pleading I saw? To play with them? To not play with them?

Personally, I loved nipple play. If someone squeezed mine in just the right way, then I could almost come.

I trailed my hand down her cheek, along the long column of her neck, across her collarbone, and to her breast. First, I cupped it.

She arched into my touch.

I squeezed.

Her eyes drifted shut.

"Eyes on me. I want you looking at me when you come."

Michael chuckled at my command, but Caressa obeyed.

I took her nipple between my index finger and thumb.

It hardened at my touch.

I squeezed.

She jerked.

Michael chuckled again. A throaty sound that shot straight to my flaccid dick. Almost demonic.

Huh, apparently, he had a whole sadistic side I'd no idea about. Well, things were about to get very interesting.

"Please." Caressa sighed the word.

Michael's rubbing intensified.

Caressa struggled to keep her eyes on me. Good girl she was, she continued to obey my command.

I moved my fingers to her other nipple and squeezed. Hard.

Her entire body tightened like a bowstring, and an inarticulate wail escaped her lips.

Michael stilled his frottage and angled his wrist, sinking deep inside her.

Damnit, I wanted to be the one doing that. Feeling her heat as she contracted around me.

I had the next best thing, though. I gently massaged her nipple as she whimpered and tried to pull away.

Michael shushed her, holding her firmly in place.

She stilled.

This time, when her eyes drifted shut, I didn't say anything.

Michael eased his fingers from her.

She pulled her legs tight to her chest.

Then, to my utter shock, he held out his fingers to me.

I inhaled deeply, then took a tentative lick. Doing this felt wildly inappropriate, wildly intimate, and yet wildly right. This moment was cementing the three of us together. Whatever happened in the future, we had this bond. This shared experience.

As I sucked on his fingers, Michael's eyes drifted shut on a moan.

Oh, like that, is it?

"Caressa baby."

She'd likely hate the nickname, but Michael'd secured sweetheart, and I wouldn't try to wrestle that away from him.

"Leave me alone." Said with no heat or malice. More like a plaintive whine.

"Sure. After. But our man is primed and ready to go." Now, I couldn't see Michael's erection, but given the odd thrust of his hips against Caressa's back, clearly he sought friction.

"He can jerk himself off. Or fuck me. I don't care." Said on a groan full of exhaustion.

"Won't you be sore?"

She cracked an eye open. "Never too sore for Michael's cock."

Well, okay then.

God knew she'd be wet enough.

"Or I can jerk him off."

Caressa's grin turned wicked. "Another time. I want

to be coherent for that."

As Michael positioned himself behind her, she lazily hooked her leg over his, opening herself.

Her scent wafted up to me, and my body tightened once more. Jesus, was I seriously getting hard again?

Yep. Yep, I was.

I palmed my cock. I wasn't old, by any stretch of the imagination, but refractory periods were a thing.

Caressa gasped as Michael thrust into her with one swift movement.

He clasped her hip as he thrust into her repeatedly.

Her head fell forward with her hair covering her face.

With one hand I stroked myself—with the other, I twisted her nipple.

She tried to bat my hand away but proved particularly ineffective, and eventually, she rested her hand upon mine.

So tiny. So smooth. So delicate.

Wordlessly, she arched her back and thrust her breast into my hand.

I tweaked her nipple harder.

Her breathing stuttered.

"She's coming, Michael." *And so am I.*

"Let her. I'm right behind."

Said through gritted teeth as he was likely chasing his own orgasm.

Caressa arched back and nearly hit Michael with her head.

He grunted.

She keened.

I moaned.

Just…just…

Cum spurted over my fist.

Michael let go a triumphant howl.

Caressa shuddered, then went limp again.

Okay, well, that was about the fucking sexiest thing I'd ever done.

And that was saying something.

Chapter Twenty-Five

Caressa

As I drifted back to sleep, the vague notion of cleaning up flittered through my mind but was gone the moment Michael pulled the blankets over us and he tucked me into his side.

Cole and I still clutched each other's hands, and we stayed that way until morning.

Although he had blackout blinds, a must for someone who worked such crazy hours, a little light filtered between the slit in Cole's drapes.

Both men slept soundly, even as morning's light crept in.

As far as I could figure, this room had the same floor-to-ceiling windows as the living room and also faced out toward English Bay. On a sunny day, Cole would be able to see the North Shore Mountains. Those majestic peaks that always called to me. So distant from the realities I'd endured. The Downtown Eastside, the college, and, eventually, Africa. Mountains said decadent to me. Somewhere the rich hung out. Somewhere the adventurous climbed. I strove to keep things small and self-contained in my world. I never stepped out of my little box.

Until last night.

What have I done?

Rousing Cole from slumber with a hand job had been a sleep-filled dream. Whether I'd been conscious or not when I started, finishing had been particularly important. Of course, with Michael rubbing my clit with the determination of an Olympic athlete, keeping my focus on Cole had been challenging.

Who knew Michael could be so…bossy?

I liked it.

And was deliciously tender in all the right spots.

Not to mention sticky. Even with the covers pulled up, I couldn't escape the smell of sweat and sex and cum.

Oh, and I was pretty damn impressed with Cole's stamina. Two orgasms? Lovely.

Still, my bladder was demanding attention, and as much as I wanted to stay in bed all day, surely, I had things to do. Like, presents to wrap or…

Nothing.

Michael'd done everything.

Except the dinner.

I pulled myself up to Cole's ear. "I'm going to defrost the turkey so we can have dinner tonight. Is that okay?"

He cracked one bleary eye. "Whatever you want. You know that."

"Do you need a heating pad or an ice pack?"

His eye drifted shut. "Zoey'll be here at eleven."

A quick glance at the clock showed barely eight. "I'll make sure you're up and showered with plenty of time to spare."

"I love you…" The words petered out, and soon his breathing was back to heavy and deep.

Huh, suck him dry with a couple of orgasms, and he's putty in your hands.

Good to know.

I shifted back to Michael. "I need to get out."

He came instantly awake. "Uh, yeah." He rubbed his eyes. "What time…"

"Eight. You can go back to sleep. I have to pee."

Half a second later, he hopped from bed and stepped out of my way.

When I tried to move past him, though, he snagged me around the waist and pulled me in for a tight hug. "Are we good?" He whispered the words into my ear.

"We're fucking amazing." With that, I pecked a kiss on his cheek, slipped from his grasp, grabbed my robe, and fled the room.

Undoubtedly, I could've used the master bathroom I'd spotted last night. No doubt it would be as luxurious and well-appointed as the rest of the house. But I needed a bit of space this morning. I stopped by the bedroom we'd been using. I grabbed my toiletries and headed into the en suite.

The hot water cascading down my body revitalized me while soothing at the same time. I might've just lain there last night, but my body had been put through a workout. Michael's enthusiasm was expected, but Cole's participation had been welcome.

I'd anticipated nerves. I'd worried about a need for modesty. I'd expected awkwardness.

None of those things happened.

Curling up with Michael at my back and Cole in front of me had reminded me of our time as children—a comfort. There had never been anything between us back then. Just three scared kids seeking solace in a world we didn't understand and that terrified us. Last night, though, had been completely different, and yet touchingly the same.

And I hadn't had a nightmare.

That fact wasn't lost on me. I'd had very few nights free of terror since returning from Africa, and I'd worried after the incident in the hospital that normal sleep would elude me.

It hadn't.

Instead, I'd found comfort in the arms of the men I cared for.

The men I loved?

Sure, I'd pronounced my love to Michael. And in most ways, I felt the same with Cole. But how would it feel to take him inside me? To have a bond that I considered sacred? I viewed very little in religious terms. The two organizations I'd worked for were secular. And none of the three of us had grown up in a religious household. And yet, to me, certain things were…sacred. The intimate bond between people was one of them. And I was under the impression that Cole wanted inside of Michael as much as he wanted inside of me.

That thought intrigued me. How far on the continuum would Michael go? I'd noticed a few women over the years. I wasn't necessarily attracted by looks, for sure. But a kind-hearted soul went a long way to rise in my estimation. But I'd never brought a woman to my bed. Maybe if I had, my life might've been simpler.

Or more complicated—women were just as messy as men. People were chaotic. Even the calmest, most rational person could lose their shit.

Michael hadn't really. Yet, anyway. But from experience I knew certain things could tip him over the edge.

Cole, on the other hand, felt things acutely. He hid

it well, but he could be easily hurt, and when warranted, and sometimes not, he could lash out.

Only at me once. Africa hadn't been the tipping point for him. No, that had come earlier.

Franklin.

And now the man was back in my life.

Breaking my contract with St. Paul's wouldn't be difficult. I could claim working in a hospital too closely resembled the work in Africa and I couldn't be at my best. If they leveled a financial penalty, Cole'd pay it. Then I could find an undemanding job. Homecare. Visiting nurse. Vaccination clinic. Family doctor's office. Plenty of places where I could do good.

And not run the risk of running into my lying, cheating scumbag of an ex.

Fucking Franklin.

I sighed as I worked the handful of shampoo into my hair. I'd need a lot. How many times had I considered chopping it all off? I'd tried one of those computer programs where I could change my appearance. Various options appealed, but I'd really liked the sleek bob cut with bangs and a pair of glasses. Knowing I'd have to get a perm to straighten my hair and my eyes were perfect, I'd dismissed the picture.

Plus, in my heart, I knew I'd never change. Cole and Michael loved my hair the way I wore it. Little comments over the years—all incredibly memorable.

You're dawdling.

Yeah, I was. I doubted I'd go through Cole's entire supply of hot water, but I had best not find out the hard way. As the conditioner sat in my hair, I shaved my underarms. I didn't bother with my legs. The hair was only fuzz, and I refused to conform to society's views of beauty. Okay, except underarm hair. For guys, and women who chose that option, I'd accept it. Just…not for me.

I rinsed off completely, then I took just one more moment to let the hot water sluice over my back. Nursing wasn't an easy profession, and I dreaded what was to come. Yet I'd never considered another vocation. I might've been smart enough to get into med school, but the length of time overwhelmed. But a four-year degree with practical experience had drawn me to nursing. I was fucking good at it.

I just didn't know if I could face Franklin over and over again and not lose my mind.

After I shut off the water, I stepped from the shower in a billow of steam. Huh. I hadn't realized I had the temperature turned up so high. Glancing in the mirror, I found my skin a deep pink. Not good for dry skin. Damn. Still, I dried off and located the oatmeal skin lotion Michael used to ship by the crate. Along with a store's worth of sunscreen. But he'd been right—I looked terrible with a tan, and I really didn't want to develop melanoma later in life. Cancer scared me. I'd done a rotation in an oncology ward. The thought of being that helpless had worn on me, and I'd been happy to move on.

By the time I slathered on the lotion, I was a bit cooler. I put on the robe and headed into the bedroom.

Michael sat on the bed.

"Sorry." Good Canadian I was, I apologized. Even when I hadn't done anything wrong.

He squinted. "I almost joined you—"

"You would've been welcome."

"—but I thought you might need time to process

everything that happened." He drew in a deep breath. "I know I did."

And given we were up a flight of stairs, Cole wasn't likely to interrupt us.

Part of me felt guilty at that thought, that we were doing something without him, and part of me liked having a few moments alone with Michael. Plus, hadn't we agreed we could do things without each other? For me, that reassured. I'd hate to think of the two men sitting miles apart on the couch watching sports while I worked a twelve-hour shift, came home exhausted, crashed, then went back to do it all over again. I liked knowing they could be affectionate with each other. Or even fuck each other—if overcome by the urge.

As long as I got the juicy details later…

I'd towel-dried my hair and lightly applied gel, but damp strands clung to my head and back. Selecting clothes for the day wasn't tough. I planned to cook and…

"Shit."

Michael's head snapped up.

"Can you grab the turkey out of the freezer and put it in the fridge?" The bird was small and would hopefully thaw by tonight.

"Of course." He still wore his robe and apparently had no problems padding down to the kitchen nearly naked to take care of the turkey. I should've done that last night, but with everything that happened…it'd slipped my mind.

Fortunately, Cole hadn't gone overboard, and the turkey was the perfect size for a family of four.

Family.

Was that what we were? I, of all people, knew that families came in different shapes and sizes.

By the time Michael returned, I'd applied deodorant and wore my plain cotton underwear and my serviceable bra.

He entered the room, moved over to me, pulled me against him, and kissed me hard. After a moment, he pulled back. "I know I keep saying that you're beautiful. And I know that pisses you off—"

"It does."

"—but it's the truth. And Cole feels the same way. We're not talking about the outer beauty, although you are stunning. We're talking about what's in your heart."

Disquiet settled over me. Michael wasn't known for his effusive praise. He used words judiciously. But he also spoke the truth as he saw it. If he said he saw beauty in my heart, then I at least owed him the decency of listening.

Even if I only felt darkness in my heart.

And in my soul.

Michael tipped my chin up so I could meet his gaze. "What is it? What are you not telling us?"

I didn't miss the *us*. Not long ago, he would've said *me*. Now, though, he'd banded together with Cole. Now I had two men I needed to deceive.

Or you could just tell them the truth.

Yeah, that didn't feel like a viable option.

"I'm fine, Michael. You have to trust me." I was being manipulative. And I didn't care. Trust was a critical word in our relationship.

We both knew it.

His hazel eyes, flecked with green this morning, probed me. "I do trust you, Caressa. But I also feel like you're not being honest. Secrets have never worked. Even…" He cleared his throat. "We found out about him

247

eventually. If he's the reason—"

"He's not." Here, at least, I could be honest.

"If you say so."

"I do."

"Well, that'll have to be good enough. But you've just confirmed you're hiding something."

Oh fuck.

Cole might be whip-smart, but Michael was more of a *slow and steady wins the race* kind of guy. He sat back and observed. Sometimes he withheld comments for extensive periods of time. Then he'd speak, and I'd be forced to acknowledge he'd caught everything going on around him. His quiet certitude matched Cole's bluster.

And they'd both captured my heart.

I sniffed. "You smell like sex."

He laughed. "Yeah, we didn't do a great job of cleaning up. I've stripped Cole's sheets and put everything into the washing machine. We'll have to put on fresh sheets. And I don't care what he says about his cleaning crew and how discreet they are. I don't want someone else cleaning up after me."

"After your cum." I grinned.

He winced. "Yeah, okay. Exactly. I've never had someone do that for me, and I'd offer to do the cleaning myself, but I suspect that'd piss Cole off, and—" He glanced around. "—this is a fucking big house."

I touched the tip of his nose. "I love that you'd offer. I could help—"

A quick shake of the head. "No way. Absolutely not. You work, and we take care of you. That's it. I don't even want you cooking today."

Here, I could put my foot down. "Cooking relaxes me."

He squinted. "Absolute bullshit. I know you. Five years hasn't changed that. I don't believe you learned to decompress in Africa while cooking."

Damn. He wasn't wrong.

Still… "You'll help?"

"We both will. Now, we need to get moving. Zoey's going to be here soon."

"I'll make breakfast."

He winced.

"You need to shower. You can help me when you're out."

"I'll take the quickest shower on record."

I laughed. "Not when you see that showerhead." I kissed his cheek, then I squeezed his ass. "I love you."

He sobered. "We're doing the right thing?"

"Are you having doubts?"

The snicker that escaped was pure Michael.

"Right. You second-guess everything. How could I have forgotten?"

This time, he gently patted my ass. "I'll meet you downstairs in a few minutes."

Only after he was safely in the shower did I realize he hadn't actually answered my question.

Breakfast consisted of whole-wheat toast, scrambled eggs with cheese, green peppers, and onions, as well as turkey bacon, coffee, and orange juice.

Cole poked at the turkey bacon, but Michael dove right in. He'd mentioned he didn't do bacon, so anything vaguely resembling was a treat.

"You don't have to eat it." I made a grab for Cole's bacon.

He playfully smacked my hand away. Then he mock scowled. "I have a nutritionist. She lets me have *some*

249

bacon."

I arched an eyebrow.

"Yeah, okay, only a couple of slices a week. I mean, I appreciate her efforts, but do I really need to eat so much green stuff?" He poked a piece of green pepper with his fork. "I feel like a rabbit sometimes."

"Well, if you want to fuck like bunnies…"

His pupils dilated. Then he took a big mouthful of eggs—including several pieces of veggies.

"So I'm thinking turkey, mashed potatoes, asparagus with cheese, cranberry sauce, stuffing, and sliced carrots in a light covering of butter."

"Oh my God." Cole sighed.

"Only if you let us help." Michael gave me a pointed look.

"Don't you have work to do? And Cole's got rehab—"

"The work can wait." He slashed the air. "You come first. We only have two days left of work before we're off for just over a week."

"No work between Christmas and New Year's?" Cole glanced eagerly at Michael.

Michael shook his head. "Several of those days are weekends anyway, so it didn't make sense. Plus, those guys have been working flat out on that building for months—they deserve a few days off."

"So do you." I eyed him.

He ducked his gaze.

"Ah, so the workers are off, but the supervisor keeps working?"

"Just some designs I need to look over for our next project. The architect has done some preliminary designs, and I want to see what she's done so far. Better to be consulted early in the project before she gets her heart set on things she can't have."

"I thought architects got everything they wanted." I'd heard Michael complain about this before, and I enjoyed riling him up a bit.

He glared.

Cole and I burst out laughing.

The lock on the front door disengaged, and someone opened it.

I cast a questioning look at Cole.

"Hey, Zoey." He yelled her name.

"She has a key?" I pitched my voice low.

"You want me to get up and let her in each time she arrives? And have to trudge over to the front door and lock it each time she leaves?"

Okay, fair point. I just didn't like the idea of anyone having a key to Cole's house.

Except me. And Michael.

"Oh, and I've invited Donovan for dinner. I apologize in advance, but I asked him weeks ago." He pointed to his leg. "Before all this shit happened. I could cancel—"

"Of course not." I met Michael's gaze before turning back to Cole. "Your friends are always welcome. This is your house."

"Our house."

He muttered the words under his breath as Zoey breezed into the room.

She examined his plate, snagged the turkey bacon, and shoved it in her mouth. She'd barely swallowed before she bumped his shoulder. "Let's go, lover boy. We don't have all day."

Lover boy?

Was she speaking from personal experience or Cole's reputation? Or had she somehow divined our new arrangement? And, finally, what was with removing food from Cole's plate? That felt way beyond professional and veering into the personal in a way I wasn't comfortable with.

Still, Cole didn't seem to mind. So I'd hold my tongue.

Then, brazen as anything, she slid her hand along his spine. When she hit his lower back, she evidently pressed hard as he winced and shifted.

"If you sat straight, that wouldn't hurt."

In that exact moment, I couldn't remember enough about anatomy class to know if she was right or not. Still, she had a point—Cole'd been slumping over his food.

She slapped him on the back. "Time to make you sweat."

Cole caught my gaze, and for just a moment, his naked panic was clearly evident.

Then, as if nothing had just happened, he snagged his crutches and rose. Easier than before, but still a struggle.

I held myself still as he made his way out of the dining room and into the living room.

"Did you see…" Michael's question hung in the air.

Still a little winded, I nodded. I couldn't recall ever having seen such naked panic on my friend.

"I don't think Zoey's the issue." Michael picked up his last piece of toast. He examined it, then tossed it back on his plate.

"No, I don't think so either." I pushed around my eggs with my fork. "He's worried he's never going to recover. Which is ridiculous."

Michael rose and snagged the plates and cutlery while I downed the dregs of my coffee. He cleaned off the plates and put them in the dishwasher.

"Might as well turn the dishwasher on, even though it isn't full." I ran through all the dishes I'd use while preparing tonight's meal. "And do we know if Donovan has any food allergies?"

Michael pressed some buttons, and the machine binged and then started churning. "I'm going to assume if he did that Cole would've said something." He scratched his scalp. "I've seen Donovan a few times over the past few years. I got the sense he's still tight with Cole."

"Well, obviously. Since he's coming for Christmas dinner." I wiped down the counter and got out several cutting boards.

"I wonder if they'd planned to invite anyone else?"

I shot Michael a sharp glance.

He held up his hands. "They're both attractive men. Both single, as far as I can tell…"

"Perhaps. Although I get the feeling Cole planned to ask us, but then things kind of cascaded into chaos."

Michael moved close, pulled me into his side, and nuzzled my neck. "Oh, we're chaos, are we?"

I giggled. "Yeah, I think we are."

"Fair enough." He nipped my ear. "What can I do to help?"

"Can you peel? Then, while I prepare the turkey, you can do your work."

He stiffened.

I turned to meet his gaze. "If you do it now, then can you have some time off between Christmas and New Year's?"

"Sure, but…"

"But?"

"I don't want to leave you alone."

I pointed to the high-top table with two barstools that Cole normally used when eating a meal alone. Or at least that's what I assumed. Maybe he ate there with his dates. The faceless women, and apparently men, who stayed the night.

Michael sighed. "All right. But just for you."

"And for Cole. I'm off tomorrow but then working the next five days. He needs company."

"We don't need to be in each other's pockets." He scowled. "I think it'd piss him off to have me always around."

"You don't know that." I elbowed him in the ribs. "You're more interesting than you give yourself credit for."

He considered. "Well, we can spend our time thinking up devious ways to pleasure you."

Heat rose in my cheeks. "And hopefully, keep each other occupied while I'm working my ass off."

"You don't mind?"

"If you guys get busy? Hell, no. Just…" I met his gaze. "I want details."

Chapter Twenty-Six

Michael

I want details.
Caressa's little admonishment carried me through the morning.
Admonishment?
Request?
Command?
All those came to mind as I spun her words in my head. Because, frankly, just the thought of messing around with Cole short-circuited my brain.
I managed to peel the potatoes and carrots without injuring myself. Then I washed the asparagus, not my favorite vegetable, and shredded cheddar for Caressa to use to make the cheese sauce. Something that made the thought of consuming the veggie just a little bit more palatable.
Undoubtedly by nefarious design.
She and Cole loved the little green fuckers.
At least we all hate Brussels sprouts…
As she organized stuffing and scoured recipes for preparing the bird, sounds of Cole and Zoey filtered through to us.
Cole wasn't a whiner by nature, but he was sure giving Zoey a hard time.
Periodically, Caressa and I would glance at each

other. Wondering if we should intervene. Wondering if Cole was okay. And for me, wondering if she'd notice if I loaded some gay porn to run in the background while I worked away at the designs.

Pamela Strickland was one of the best architects in Vancouver. That being said, she could be a tyrant to work with. Most of the time, I was okay with that. We wanted the same thing—the perfect building. Sometimes our vision on how to achieve that perfection clashed.

I hovered my fingers over the keyboard.

Then I eyed my phone. I could shut down the Wi-Fi and stream the porn on my phone. That way it couldn't be tracked back to Cole. And this was my personal cell, so although the data rates would be ridiculous with the overage charges, no one would need to know.

Or you can just google gay sex.

Well, that was true. I mean, I understood mechanics. I'd even dated a woman who'd brought a strap-on to my condo once with a bottle of lube and an explanation of the prostate. Needless to say, I'd ushered her to the door, deleted her number, and resigned myself to jerking off alone for the next few months.

What had I been so scared of? She hadn't said we *had* to do it. Pegging was something she'd enjoyed with her last boyfriend, and she'd thought I might. She'd claimed I came across as liberal and accepting.

Sure, I was accepting. If other guys wanted their prostates pegged, all the more power to them.

I just hadn't seen myself as one of those guys.

Are you now?

I didn't have an appropriate answer for that.

"Keep him on the straight and narrow. No funny business."

Glancing up, I found Zoey in the entryway to the kitchen, leaning against it.

She appraised both Caressa and myself. "Just friends, eh?"

"None of your business." Caressa's tone took that haughty tenor I loved so much.

I smothered a smile.

Zoey winked.

Fucking winked.

Then she hefted her bag over her shoulder. "I'll see myself out. And I'll be back the day after tomorrow."

"At least you're not coming on Christmas." Caressa's mutter certainly was loud enough for me to hear, and judging by Zoey's amused expression, she heard it as well.

"Oh, I'd be here, if I thought it'd do any good."

"You get paid double overtime?"

Ouch.

My girlfriend wasn't pulling her punches.

Zoey eyed her. "I do whatever it takes to get my patients healthy. If that means riding them hard, then I ride them hard. If that means curtailing their extracurricular activities, I won't hesitate to do that either. His recovery is my sole focus."

Caressa sighed. "I apologize."

"Don't." Zoey fluffed her bangs. "I'd be just as protective if that was my 'friend.' "

Damn woman used air quotes.

Caressa flinched.

"Look, it's no skin off my nose what he does in his spare time. As long as it doesn't jeopardize his recovery. Blow jobs and hand jobs are fine. No fucking and nothing that'll jostle him. On that note, I'm off. I have a hockey player just dying for me to get my hands all over her."

I didn't ask if she was referring to her personal life or another client. In the end, I wasn't sure it mattered.

A silence descended once the front door lock clicked shut.

"That went well."

No missing Caressa's sarcasm.

I rose and moved to her. Leaning against the counter, I tipped her chin up. "What's wrong?"

"What if she reports what she thinks she's seen in her clinical notes?"

"Do you really think she'd do that? Would you do that?"

"Of course not."

"So give her some credit. And what has she really seen?" Not much, although I couldn't be certain Cole'd kept his mouth shut. Not that he was bragging, nor was he known for being indiscreet, but she'd worked him pretty hard.

Cole appeared in the entryway where Zoey had stood only minutes ago. "I need a shower." He scrutinized us. "Hey, what's up?"

"Zoey seems to know an awful lot about us." Caressa met my gaze before turning to face Cole.

He shrugged. "I didn't say anything, but…well…" He considered. "She's an intuitive woman—it's why she's so good at her job. And in the end, it's no one's business but our own." He grinned. "Now, anyone want to join me in the shower?"

Caressa grunted and pointed to the tablet and the pile of spices and other food stuff on the counter.

"You can't be planning to spend the whole day at

this."

Whine much?

Except hadn't I had the same thought? That I didn't want her slaving away in the kitchen?

"Caressa and I could go for a walk later."

Cole shook his head. "Not unless it warms up significantly. Zoey said it's sheer ice. She had to wear spikes on her boots."

Together, Caressa and I both looked up through the kitchen window. It faced the front yard and street, but most of the view was hidden by a tree and the slatted blinds. No one could wander by and happen to catch a glimpse of Cole Hamilton.

The tree was covered in ice.

"Will Donovan be able to make it? And should Zoey really have come?" Caressa squinted, trying to look up at the sky. "And what's the forecast?"

"Snow later tonight." Cole shrugged. "Zoey has winter tires, and the roads are mostly clear. Not like that storm last year, thank God. And Donovan won't risk it if he can't make it safely."

"Well, here's hoping it's safe." I nodded to Cole. I wasn't sure I really wanted a fourth, we three had so much to talk about, but I didn't want the guy to be alone either. Although, technically, we were only at the twenty-second.

"We'll play it by ear." Cole sniffed his pits. "God, I reek. On that note, I'm out of here."

He didn't again ask for company as he took off.

I turned to Caressa. "I don't want you spending all your time cooking either. This is one of only three days off. You deserve a break."

"You can give me a massage while the turkey

cooks."

"Fair enough." I hesitated. "Are you okay?"

She gazed up at me. "I'm feeling…unsettled."

"Zoey or Donovan or…" I couldn't finish the sentence. *Am I causing you distress? Is Cole?*

"Kiss me."

A request I'd never deny.

I gathered her into my arms and lowered my mouth to hers.

She twined her arms around my neck and pulled me closer.

As she opened for me immediately, our tongues tangled. Both of us fought for dominance in one moment, then submitted to surrender in the next.

She raked her fingernails along my scalp in the way I loved.

My cock sat up and took notice as she rubbed sinuously against me.

I stroked my hand along her cheek and lower still. As I brushed my fingers along her pulse point, I felt the steady beating of her heart.

When I cupped her breast, she gasped into my mouth.

"I want you, Michael. I *need* you."

Who was I to deny her?

"Bedroom?" I calculated whether Cole's was closer or if we'd be better off going upstairs. Of course, a perfectly acceptable leather couch sat in the living room, but I couldn't imagine that'd be comfortable for her. But if I lay underneath and she rode me? I didn't care about my bare ass on the couch and—

"Fuck me now, Michael."

She pushed me away and reached for the snap of her

jeans.

Well, okay then.

By the time she had her jeans and underwear removed and tossed aside, I had my T-shirt off and my own fly lowered. I tugged down my jeans and was going to remove them, but she snagged my cock in her cold little hand.

"You can do me like this."

I could appreciate the carnality, and the decadence, of fucking in the kitchen while half clothed. That excitement overtook us, and finding a flat surface proved too much of a hassle.

Caressa turned her back to me, tucked her hair out of the way, spread her legs, and stuck her ass out.

My cock leaked a drop of pre-cum onto the floor.

Going to have to clean that up.

I advanced toward her carefully.

She whined with impatience.

I pressed my chest against her back, reveling in the warmth. Then I snaked my arm around her waist and lower still.

"Just fuck me, already."

"Not until I'm sure you're ready." Her scent wafted, but the smell of her shampoo lay heavier than any proof she was wet enough for me to sink into. She might not care, but I fucking did. I wasn't going to hurt her.

When I rubbed her clit, she bucked. I continued to massage it with my thumb as I sank two fingers into her.

So ready. So warm. So wet.

I'd been with few women who could be so ready for action so quickly.

Need to remember that in the future.

I twisted my wrist in just the right way and hit her

rigid G-spot.

She keened.

Finally, I eased my fingers out of her.

She wailed.

I gave myself a couple of good pumps, then lined myself up.

"Holy shit, that's fucking hot."

Both Caressa and I turned to find Cole staring at us.

He leaned on his crutches and gazed at us through hooded lashes. He licked his lips.

My cock jerked in my hand.

"Man, I want to fuck you so badly." His gaze was on me.

I clenched. "I want that too." Then, reluctantly, I indicated his leg with my chin.

He grimaced.

Caressa glanced over her shoulder at me, then turned back to Cole. "I have an idea."

"I like ideas." His blue eyes shone.

Two minutes later, Cole sat bare-assed on the kitchen counter. A footstool and a strong hand from me had gotten him up there. His jeans were around his knees, and his cock jutted up from a nest of black curls.

"Now." Caressa gave me an appraising look. "You're going to fuck my pussy. I'm going to fuck Cole with my mouth. He's going to tell us all the dirty things he's going to do to us once he's healed."

Cole licked his lips. Then he caught my gaze. "Did you know she could be this bossy?"

"Is there a right way to answer that?"

Caressa poked me in the ribs. She snagged my cock, which had softened, and tightened her grip. "Call me bossy again, and you'll regret it."

Blood rushed to my cock. "Whatever you say."

This time, when she turned, I was quick to plaster myself against her. As much as I was in a hurry, I could also be patient. This was the first time she was blowing Cole. I didn't want her to feel rushed.

I needn't have worried.

She licked and nibbled her way up the vein in his cock. She swirled her tongue around the head. She hummed.

Then she took him down nearly to the root.

When she pulled back, I positioned myself and thrust into her.

She grunted.

Cole grinned.

As Caressa went to work on his cock, I did everything in my power to get her off. Her pussy sheathed me as I pushed in an out, driving her higher.

"I…" Cole cleared his throat. "I want to be fucking you, Michael."

Our gazes met and held.

I continued pumping in and out of Caressa.

"Hard. I mean, not the first time. But once you're used to taking my cock? Hard and fast."

My balls grew heavy.

"And Caressa will watch. She'll want to be involved, but this time it's just us. You and me. I'll take you. Claim you. Own you. Your ass will only ever be mine."

That's good to know.

"Or another time, maybe I'll let you fuck me."

My ears perked, yet I maintained my steady rhythm as my fingers dug into Caressa's hips.

"You'll be fucking me…" His breath hitched. "And

maybe I'm fucking Caressa. With my mouth. Or my cock." He stroked her hair. "Would you like that, baby?"

She hummed her approval and clenched around me.

Well, good to know.

I wanted to speak. Wanted to tell him how much I wanted him. Wanted to tell Caressa how much I loved being inside her. I held my tongue, though. Caressa'd given us our marching orders, and I intended to obey them. Because it'd be all the sweeter when I took my turn at giving the commands again. Last night had been hot, but we'd still been exploring each other. When all the barriers came down? I couldn't even imagine how much pleasure we could wring out of each other.

Caressa moaned and stuttered.

I redoubled my efforts. Then I insinuated a hand between her thighs and unerringly located her clit.

Three flicks later, and she stiffened.

Cole groaned.

I continued my steady rhythm, even as she contracted around me.

"Fuck." Cole let the expletive fly as he flung his head back and banged it on the cupboard.

I'd bet serious money he didn't feel it.

Caressa continued to fellate him, even as my orgasm overtook me. With one final thrust, I spilled into her.

Careful not to collapse on her, I pressed myself against her, partially using my thighs to hold her up as she turned boneless in my arms.

She pulled off Cole's cock with a little pop. Then she turned her head and laid it on his thighs.

I stroked her damp hair out of the way as I pressed little kisses to her shoulder blade and neck.

Cole's left leg flexed.

Quickly, I pulled Caressa back.

She moaned, but I gathered her into my arms.

I chuckled. "I don't know if that was Zoey approved."

"She said blow jobs and hand jobs." Caressa managed a coherent whisper. "We didn't fuck."

Cole chuckled. "No, we didn't." He met my gaze over Caressa's head. "Something to plan for the next time."

My insides clenched deliciously. Yeah, I was definitely googling *anal penetration* on my lunch break tomorrow. Because, apparently, I didn't just need to know how to receive.

Can I do it? Can I fuck Cole? I wasn't sure I knew the answer—but I damn well intended to find out.

Chapter Twenty-Seven

Cole

I was sore in all the right places as I lounged in the living room, looking out over the darkening western skies.

After a second shower, Michael'd insisted I relax on the couch and had brought me a sandwich.

Which I'd consumed in about six inelegant bites. Then I'd sipped some milk, and by the time he took away the plate and glass, I was half asleep.

I dozed most of the afternoon while the smells in the kitchen wafted in. They surrounded me, enveloped me, and kept me in warm and happy dreams. I also might've felt vaguely guilty, but at one point Caressa stretched out beside me, with her head in my lap, while Michael gave her a thorough massage.

Her groans alone nearly had me coming in my pants again.

Jesus.

"Hey, buddy."

I'd been so far into my contemplations on the fading sky that I hadn't heard Donovan enter.

He handed me a glass of eggnog and settled on the chair across from me with some kind of amber liquid.

"Scotch?"

"Nah. I'm staying sober tonight. Those roads are

treacherous. If they get worse, I might need to bunk down in a spare room. You've got one of those, right?"

I snickered.

"And I won't be interrupting your fun?"

I cocked my head.

"Hors d'oeuvres." Caressa entered the room with Michael behind her.

Both carried trays as well as drinks for themselves.

"Turkey will be ready in about thirty minutes." Michael handed me a napkin.

I took it and snagged a couple of spring rolls off the plate.

Caressa clucked her tongue. "Not too many. You need to leave room for dinner."

The teasing admonishment not to act like my mother was on the tip of my tongue, but given the parental history for all four of us, or lack thereof, I decided not to make a snarky comment.

Caressa indicated Michael should sit next to me, then she plopped down on the far end of the sectional and tucked her feet under her. She had a nice glow from the heat in the kitchen. Or at least I assumed that was what the pink color was caused by. It might just as easily have been something she did with Michael.

When I thought about the scene I interrupted this morning…

I shifted.

Michael's gaze shot to my crotch.

Jesus. Can you be any more obvious?

A poker face, he did not have. His cheeks pinkened.

Donovan, facing us, glided his gaze from me to Michael to Caressa. And then back again, finally settling on my crotch as well.

Remembering the kitchen was bad enough—remembering what a talented tongue Donovan had?

Jesus. Can I be more obvious?

"Cole said you two have moved in."

Caressa coughed.

"Uh, yeah." Michael indicated the three of us with his hand. "Cole needed us, right?"

"Did he mention that I offered to move in to help?"

Caressa's glare carried ice all the way from the other end of the couch.

"You're a bad influence." I tried to convey as much of a *shut the fuck up* vibe as I could.

"Oh, I can behave. When I need to." He sucked a small block of cheese and a sliver of pepperoni off a toothpick. Then, as he chewed, he waggled his eyebrows and grinned unrepentantly.

"Donovan, you've never behaved." Caressa shifted, turning her attention to my friend. "You were a bad influence on Cole ten years ago. Something tells me times haven't changed that much."

With a continued grin, he clutched his heart. "You wound me."

"Oh, shut the fuck up."

Yet I heard the laughter in her voice.

I wanted all her giggles. I wanted her to relax and just have a good time. I wanted to take away all the pain from her life.

But I also knew I couldn't do that. Caressa still had dark demons she needed to confront. The question remaining uppermost in my mind was whether she'd accept my help to do it. Accept Michael's help as well. Or would she feel she could only tackle the darkness herself? She was just willful enough to try.

Suddenly, Caressa leapt up and padded back to the kitchen.

She needs slippers. Her feet will get cold.

Oh good God, I sounded like a parent.

Or a caring lover.

"I'd better go help." Michael rose as well. He inclined his head toward Donovan. "Glad you're here. Maybe you can keep him in line." He gave me a pointed look before heading out.

Donovan whistled—low so no one else could hear. "I knew you had the hots for Caressa. About five years, if I don't miss my mark."

"You rarely do." I kept my tone dry. I hadn't realized I'd been that obvious—but my friend had always been perceptive in ways many others weren't. That made him very good at his job. "How are the stunts lining up? I should be able to return—"

He wagged his finger at me. "No way are we veering off that topic so quickly." He made a show of glancing over—I assumed making certain we weren't being overheard. He leaned in. "You get a piece of that fine ass yet?"

Part of me bristled about Michael being reduced to a *fine ass*.

Part of me acknowledged Donovan was absolutely right.

Michael had a very fine ass. One I'd be happy to claim any day now.

I pointed to my thigh.

My friend winced. "Yeah, fair enough."

I considered telling him about the debauchery in the kitchen earlier. Not so long ago, I would've shared all the details. And more. Donovan knew my predilections in a way Caressa and Michael couldn't conceive.

Donovan cocked his head.

"I'm not sharing."

He pouted.

"It's different." I'd seen people over the years—men, women, and both—but I wouldn't have labelled it dating. And none had stayed around long. They'd known the score when they got involved. I didn't do long-term.

Or I hadn't.

Because I was waiting for Caressa and Michael.

Well, maybe not Michael in particular. He was just a lovely bonus.

"Oh my God, you're blushing."

I could rarely catch Donovan blushing. Whether because of his dark skin color or because the man just didn't have thoughts he wasn't always willing to share, I wasn't sure.

Still, heat rose in my cheeks.

He moved over to the couch, tucked himself against me, and threw his arm around me. "About bloody time. You're due for some enjoyment out of life." He pitched his voice to a whisper. "You've spent five years worrying. I hope you spend at least that long enjoying yourself."

Five years?

I planned a lifetime.

Except...

"How is this going to work?"

He pulled back.

I turned my head to meet his gaze.

Slowly, he nodded. "Yeah. As progressive as the world is, I don't think you can come out as a legitimate throuple. Or triad. Or ménage."

He was right, of course.

I hated when he was right.

"You can talk to Kelci and Elouise about what it's like to come out as gay."

Huh? "They're lesbians. Elouise is an Academy Award and Golden Globe nominated actor. I don't see how my life compares to hers."

"Well, if you and Michael came out as a couple—with your best friend Caressa always hanging out—that might throw suspicion."

"Or land us in all kinds of hot water." I ran a hand through my overlong hair. "There isn't a solution. We can't come out."

"So you're going to live the rest of your lives holed up in this house? An impressive house, to be sure, but it'll become a prison. To all of you. Have you thought about that?"

"Truthfully? No." Which was my mistake. I'd just been so stunned when they agreed to be mine. And I agreed to be theirs. Nothing was ever going to take them away from me again—not Africa, not work…and certainly not nosy journalists and a general public who didn't, despite their belief to the contrary, own me.

"Dinnertime."

Caressa appeared before us.

Better make those loud slippers.

She gazed between Donovan and myself.

Seeing my friend's arm around me and being snuggled by my side, she might've misinterpreted things.

"Are we a fourth tonight?"

No missing the bite in her tone.

"Oh, you bet—"

I elbowed Donovan in the ribs.

He shrugged sheepishly.

Caressa smirked. Then grabbed my crutches.

I was loath to have Donovan see me in such a weakened state, but I was better than I'd been a week ago.

Hopefully, he'd notice the improvement.

He didn't. He kept his gaze on Caressa. And now Michael, since he'd appeared.

I knew Donovan. Intimately. Numerous nights, usually shared with other people, and we'd wound up fucking each other. The affection I felt for him was filial. Not romantic. Never that. And Donovan wasn't eyeing Caressa right now.

He only had eyes for Michael.

I might've accidentally tapped his shin with my crutch.

Spinning to face me, he yelped in protest.

I arched an eyebrow.

He grinned unrepentantly.

Someday, my friend. Someday, you'll meet someone who'll knock you on your ass. Someday, you'll feel a need to protect as fierce as anything you've ever endured. And, finally, someday, you'll meet someone with the capacity to break you. And you'll almost hope they will.

Whether I conveyed all that in one long look, I couldn't be sure.

That being said, Donovan was on his best behavior through dinner. No more innuendos or inappropriate comments or questions about how we'd face the future as a triad. A true triad, as far as I was concerned. We would fall down if any one of the pieces were removed.

Or so you tell yourself.

Caressa and Michael were a couple before you. They're capable of going on without you.

But I'm not capable of going on without them.

More peril to you.

I wasn't enamored with my inner voice tonight. He was being downright bitchy.

Because of the doubts Donovan'd planted in my mind.

Not that I hadn't contemplated all these things. But they'd been passing thoughts. Something to be dealt with far in the future.

Then, without warning, things took a turn.

"So who are you taking to the gala?"

Donovan's words caught me off guard.

"Uh." I scrambled through the thoughts in my mind to find a coherent answer.

"Gala?" Caressa sipped her water.

None of us had chosen alcohol tonight. In fact, none of us were big drinkers. Coming from families with dysfunctional adults, Caressa, Michael, and I had made the decision we'd never let ourselves lose control—most especially to a mind-altering substance.

"There's a fundraiser every year for a shelter in the Downtown Eastside. Cole's a benefactor."

And again with the heated cheeks.

Caressa and Michael both appeared impressed. I was a little surprised Michael didn't know.

Did you ever tell him?

Well, that was a good point. I tried to downplay all of my charitable works.

I cleared my throat. "I'm sure I've asked Julie. I always take Julie."

Always being the last three years since I'd taken on

the role as benefactor. I disliked the amount of money spent on the gala, but we raised magnitudes of that—some of which we wouldn't have gotten through traditional fundraising. Many of the cast and crew from *VJ* showed up to support me and to schmooze with the elite of Vancouver. And we also gave away a handful of tickets to fans and underprivileged kids. Kept the evening more real—and provided donors an opportunity to see where some of their money went.

"I think Julie's accompanying Seamus. Val's got an important meeting in LA that he can't miss, but he wants Seamus to get out for the night. They're pretty involved with their son."

Val was a producer on our show, and his husband Seamus was a production assistant. They'd recently taken in a young boy whose mother died and whose father couldn't cope. Adoption wasn't in the cards, but they loved that little boy as if he were their own—always knowing he could be taken from them at any moment.

"Why didn't Julie say something?"

Donovan pointed to my leg. "I think she wasn't sure you'd be able to make it and she wanted Val to be secure in the knowledge Seamus would have someone to watch out for him."

Fair point. Seamus was from a small town in Newfoundland, on the other side of Canada. He couldn't hide his accent…or the fact he still found the big city and bright lights a little intimidating.

"I think you should take Caressa, and Michael can come as my date."

Michael coughed.

"Or you can take Michael, and Caressa will be my date. I mean, coming out as bisexual would definitely get tongues wagging. You might raise more money if you hinted at a revelation that night."

Caressa glared across the table at Donovan. Then she pivoted to Michael who sat beside her.

He was turning a worrying shade of red.

"Is he choking?" The words left my mouth as panic set in.

"No." Caressa stroked his back. "He's getting air in and out. He just needs to cough."

My panic receded as I heard Michael wheeze.

Okay, by a fraction.

Then Michael did cough. Whatever came up, he managed to catch it in his napkin.

By now, he was a disturbing shade of puce.

He rose, a little unsteadily. "Uh, sorry." He bolted.

Caressa laid her cloth napkin beside her chair and rose. She glared at Donovan.

My friend held up his hands in surrender.

She followed Michael from the room.

"Does this mean I won't get dessert?"

I smacked him on the upper arm.

Hard.

He chuckled.

About ten minutes later, my lovers returned to the table.

Caressa carried an apple pie while Michael had the slices of cheesecake from the night before that we'd never gotten around to eating.

Since we only had three, I was willing to forgo mine, but Donovan indicated he was only interested in the homemade pie.

We settled down to eat our dessert. And as much as we tried to resume our normal conversation with our friendly banter, Donovan's big mouth had laid a pall over our evening together.

That and the fact the weather had gotten nasty again had him bidding us farewell after dinner.

Caressa closed the door after he'd left. She turned her back and slumped against the door. Then she met my gaze. "Your friend."

"Hey, you've known him almost as long as I have."

Michael snorted. "You guys met in theater school. You've been tight ever since."

And he was likely aware I'd gotten Donovan the stunt coordinator role on *VJ*. I'd made very few requests when I started the show, I'd still been relatively unknown, but I'd known having Donovan on the show would take it to a whole new level.

He'd proved me right and earned his stripes. And he did some of the big action films during our hiatuses. Heck, he could probably start bringing in more money if he shifted to just doing the Hollywood films, but he stuck with us. Not just loyalty to me, although that played a part in it. No, he was loyal to *VJ*. Now I'd gone and fucked that up by getting injured.

Michael extended his hand, and she grasped it.

I clung to my crutches, the anger and frustration boiling inside me. "Fuck."

Caressa, while still gripping Michael's hand, stepped up to me. She cupped my chin in her palm. "It'll be over soon."

She can read my mind.

Well, thank God not everything.

No, I still had some secrets.

For how long?

Let's not worry about that now.

She scratched my chin. "You need a shave."

"I thought stubble looked distinguished." My character was clean-shaven, and frankly, so was I.

Usually.

I glanced over at Michael. He was a bit less meticulous with his grooming—good old electric shaver was good enough for him. I always used a blade.

"Why don't we do it now?"

"I can shave him." Michael made the offer, but he didn't look overly enthused. Just…like he was offering to be helpful. As he always was.

Caressa squeezed his hand. "If you don't mind cleaning up the leftovers, I can give Cole a proper shave. Then, I think, bed. I'm wiped."

We'd barely hit eight, but I couldn't argue with her logic.

More time in bed.

Yeah, I'd always be down for that.

"Happy to do dishes." Michael pressed a kiss to Caressa's cheek.

Then he gently eased her aside, stepped right up to me, grasped my cheeks in his hands, and drew my mouth to his. Without preamble, he thrust his tongue into my mouth.

My hands tightened on my crutches.

Michael growled as he pulled back. "Get better so I can fuck you. Or so you can fuck me." He reached down to cup my cock.

I thrust my jeans-clad erection into his fingers.

He pulled back with a Cheshire grin. "I think we're going to have fun tonight." He pivoted to kiss Caressa, then he headed to the kitchen.

Humming.

That out-of-tune song went straight to my hardening dick. I glanced at Caressa.

She held out her hands. "I've already given you a blow job today. How about we just focus on getting you shaved?"

My cock wasn't thrilled at that suggestion, but then the thought of being in such close proximity had advantages I was only now contemplating.

"Can I be naked?"

She snorted. "Whatever floats your boat. I'm going to throw on some pj's, and I'll meet you in your bathroom in a few." She turned and headed up the stairs.

Well, phooey. I'd hoped for a show. Maybe a chance to grab a breast. Twist a nipple.

You can do those things through clothes.

True. But she was clearly erecting a barrier. And I had to respect it. I might not like it, but I had to honor her wishes.

Five minutes later I sat on a towel on the closed toilet-seat lid.

And cursed the fact I hadn't thought to raise the temperature in the room. I made boatloads of money, and our electricity was obtained through the clean energy of a hydroelectric dam, but I still couldn't bring myself to raise the temperature much above tolerable. And although I used the air conditioner in the summer, I did so sparingly. I still paid all my own bills and kept track of all my expenses.

My accountant had offered to take over some of the responsibility. I trusted her implicitly, but I couldn't do it. I needed to know exactly how much I was making. What I'd saved, what I'd spent, and what I'd donated.

Fuck.

The gala.

I still didn't have a solution.

And fuck Julie for being so accommodating and agreeing to accompany Seamus.

Fuck Seamus for not being strong enough to go on his own.

That's mean.

So what? I feel like being mean.

Yet the redheaded Newfie was one of my favorite people in the world, so the burst of annoyance fizzled long before it settled.

Oh, I could invite Lisette. Surely, the director would want to put in an appearance.

Except she had a new girlfriend. A much younger woman, no less. So, yeah, that was probably not a road to try to go down.

Caressa breezed into the bathroom. Then she stopped, slowly spun, and faced me—slack-jawed.

Yeah, I'd felt the same way the first time I stepped inside.

"Holy shit, Cole."

"Yeah."

"This is bigger than the apartment you shared with your dad."

"Well…" Truthfully, I hadn't done the full calculations. The shower fit four comfortably with multi-jet sprays and, thankfully, a bench. That had proved incredibly helpful in the last week. I could sit and get myself pretty clean.

The soaker tub with jets fit three comfortably.

Again, I knew this from personal experience.

The double vanity was pretty sweet as well.

Too bad it isn't a triple.

True. But Caressa wasn't fussy like that. She didn't spend a lot of time in front of the mirror. She rarely wore makeup. While Michael and I shaved, she wouldn't even likely be around. In fact, given the chaotic nature of all our schedules, the likelihood of all of us needing to be in here together felt remote.

I pointed over to the far corner.

She poked her head. Then she turned and grinned. "A water closet."

"For maximum privacy."

"Huh." She wrinkled her nose. "I've shared facilities with people for so long that I can't fathom what it's like to have something of my own."

"Well, Michael hasn't had to share for a while. You can both also nab bathrooms of your own upstairs—so you can find privacy if you need it."

She ran her hand along the rim of the bathtub. "Any of them have jets?"

"I, uh…" I tilted my head. "I have no idea. I've only ever used this one. Guess you'll have to go exploring."

"Sounds like fun." She headed over to my sink and dipped her fingers in the water gathered in the basin. "A little tepid."

"It'll do."

"True."

She grabbed a washcloth and ran it under the other tap. Soon, steam rose.

"Good grief."

"If it's not going to burn my hand, then it's not going to burn your sensitive face." She rolled her eyes to accompany that comment.

Well, fine then.

When she pressed the washcloth to my face, though,

I involuntarily hissed. "Holy fuck."

She grinned unremorsefully. Then she set the cloth aside, put some shaving cream on the brush, and coated my neck and cheeks.

As much as I wanted conversation, I was happy to let her work in silence. And since she'd snagged my straight razor, I held as still as possible.

But predictably, my cock enjoyed her nearness.

As she wiped away the last of the cream, she glanced down at my crotch. "We're going to have to do something about that."

Oh God, I hoped so.

Chapter Twenty-Eight

Caressa

Although I didn't have a ton of experience with cocks, I knew enough to appreciate Cole's was a bit on the large side—more girth than length. That, while Michael's was longer and slenderer.

For the first time in my life, I actually thought about how each would feel inside me. Sure, I'd had sex before. This wasn't my first rodeo. But this was my first time with two men. And although sex was off the table with Cole right now, that wouldn't always be the case.

I needed to google *double penetration* and figure out if that was something I'd be interested in or if we'd be sticking to one at a time.

My cheeks heated.

Cole reached out to snag a tendril of my hair. "I love when you blush. When you've got color in your cheeks. Dare I ask…"

I swatted his hand away. "No, you may not." I snagged his crutches. "I'm going to see how Michael's faring. I didn't think it would take him this long."

I'd gone very slowly and carefully, we'd been at this for about twenty minutes, so I would've thought Michael'd be done.

Perhaps he was showering? Although we'd had one after our bout of erotic lovemaking in the kitchen. After

I'd scoured the counter. God knew I'd never be able to be in that room again and not think about... I cocked my head. While Michael'd been fucking me, I'd been fucking Cole with my mouth. Did that count as double penetration?

Hello, Google, here I come.

Tomorrow.

Exhaustion had set in about the time Donovan left. I didn't want to think about the new dilemma he'd raised—Cole dating. Cole being seen in public. Cole unable to acknowledge both Michael and myself. I tried to think of another famous triad, but I came up blank. Threesomes with minor celebrities didn't appear to be a thing. Or if they were, I'd no idea.

Given you've lived under a rock for the past five years, would you even know?

Okay. Valid point.

That being said, when Donovan suggested people Cole could speak to, he hadn't volunteered any throuples.

Crap.

Things were getting a shit ton more complicated.

Once Cole was securely on his crutches, I headed out of the bathroom and into the bedroom.

And stopped short.

Which caused Cole to knock into me.

I turned to help him, but he righted himself.

"Okay, what was that?" His brow furrowed.

I stepped aside to let him see.

That brow unfurrowed pretty fucking quickly and became a massive smile. "Holy shit."

Michael'd turned down the bed. He now lay on the center. Stroking his very erect cock.

My man was just full of surprises.

Cole whistled.

Apparently, he was impressed as well.

Michael scooted over to the left side of the bed, leaving Cole's spot empty for him.

He moved in that direction, and I followed, helpfully taking away his crutches.

"Zoey says I can move to a cane as long as I keep up my exercises and not walk very far."

I eyed Cole.

"She says I can heal in another three weeks. If I do everything she tells me to do." He lay down. "And I've been good."

"No fucking," I reminded him.

He winced. "Yeah. But soon…"

We'd have to be creative—that was for sure. He wouldn't be able to lie on his side for another couple of weeks.

Of course, apparently, being creative was Michael's middle name. He patted the spot beside him.

After securing the crutches, I wended my way to the far side of the bed and crawled in beside him.

He pressed a kiss to my nose. "I'm going to give Cole a blow job."

Cole let out a strangled sound.

Michael and I both glanced over at him.

He met Michael's gaze. "I'm not going to ask if you're sure because you're mature enough to make up your own mind." He palmed his growing erection. "But what's Caressa going to do?"

"Huh." Michael gave me a thorough perusal. "Well, she needs to get out of her pj's."

True. Given I was the only one wearing clothing and

tonight definitely involved parts I wanted uncovered. I yanked my pj's top over my head and shimmied out of the bottoms—throwing everything off the side of the bed.

Cole whistled.

Michael grinned.

I flushed. "They're just breasts."

"Oh, baby, they're so much more than that." Cole eyed me as I widened my thighs. "One day I'm going to eat out that pussy, and you're going to scream."

Michael's grin widened. "Oh yeah, she loves that."

I smacked him playfully.

He chuckled. Then he scooted back and knelt next to Cole's thighs.

Their gazes locked.

Cole's cock bobbed—angry, red, and leaking a drop of pre-cum.

Michael leaned over and lapped it with his tongue.

I held my breath.

He grinned.

Cole returned the smile.

"I feel like you guys don't need me at all." Jokingly, I started to rise.

Cole snagged my arm and tugged.

Not hard or anything. But just enough to catch me off-balance.

I fell against his chest.

He *oofed.* Then he pulled me in and grasped my hair, using it as leverage to lower my mouth to his.

The first brush of lips was a mere whisper. The second was more forceful. On the third pass, he opened his mouth, and I took full advantage. I thrust my tongue in his mouth and sought the recesses. I made sure to claim him.

He was mine.

I was his.

He moaned.

Ah. Michael'd taken him in his mouth.

Or at least I assumed. I wanted to look so badly, but Cole firmly gripped my hair, essentially holding me in place.

Our kissing morphed into something less frenzied. More seductive.

He trailed his hand down my neck to my chest.

I wasn't surprised when he palmed my breast. And didn't startle when he tweaked my nipple. This time, I hummed my approval.

He pulled back, and our gazes met.

"I want you so badly that I think it's going to break me."

My heart ached. I understood. He wasn't just talking about sex. He was speaking of the power of intimacy. What we could get from each other in terms of not just pleasure, but of bonding.

"Soon."

Blasted injury.

His eyes rolled back, and his lids drifted shut as he let out a long moan.

To my surprise, his grip on my nipple tightened. Not painfully. Just enough so I was fully aware he had ahold of me.

I peeked over my shoulder and grinned.

Michael was enthusiastically fellating Cole. For a guy who'd never done this before, he sure appeared to be doing a good job.

Or at least I assumed he'd never done it before. He

certainly hadn't shared if he'd had any adventures with men.

He glanced up, caught my gaze, then redoubled his efforts. He held the base of Cole's cock and bobbed up and down for all he was worth.

Cole whimpered. He moaned. Little inarticulate sounds came from his mouth.

I had to smile. I wasn't used to seeing him like this because he was one of the most articulate men I knew. Except when he was exceptionally angry. But that didn't happen often. Cole was a man who held tight control over everything. He attempted to keep control over everyone as well.

Part of me reveled that Michael was able to undo him so quickly. So expertly.

"I'm coming, Michael. If you don't want…" Cole's voice trailed off.

Michael just kept sucking.

Cole's body jerked as the orgasm overtook him. His grasp of my breast released as he pressed the heels of his hands to his closed eyes. His breathing was labored as he struggled through the obvious ecstasy and agony. A deep flush overtook his chest, neck, and cheeks. Sweat sheened down his forehead. He looked, in a word, debauched.

Eventually, Michael pulled off. He gently laid Cole's spent cock back in the nest of black curls.

Then he turned his attention to me. "If I fuck you from behind, he can see into your eyes when you come."

Arrogant much? The assumption I'd orgasm was a little egotistical. Except this was Michael. He'd do everything in his power to ensure I climaxed before he did. Hell, if I *didn't* come, he likely wouldn't either. He was just that kind of gentleman. Vigorous and enthusiastic lover, obviously. But also a kind soul who'd always put others ahead of himself.

Cole and I would need to work on him to ensure he dedicated more time to himself. To his pleasure. To his enjoyment. Somehow, I suspected things would be very different from now on.

"Yes, please."

"You guys don't use condoms?"

Cole's question caught me off guard. "Uh, no. Neither of us have ever, you know, and we've both been tested…"

"Ah."

I tried to figure out how I was supposed to interpret that. Michael'd just had Cole come in his mouth—I had assumed Cole was safe, but that was a pretty big assumption.

"The studio does a full physical at the beginning of each season. Mine was six weeks ago. I'm clean."

I didn't miss the fact he didn't add he'd never gone bareback.

"You want us to forgo them entirely?" Michael trailed a hand along my shoulder. "That's an enormous commitment. That means no cheating. No one but the three of us."

"I'm one hundred percent behind that." Cole met my gaze.

"Yeah, me too."

I, in turn, faced Michael.

He nodded. The flecks of gold in his eyes sparkled as he indicated he was going to move behind me.

Apparently, the conversation had been concluded and…doggy style twice in one day?

New record for me.

This morning I'd been solely focused on giving Cole the best blow job I could manage while Michael drilled into me. This time, though, I suspected it would be more about my pleasure. About what my lovers could wring out of me.

Michael positioned my hips as Cole snagged a pillow and laid it under me.

I cocked my head as I got on all fours.

"You might not be able to support yourself. I want you to have a soft landing."

His words caught me unprepared because, in fact, I'd never done it like this before. Most of my encounters had been nice, staid, and missionary style.

Michael raked his fingernails along my back, curling them in toward the base of my spine.

I purred in pleasure.

He drew his index fingers up the insides of my thighs from my knee to my ass.

I sighed.

He positioned himself over me, slid his hand around my waist, and delved into my pussy.

I met Cole's gaze and enjoyed when his pupils dilated. Apparently, my man enjoyed being a voyeur. Even his cock plumped a little.

Tempted as I was to give him another blow job, I wanted to entirely focus on Michael.

Speaking of Michael… His finger brushed my clit, and I jerked.

"Shush." He said the word quietly into my ear. "You're going to love this."

I already did.

His magical fingers did all kinds of wonderful things

to my insides as he massaged me. Maintained a maddeningly slow pace, and my body slowly came to life.

"Get on with it." Said through gritted teeth.

"All in good time." The words came not from Michael, but from Cole.

I had the distinct impression the guys watched each other closely while Michael slowly, and I meant slowly, increased the pace.

"Michael, for fuck's sake—"

He withdrew his hand.

"That's not what I meant." I nearly wailed at the loss of contact.

After spreading my thighs, he nudged my pussy with his cockhead.

"Oh, just do it already." I wasn't sure I could put any more exasperation in my voice, but I'd be willing to try. This teasing and tormenting might amuse the two men in my life, but it did nothing to sate the hunger burning low in my belly.

He thrust into me, nearly jolting me forward.

I pushed back.

He pressed in.

Finally, that feeling of fullness warmed me from within.

Michael began his unrelenting barrage of thrusts. Sometimes, he liked to ease into our lovemaking. Other times he dove in and just went for it. This, apparently, was one of *those* times.

I hung my head as he drove me higher and higher. My body sought release, but part of me wanted to stave off the climax for just another minute.

"Look at me."

My gaze shot to Cole. I wasn't sure he meant me, but when our gazes locked, I felt his command down to the depths of my soul. This man owned me. As much as Michael did. And I was powerless to disobey as his blue stare bore into me.

"Michael?" A casual question. Cole looked relaxed, but I caught the tic in his jaw.

"I want her to come."

No missing the pleading in his voice.

Cole leaned toward me.

I wanted to protest about his leg, but he unerringly reached for my nipple.

That squeeze shot straight to my core, and the overload of sensations sent my body right over the cliff and soaring toward my beloved ocean.

"Thank fuck." Michael continued to thrust until, a moment later, he held himself still.

Knowing he was emptying himself inside me did all kinds of lovely things to me.

My arms gave out, and I pitched toward the pillow.

Michael pulled out and snagged me around the waist before I fell. He pulled me back against his chest.

"Fuck, you two are so hot." Cole palmed his cock.

"Do it," Michael growled.

Even as he held me tight, Cole jerked himself. He tugged viciously as he chased a second orgasm.

Michael slid his hands to my chest and cupped my breasts.

My nipples, already sensitive, sent a message to my core.

A message I wasn't up to acting on, but one that sent a potent echo through me of the orgasm I'd just enjoyed.

Still, Cole held our gazes. His eyes would dart to

mine, then away, then back again. His jaw clenched as his movements became frenetic.

"Come, Cole. Join us." I uttered the words softly, but they appeared to be the right ones.

He bucked up, held himself taut, then spilled all over his hand.

"Fuck me." Michael whispered the words in my ear.

"I thought we just did that." My tone was a little wry.

"God, I love you so much." He laid his hands on my belly. "I'll never get enough of you."

Cole cracked his eyes open as he continued to nurse himself through his release. "That goes double for me."

I giggled. "It's not a competition."

His expression sobered. "No, it's not. This is a true partnership—between the three of us."

Holding my hands to Michael's, I squeezed. "Yeah." I sniffed. "Now, clean up and then bed? Cooking turkey was fucking exhausting."

Cole chuckled.

Michael coaxed me to lie down while he went to the bathroom. He was back a minute later with a couple of washcloths.

Although a small part of me rebelled at having someone care for me this way, I let Michael do exactly that. He cleaned my mons while giving me little kisses and caresses. He took just as much care with Cole, and soon he tossed the washcloths into the dirty laundry hamper in the walk-in closet and climbed back into bed.

Again, I found myself between my two men.

"Is it always going to be a Caressa sandwich?"

Michael grasped a lock of my hair in his fingers and twirled it. "We're protective of you."

"I don't think any boogeymen are going to sneak in during the night to try to steal me away."

Cole tapped my nose. "I promise you—as soon as I'm healed, I want a Cole sandwich."

Michael hummed his approval. "And I'll take a turn as well."

I started to shift, but he put a hand on my hip. "Not tonight, sweetheart. Just rest, okay? Plus, I have to be up early. Two more days and then I'm off for a week." He pressed a kiss to my shoulder blade. "And I know you're working, but we'll have dinners and massages ready for you when you come home."

"I'm seeing the psychologist on Tuesday. Christmas Eve, no less. But she's got an opening, and I didn't want to wait." Because I might've chickened out. Because I might've found an excuse.

Because a child died on my watch and I hadn't even begun to process that.

Cole caressed my cheek. "We'll get through this—whatever this is."

When I couldn't hold his gaze any longer, I let my eyes drift shut.

After a long moment, he flipped off the lamp.

Sleep claimed both my men long before it claimed me.

Chapter Twenty-Nine

Michael

When my boss let everyone go at noon on Christmas Eve with a promise to pay us for a full day's work, I did a little jig inside. And bolted to my SUV.

Caressa'd be at work, but Cole'd be home. This would be our first chance to really talk without our third.

He'd texted me about an hour ago that things had gone well with Zoey and he'd been liberated from his crutches. He'd sent me a picture of the cane his physiotherapist had gifted him.

Talk about badass. Black lacquer with fiery red and orange flames and a phoenix coming up through the flames. Well, it suited Cole. I'd pick something more sedate for myself, but if one was the biggest television star these days, why not make a splash?

I texted him I was on my way home and barely had the vehicle in gear when he texted back, asking if we could go shopping. I shot back a *sure* and laid on the gas to get over the Burrard bridge and on to Cole's house.

This neighborhood never ceased to take my breath away.

Cole had come so far.

And, now, thanks to him, I'd come far too.

With Caressa no less.

But the knot in the pit of my stomach tightened.

Sure, we were good now. But for how long? Donovan'd made a great point—we couldn't be out as a throuple. Hell, was that even the right word? And we were good for now. But what would happen when Cole went back to work? When Caressa's schedule was even more hectic? When I had to spend more time in the office or risk bringing work home with me?

And, while we were on *what ifs*…what about my condo? Should I sell it? Rent it out? Keep it in case I needed an out? In case Caressa did?

We couldn't be asking Cole to support and care for us forever, could we? If I'd taken one lesson from my parents' disastrous marriage, it was that nothing ever lasted. Okay, they'd stayed together. Only to die in an apartment building fire because they'd been too drunk to react to the fire alarm.

That'd only happened four years ago. Yet I hadn't spoken to them since the day I graduated from high school and moved in with Caressa and Cole into the first proper home I'd ever had.

And as much as I loved my downtown condo, it didn't fit my idea of a perfect home. The thing was the best I could do while living in Vancouver and making the salary I did. I'd always thought, in the hypothetical, that if I married and we wanted a baby, hopefully myself and this phantom woman would either be able to afford a two-bedroom condo or we'd move out into the suburbs. Maybe get a townhouse. But that would mean a long commute for me and less time with this imaginary family.

And although I'd imagined the scenario plenty of times, I had always been careful to never impose Caressa into the dream. That was just setting myself up for disappointment. And never, not in a million years, had I considered I might have a husband. I was straight. No guy had ever turned my head.

I shifted in my seat. Somehow, the thought of being with Cole was coming into my consciousness more and more.

And I might've streamed some gay porn on my personal phone during lunch yesterday while I sat in my SUV. I might've been tempted to jerk off as I watched one guy drill another. I also might've googled safe sex practices. Grateful we'd had the condom discussion the night before last, I now sought to understand how to keep things safe while, uh, having fun.

I pulled up in front of Cole's house.

Our house.

That thought nearly took the breath from my lungs. Soon I'd need to bring over more clothes. More…stuff. And we'd need to pack up Caressa's few remaining belongings and bring them as well. Although we hadn't rejoiced at the idea, we'd taken Cole's advice and staked out our own bedrooms with en suite bathrooms. Yeah, I could admit there would likely be times when I'd want privacy. I'd never lived with someone while in a romantic relationship. Neither had Caressa nor Cole. Unchartered waters for all of us.

Cole exited the house, locked the front door, and gingerly walked over to the SUV.

Okay, that was quite some cane. No missing that or mistaking it for an umbrella.

He eased his way in, stowed his cane, closed the door, then leaned over and tugged me in for a breath-stealing kiss.

Anyone walking by could see us, and Cole likely

knew that, but he gripped my cheeks tightly as he explored the recesses of my mouth with his tongue.

My cock stirred.

I shifted.

He pulled back with a grin. Then he laid his hand gently against my bulge, squeezed lightly, winked, and settled back into his seat. He had his seatbelt on and a shit-eating grin on his face by the time I put the SUV in gear.

"So where are we going?"

I was surprised when he told me one of the most exclusive jewelry stores in all of Vancouver. I drove up to West Fourth and pointed us back toward the Burrard Street Bridge.

Cole kept up a lively chatter all the way back downtown, but my mind spiraled.

What's he up to? And why does he need me?

In the end, I nabbed a spot right outside the store. Talk about having a horseshoe up my ass. Christmas Eve? Incredibly lucky.

We entered, and to my shock, we were the only ones.

"Mr. Hamilton." A lovely brunette with a blunt bob cut and sparkling turquoise eyes greeted us.

No way that eye color came from Mother Nature.

"Zelda, lovely to see you."

They exchanged air kisses as she eyed his cane.

"A little thing. Nothing to worry about."

She gave him one long level look before nodding. "And your…"

Cole eyed me.

I blinked.

He turned back to Zelda. "An old, dear friend."

"Not so old," she said, giving me the once-over.

I felt vaguely disconcerted—like she was judging me and finding me wanting. On the other hand, I wore work boots, scruffy jeans, a plaid shirt, and a heavy wool coat.

Then she caught sight of my engineering ring, and her eyes flickered.

Ah, so observant. And apparently, I'd just gone up in her estimation.

"Well, how can I help you gentlemen?"

Two hours later, we departed. I'd had to go back twice to top up the meter so I didn't get a parking ticket.

Cole sat with the turquoise bag protectively sitting on his lap.

I turned us back again so we headed south toward the bridge. "Do you think her eye color is intentional to match the store's colors?"

He guffawed. "You know, I've known Zelda for five years, and in all that time, I'd never made the connection." He fingered the gift bag. "Yes, her eyes are strikingly similar."

"She likes you."

Cole snorted. "Everyone likes me. My credit card makes me everyone's best friend."

I didn't miss the bite. "So not in *that* way?"

"Zelda? God, no. She's got...unique tastes. We...wouldn't be a good match."

What the hell he meant by that, I had no idea.

I activated the garage door when we got home and drove my car in beside Cole's electric. "I'm glad you have a second charging station."

"Seemed the prudent thing to do. And they gave me a discount."

This time, I snickered. "Like you needed it."

Cole cut me a look as I cut the engine.

"Sorry."

"Don't be." He brushed his finger along my jaw. "My money is your money. What I have is for all of us." He gave a little shrug. "You and Caressa have always been my joint beneficiaries. Now we just get to enjoy the spoils of my labor *before* I die. Pretty fucking sweet." Without missing a beat, he opened his door and maneuvered himself out of the SUV.

I was slower to follow.

Somehow, I'd known this, and yet having him say it made things more real. I knew how much he made per episode. He hadn't been bragging, merely keeping me in the loop. Even after he paid his agent, his lawyer, and the taxman, he had serious scratch left over at the end of the day. He'd also been investing wisely, owned this place outright, and had one hell of a nest egg. Even if the work dried up tomorrow, if he was careful, he had enough so he never needed to work again.

I barely had five years paid down on a twenty-five-year mortgage.

Still, I didn't want to be a kept man, and Caressa sure as shit didn't want to be a kept woman. At some point, we'd need to sit down and discuss finances.

After Christmas.

After the gifts.

Knowledge of what the turquoise bag contained burned through me. How would Caressa react? Were we doing the right thing? Pushing too hard? Not pushing hard enough?

Cole activated the switch to close the garage door as I made my way over to him. He palmed his keys, then, as the daylight disappeared, he pushed me against the wall.

His cane clattered to the floor.

Before I could protest, he had me pressed up against the door.

"Your leg…" My words fell away as he rubbed against me.

At least the bulk of his weight rested on his right leg. Creatively, though, he insinuated his left between my thighs so he could frot against me.

I cursed our bulky coats as I clasped him to me.

Our gazes locked.

I licked my lips.

He grinned.

Our mouths collided.

The kiss was hungry, needy, and desperate. He grasped my cheeks in his hands and tugged me closer as he thrust his tongue in my mouth.

I angled myself and banded my arms around his waist so he mostly leaned on me.

We sought friction. We sought connection. We sought understanding.

Or at least I did. I wanted him in a way I'd never wanted anyone before except Caressa, and the thought of her had me pausing.

Cole pulled back and nibbled my neck. "We'll tell her."

"She's going to be pissed."

Not about the making out part. She'd likely get a kick out of that. No, she'd be pissed that Cole was doing anything to endanger his recovery.

Part of me reveled in the fact he couldn't keep his hands off me. And the rest of me knew the risk was too damn high.

"Hold my shoulder. No weight on your left leg."

He rolled his eyes, grunted, then complied.

I leaned over to grab his cane. "A few more weeks, Cole. You've waited this long—you can manage a few more weeks."

Another eye roll.

"Just you watch yourself. I'll tell Zoey." I'd thought to threaten to tell Caressa, but we'd already committed to doing at least part of that. No, Zoey was the genuine concern for Cole.

His grumbled, "fuck, no," was all the confirmation I needed.

I unlocked the door and was heading toward the alarm keypad when I was hit by the most amazing smell.

"What the…" I was confused.

Cole caught my gaze and shrugged. "I don't think it's the caterer's day, but I'm all turned around."

He had a caterer? Someone who cooked the meals in house? God, the things I hadn't even conceived.

We shucked our boots, hung up our coats, and ambled into the kitchen.

A pot of tomato sauce heated on the stove, the spicy aroma filling the air. A pot of water for pasta sat waiting to boil. The package of spaghetti rested next to a chopping board filled with onions, mushrooms, and shredded cheddar cheese. Finally, a container of meat was right there, waiting to be browned.

"This is Caressa."

Cole nodded. "Yeah. So where is she?"

We held still for a moment before a rhythmic tapping caught my attention.

I cocked my head.

Cole shrugged.

We followed the tapping all the way to the dining room.

Caressa sat on the end chair with her foot propped on the table. The image jarred because she was always so respectful of other people's things.

I couldn't fathom how expensive this table was, but certainly more than I'd paid for every piece of furniture I ever owned.

We rounded the table, and I stuttered to a stop.

Cole halted as well.

The tapping sound was Caressa hitting the handle of a whip against the tabletop.

A whip? What the actual fuck?

A pair of metal handcuffs accompanied the whip with something that looked like a riding crop and something I thought might be…a flogger?

My mind wouldn't compute what lay before me.

Was Caressa suggesting we…get kinky?

I mean, I was a pretty open-minded guy. And I'd just viewed plenty of gay porn, and some involved bondage but…

"Cole?" Caressa continued to tap the whip handle.

He cleared his throat. "I see you went investigating."

Holy fucking shit. This was *his* stuff?

And yet why didn't *that* surprise me?

Cole eased himself into the chair next to Caressa's.

I sat on the opposite side.

"What did the psychologist say?"

Huh? Oh, right. Maybe that would explain why Caressa was home early.

I was still eyeing the whip and wondering if Cole wielded it or if people used it on him. Men? Women?

More than one? And where had Caressa found this stuff? In a box under Cole's bed?

The locked room.

Oh God, had he left it unlocked?

Fuckety fuck, fuck, fuck.

I hadn't asked, but my engineering brain had figured the approximate dimensions that weren't accounted for when Cole gave me the tour.

Actually, I couldn't say for certain if the room had been locked or not. I'd assumed it had, and asking would've been gauche, so I hadn't.

Wow, talk about a missed opportunity.

Or…would he have shared the contents of the room? Let me know what he got up to? If he had, would I have been so willing to move into his space with Caressa? To allow him further access to our bodies and our hearts?

I eyed the turquoise bag Cole had placed on the table.

Caressa had to recognize the name of the jeweler.

What would she think of the three matching platinum bands?

We might only ever wear them in the house, but Cole'd convinced me we needed a tangible reminder of our arrangement.

Hadn't taken much arm twisting to get me to agree.

I'd known, in my heart, that Caressa'd be the toughest nut to crack.

She stopped the tapping. "Things didn't go well." She waved again before either of us could speak. "The hospital's launched an investigation over the baby's death. They wanted to put me on administrative leave, but with Christmas tomorrow and them already being woefully understaffed…" She let the words trail off.

"Anyway, the psychologist felt, after our session, that I needed some time off. I have until tomorrow morning to get my proverbial shit together."

That sounded not just like a tall order, but damn near impossible. As if a baby dying wasn't bad enough, she still had Africa shit to sort through, and I had no doubt we hadn't heard the last of Fucking Franklin.

And Cole still wasn't fully healed.

Yet none of this felt insurmountable.

We'd found our way back to each other. We'd find a way to conquer all the problems that lay before us.

Cole stretched his arms out—one to Caressa and one to me.

I grasped his hand quickly, holding out my other to Caressa.

She eyed us both for a long time before clasping our hands.

Does she think I knew about Cole's...hobby? That I should've warned her?

"We're in this together." Cole squeezed our hands. "Whatever's happening, you come to us. You hear? You're not alone anymore." His gaze fell to our joined hands. "None of us are."

The weight of that settled in my chest, heavy and secure.

I couldn't have said how long we sat there.

Unspeaking.

Unmoving.

Unyielding.

Eventually, Caressa let go. "I have to see about dinner." She pointed to the bag. "And tonight, once we're in bed, you can give me my Christmas present." With that, she left.

Cole met my gaze and arched an eyebrow.
I indicated the BDSM equipment.
He grinned wickedly.
Oh yeah, this is going to be fun…

A word about the author…

USA Today Bestselling author Gabbi Grey lives in beautiful British Columbia where her fur baby chin-poo keeps her safe from the nasty neighborhood squirrels. Working for the government by day, she spends her early mornings writing contemporary, gay, sweet, and dark erotic BDSM romances. While she firmly believes in happy endings, she also believes in making her characters suffer before finding their true love. She also writes M/F romances as Gabbi Black and Gabbi Powell.

~*~

Visit Gabbi Grey online at:
www.gabbigrey.com